One moment, Vince and Harley were joking. The next, they weren't. And after that? Her lips were pressed to his.

His eyes widened and then slowly drifted closed as he deepened the kiss.

Only to have her pull away and announce, "Time."

He blinked. Disoriented. The willing woman in his arms was gone. Walking away from him. A swing to her step.

"Hang on." He jogged to Harley's side. "What just happened there?"

Harley wouldn't look at him. She reached the crosswalk and looked both ways, more careful crossing the road than she was with her affections. "I got carried away in my role as your plus-one and you got a freebie."

Vince wanted to haul Harley back into his arms and kiss her as senseless as she made him.

Not the wisest thought I've had today.

But certainly one of the best.

If only they weren't in Harmony Valley...

Dear Reader,

Welcome to Harmony Valley!

Just a few short years ago, Harmony Valley was on the brink of extinction, with only those over the age of sixty in residence. Now the influx of a younger generation is making life in Harmony Valley more fun and definitely more interesting for its gray-haired residents.

I hope you enjoy Vince and Harley's touching journey to a happily-ever-after—which begins with a harmless invite to a family wedding—as well as the other romances in the Harmony Valley series. I love to hear from readers. Check my website to learn more about upcoming books, sign up for email book announcements (and I'll send you a free sweet romance read) or chat with me on Facebook (MelindaCurtisAuthor) to hear about my latest giveaways.

Melinda Curtis

MelindaCurtis.com

HEARTWARMING

Marrying the Wedding Crasher

——

Melinda Curtis

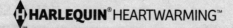

Recycling programs for this product may not exist in your area.

ISBN-13: 978-1-335-63353-8

Marrying the Wedding Crasher

Copyright © 2018 by Melinda Wooten

This edition published by arrangement with Harlequin Books S.A.

For questions and comments about the quality of this book, please contact us at CustomerService@Harlequin.com.

® and TM are trademarks of Harlequin Enterprises Limited or its corporate affiliates. Trademarks indicated with ® are registered in the United States Patent and Trademark Office, the Canadian Intellectual Property Office and in other countries.

Printed in U.S.A.

Award-winning *USA TODAY* bestselling author **Melinda Curtis** is an empty nester married to her college sweetheart. She's lived in three states in the United States—California, Georgia and Texas—and plans to move to a fourth when Mr. Curtis retires (because all their children live in Oregon). She and her husband are constantly remodelling something—their house, their parents' homes, the abodes of their children. Check out social media for before/after pictures.

Melinda writes sweet contemporary romances as Melinda Curtis (Brenda Novak says *Season of Change* "found a place on my keeper shelf") and fun, sexy reads as Mel Curtis (Jayne Ann Krentz says *Fool for Love* is "wonderfully entertaining").

Books by Melinda Curtis

Harlequin Heartwarming

Dandelion Wishes
Summer Kisses
Season of Change
A Perfect Year
Time for Love
A Memory Away
Marrying the Single Dad
Love, Special Delivery
Support Your Local Sheriff

Visit the Author Profile page at Harlequin.com for more titles.

To Anna J. Stewart and Cari Lynn Webb.
Thanks for understanding, making me
laugh and keeping me strong.

CHAPTER ONE

VINCE MESSINA CONSIDERED himself a survivor.

He didn't think he'd survive his little brother's wedding back home in Harmony Valley.

Bittersweet memories. Long-kept secrets. Family he hadn't seen in years. It had all the makings of a serious crash-and-burn.

The Texas summer sun beat down on Vince, nearly as hot as an oil-fueled ball of flame.

"You're going to come to my wedding." His younger brother Joe wasn't asking. "And you're going to bring that girlfriend of yours. It's long past time we met her."

Ah, the girlfriend.

His brothers pestered him less when they thought he was in a relationship. Hence his make-believe girlfriend, the latest of which hadn't been make-believe a month ago.

Vince's gaze drifted across the job site

to the blonde working the tile saw. Harley O'Hannigan wasn't likely to go away with him again. "She's not sure she can get off work." Besides, Harley would think he was a jerk if he asked her. But she was just the kind of woman who could hold her own against his siblings.

"What's her name?" His older brother Gabe was nearly silenced by the whir of the tile saw and the punch-punch-punch of a nail gun. "And what's that noise? Where are you?"

"They're remodeling my local Starbucks." Lying, Vince pulled his focus away from Harley. He was part of a crew working on a huge remodel in a fancy neighborhood outside of Houston. "And, no, I won't tell you her name. The last time I introduced you to my girlfriend, you stole her, Gabe."

Mandy Zapien, a girl with a heart of gold. He hoped she was married to somebody stable and had three kids by now.

"That was high school," Gabe scoffed. "There is no girlfriend, admit it. All the more reason Vince needs to come home so we can straighten out his life."

Vince's life was fine as long as his brothers stayed out of it. Not that he didn't love them.

He just didn't want to answer for every decision he'd made, every confidence he'd kept.

"The fake girlfriend is your tell." Joe sounded disappointed. "The last time you bluffed about one, you'd been clipped by a stray bullet in a bar fight."

"I wasn't actually *in* the bar fight." He'd been collateral damage, which seemed to be the story of his life. Vince set his jaw. "I'm not bluffing. There's a girl."

Correction. A woman. Wearing worn blue jeans, a burgundy T-shirt with the construction company's logo and scuffed work boots. She wiped a tile dry with a towel, examining the cut she'd made in the white marble.

"Send us a picture," Joe prodded. "We'll compare her to Sarah Whitfield. Did I tell you she was back in town? And still single?"

"Guys…" Vince squeezed the tail end of his patience.

"There is no girlfriend." Gabe pounced once more. "Which means you're in trouble. Do you need me to spot you some cash?"

"No!" Money was the last thing Vince was worried about.

Harley spared Vince a glance. She was what Texans called a tall drink of water. Long, elegant lines, delicate bone structure, straight blond hair that she kept in a long braid down her back. Everything about her appearance was at odds with her being a construction worker. That contradiction was the reason he'd asked her out. Her gentle humor and sly wit had kept him asking.

"If it's not money, how's that truck of yours running?" Joe jumped in on Gabe's fun. "I could re-bore those heads again and you'd get another fifty thousand miles."

Vince drove their father's red-and-white 1976 pickup truck. It had a weak air conditioner, cloth seats and unreliable headlights. Dad had been a mechanic who'd struggled with mental illness, made harder on the family when Mom had left them. Despite challenges, Dad had taught his three boys his trade. Only Joe had followed in Dad's footsteps. Gabe was a lifer in the military, currently on leave for Joe's wedding. And Vince—

"Messina! Break time's over."

Vince's boss rounded the far corner of the house they were remodeling. Jerry wore a frown and a sunburn from a weekend spent bass fishing. "That deck's got to be finished today."

Vince held up a hand, acknowledging the

older man. "I'm fine," Vince said into the phone. "The truck is fine. My bank account is fine. Harley is fine." This last came out like a backfire through a rust-ridden muffler.

His brothers crowed over his slip.

"Retire Dad's truck," Gabe said when he stopped laughing. "I'll reserve you a room at the Lambridge Bed and Breakfast where I'm staying."

"Bring me some of that oil you dredge up on that rig of yours," Joe said, gasping for breath. "Gas in California is expensive. And a girlfriend? Sarah is going to be so disappointed."

Vince wasn't working on an oil rig, hadn't been for over a year since it'd exploded.

He wasn't retiring Dad's truck. Other than the faulty headlight wiring, it ran like a champ.

He wasn't dating Harley, not since she'd broken up with him.

And he had no idea if he was going to go to his brother's wedding.

HARLEY O'HANNIGAN FINISHED wiping the grout from the shower tile in the master bathroom and sat back to admire her effort.

Carrera marble countertops. Chrome fixtures. White and black glass accents. It was luxury at its finest, not to mention it was bigger than the bedroom she'd had growing up and reminded her of the condo she used to rent in a high-rise downtown. That was six months and another lifetime ago.

"Harley!" The male voice, deep and angry, reverberated off the walls in the empty house and shook Harley's stomach.

She moved into the master bedroom. Most of the construction crew had left for the day, except for Vince, who was sanding the deck outside the bedroom's French doors. She wished he'd left, too.

There's a mistake I won't repeat.

"Harley!" Dan's voice was as hard as his footsteps on the wood floor. "I know you're here."

"I'm in the back."

And then so was her former boss, standing in the bedroom doorway.

On first glance, Dan looked like any other young, hipster architect, the kind of man her brother would roll his eyes at—close-cropped blond hair, neatly trimmed goatee, pink cotton, button-down and tight, white cigarette pants. He looked like the worst damage he could do was post a bad review online. But take a second look and you'd register cold gray eyes, an openmouthed sneer, and fingers flexing into fists. You'd recognize a desperate snake ready to strike.

Fear stuck in Harley's throat. Why hadn't she seen Dan's reptilian side when he'd hired her, a fledgling architect, a year ago? Suddenly she was glad Vince was still around.

"Your design can't be done," Dan said in an ominous voice that conjured images of cop dramas and crimes about to be committed. "You knew this would happen."

"Yes," she choked out, hating that she sounded scared. "And so did you. I told you not to do it." Not to steal her unfinished sketch. Not to present it to high-profile clients. Not to promise it could be built.

He'd stolen more than her architectural plans. He'd stolen her joy in the work and her confidence in her abilities.

Dan's brows dropped to the locked-and-loaded position. "The structural engineers are demanding to see the plans from you. I put them off another two weeks, but that's it."

"Give the money back, Dan." He'd won an international design award with her conceptual drawings of a playhouse with balconies that seemed to float in the sky. And then the city of Houston had agreed to pay Dan millions to build it.

"Give it back?" He choked on the words and then seemed angered to have done so. His face reddened. "I spent the advance on things like salaries and tuition reimbursement." For her.

"And on cars and a new house." An over-the-top place some other architect had designed. Dan had little talent of his own. He was drunk on new business and higher fees.

As usual, her arguments fell on deaf ears. Dan made a guttural hiss.

The fear in Harley's throat plummeted to her legs, weakening them. He'd never confronted her alone in an isolated place before. Every instinct she had urged her to run, to get out of the house and away from Dan.

Before Harley had a chance to move, Dan did. He closed the distance between them and shoved her, hard.

As she fell, Harley's vision tunneled until all she saw were angry eyes.

She couldn't catch her breath. She was

from a good home, a stable family. People in her world didn't get in physical fights.

Her legs gave out and she felt cold from her head to her toes.

She became aware of a scuffling noise. Someone might have shouted. Someone who sounded vaguely like Dan.

"Harley?" Definitely not Dan's voice.

She was incredibly thankful for whoever Not-Dan was.

Warm hands engulfed hers, not the slightest bit vengeful.

"Harley?" A gentle voice, one she should be able to identify if her head didn't feel like someone had stuffed it with thick insulation. "You're safe. He's gone."

She opened her eyes on a shuddering breath. A familiar face greeted her.

Vince. They both worked for Jerry, remodeling houses.

Vince. Friendly black eyes, a sturdy nose and black hair. That black hair. It had required a second glance when they'd first met. He had fantastic hair. The kind of hair Disney gave its princes.

Her heart was racing for the exit and her hands had started to tremble in his.

Vince's hands, not Dan's.

Vince. He drove an old truck, not a new Ferrari. He'd offered her carrots once when he'd heard she'd forgotten her lunch on a remote job site. He'd bought her a drink after work one day, which had led to him buying her dinner—more than once—and then the infamous weekend away where he'd learned she'd quit being an architect. Not that he'd understood Harley and her inability to pick herself up after one undisclosed setback. He may have been seven years older than her, but that didn't mean he could be judgmental about her carcer choices.

Note to self... I'm not safe with Vince, either.

"Hey." Vince gave her hands a gentle squeeze. "Are you with me?"

With him? She would've followed him anywhere a few weeks ago, before the let-me-tell-you-what-to-do-with-your-life debacle.

Something crashed outside.

Vince muttered what might have been an oath or a psalm. She couldn't hear over the pounding of her heart.

He moved to sit next to Harley, tucking her beneath his arm, next to his bulky tool belt. "Breathe in. Breathe out."

Sounded easy enough, but that heart of

hers was hammering against her lungs, making her pant. Vince holding her wasn't helping her recovery.

Not that she moved away from him. Not one inch.

"Like this." Vince took Harley's hand and placed her palm on his sturdy chest.

She could feel his heart beat nearly as fast as hers, but she could also feel him fill his lungs with air.

"Breathe in. Breathe out." Vince was big and warm and calm, and completely different than Dan. He'd never be a slave to fashion. He'd never take credit for someone else's work. He'd never put his hands on a woman with intent to do damage.

In a distant part of her brain, somewhere where things weren't pounding, Harley's mother recited one of her Southern lectures. *Life is hard, baby girl. You need to find yourself a big, strong man to lean on when times get tough.*

Finding big, strong men was something of a specialty of Harley's. It was finding the ones she could lean on forever that eluded her.

"That's it," Vince reassured her.

Vince was strong, too. He looked like he

could play tight end for the Houston Texans. He smelled of fresh-cut wood and hard work. And he sounded the way Disney princes should—reliable, honorable, understanding.

Two out of three...

"Your hair lies," she murmured. It promised empathy and happily-ever-afters.

She should never have broken the no co-worker rule in her dating handbook. But Vince had that hair and that smile and that self-confidence slightly older men with their act together seemed to have.

"Are you dizzy? Nauseous? Bleeding?" His fingers explored the back of her head and found—

"Ouch." She held her breath until the pain passed. "Give...me...a...minute." And then she'd ask Vince to stop touching her.

"Take as long as you need."

She was afraid she'd take as long as he let her, which just wouldn't do. She was Harley O'Hannigan. She was tough, independent and wasn't the kind of woman who expected flowers or pretty words or who waited for men to open the door.

Harley sighed and put some space between them. "Thanks."

"My pleasure."

She shot him with a sideways scowl.

"I meant…" Vince held up his hands, revealing scraped and bloodied knuckles. "I haven't had a good fight in a while." He grinned. It was lopsided and devilish, and made her girlish fantasies flutter foolishly inside her chest.

Mr. Carrots was a fighter? How had she not known this?

I didn't know him at all.

"You should press charges."

A new sensation banged around her chest. *Embarrassment.* "I can't afford the time off from work to fill out police reports or show up in court." What a flimsy fib. "Which makes me sound—"

"Practical."

There he went, being nice again. This time it sent tears to her eyes. She didn't want his pity or his kind words. That would destroy the carefully constructed image she had of herself as The Woman Who Could Do Anything.

Which in hindsight was a lie, too.

"How about we call it a day?" Vince stood and offered a hand to help her up, flashing that grin that'd gotten her into trouble a few weeks ago. "Pack your tools and let's get out of here. First beer's on me."

Harley shook her throbbing head, pushing to her feet with the aid of the wall. "Thanks for the offer, but we both know that's not happening."

"No worries." The grin disappeared and, just for a moment, she thought he looked disappointed. "But we are getting out of here. Pack up your tools. I'll lock up."

Agreeing with Vince that she'd finished for the day, Harley loaded her tools into a bucket and headed for the driveway where she'd left her tile saw. It'd been hot inside the house, but it was hotter outside in the sun. It beat down on her head as if its goal was to melt her out of existence.

Speaking of existence, the table she'd clamped the tile saw to had been upended. And dragged. And shoved half into the bushes.

"No. Oh, no." Harley's stomach fell and fell and fell, all the way to the pavement. Her bucket clattered next to it. She needed that saw to make a living.

She righted the saw, which was still plugged in, and turned it on. It ka-clunked

MELINDA CURTIS 21

a bunch of times and began smoking. She shut it off and stared at it, unable to move.

"That doesn't sound good." Vince approached her, carrying a bulky black tool bag. His eyes narrowed. "I wondered what all that racket was when he left."

"Dan… He smashed it." The same way he'd sort of smashed her.

"There are two things a man needs," Vince said. "Pride and honor. This Dan has too much of one and none of the other."

Harley nodded miserably.

Vince peered at the saw. "This is totaled. You sure you don't want to press charges against your boyfriend?"

A weight dropped on Harley's shoulders so hard and heavy she didn't correct his presumption about Dan. "I… Can't you fix it?" By tomorrow when she had to tile the outdoor kitchen? Vince was always fixing something for Jerry, their boss.

Vince set down his tool bag and examined her saw. "See those dents in the casing? When it collapses like that, parts inside get damaged."

"I can't afford a new one." She'd gone from a starting architect's salary to a tiler's paycheck. And she'd just put a new truck transmission on her credit card.

"You can take it to that shop on Polk. They'll give you money for whatever parts they can salvage and apply it toward the purchase of a new one."

She couldn't afford that, either, not without a second job. Until then, she'd be cutting tile with a low-tech manual saw and nippers. "Thanks for the advice."

Demoralized, Harley released the base from the table and carried the dead saw to her truck, returning for her tool bucket and the worktable.

If only she could figure out how to make playhouse balconies float on air.

Vince was still loading his stuff into his truck's lockbox when Harley opened the creaky door to her hot cab and climbed in. She missed her Lexus. She missed auto-start and powerful air-conditioning. She turned the key in the ignition.

Nothing. Not so much as a tick of the starter.

She missed reliability.

"Not today," she muttered. The truck was finicky. It didn't like to run when the temperature dropped to the thirties or in thunderstorms, but the day had been hot, the skies clear. "Come on, baby," she chided the old vehicle.

Don't leave me stranded with Mr. Carrots and that grin.

Vince locked up his tools and leaned on his truck, staring at hers.

Still nothing. Her backside was growing damp with sweat.

Vince came forward. He walked with the swagger of a man who knew what his purpose was in life. And, right now, that purpose was to rescue a damsel in distress.

"Pop the hood."

She did, hopping out and joining him at the grille. Not that she knew anything about engines. Her mechanical ability stopped at turning power tools off and on.

Vince tsked and gave Harley a look that disapproved and teased at the same time.

"Hey, don't judge," she said. "It runs."

"It's not running now." He drew a blue rag from his back pocket. It was the kind of scrap mechanics used to wipe their hands and touch hot engines. "You might want to spray your engine off every once in a while." He used the rag to check battery connections, hose connections and to prod the engine compartment as if he knew what he was doing.

"I barely clean my apartment. Why would I clean my engine?"

"So a mechanic can see if you've got leaks anywhere, for one thing," Vince said straight-faced. "Why don't you try it again?"

She hurried back behind the wheel. The truck started right up.

"Traitor," she accused under her breath.

Vince shut the hood and came around to her window, wiping his hands.

"Thanks." Harley gave him her polite smile, the one she reserved for helpful sales-clerks and the receptionist who squeezed her in at the doctor's office. "I owe you."

"Yeeeaah." He wound out the word and ran his fingers through that thatch of mid-night hair. "About that. I need a favor." Those kind black eyes lifted to her face.

Don't believe in fairy tales... Don't believe in fairy tales...

Despite their history, despite knowing better, silly fantasies about princely rescues and Mr. Right fluttered about her chest like happy butterflies on a warm spring day.

She should go. Instead she lingered and asked, "So what's the favor?"

The devilish grin returned, making the butterflies ecstatic. "I need a date to my brother's wedding."

CHAPTER TWO

WHEN HAD A man ever asked Harley to be his wedding date?

When was the last time she'd felt like going to a wedding?

She couldn't remember on either count.

Harley had turned Vince down, of course. The wedding was in California the weekend after next, but he'd wanted her to fly out with him this Saturday.

Take to the skies with Vince?

Thunderclouds lined the southern horizon.

There was a time when Harley O'Hannigan thought the sky was the limit. A time when everything she'd touched had turned to gold.

Daughter of a couple who owned a tile and granite outlet in Birmingham, she'd been the girl most likely to succeed in high school, valedictorian of her college class, the young architect hired to design beautiful structures for a boutique agency in Houston.

And then reality struck. The balconies she'd dreamed up for a uniquely modern theater couldn't be built with today's construction techniques. She'd only shared the drawing with Dan because unbuildable designs could be entered in architectural theory competitions. Winning those awards brought agencies and architects prestige. But Dan had done the unthinkable. He'd presented her design to a client as do-able. And they'd bought it.

She'd begged Dan to back out of the deal. But the press he'd received from the sale was amazing, and had led to more architectural business and more requests for impossible, pie-in-the-sky ideas. Instead of admitting the balconies couldn't be done, Dan had found a contractor willing to begin construction with the interior still up in the air. Literally.

Backed into a corner where all she could do was put Fail on her résumé, Harley had quit, only to be told she'd signed a noncompete clause when she'd been hired. Oh, and since her employment package included the firm paying her college debt, she couldn't work as an architect if she didn't work for Dan. Not for four more years. He'd told her he'd reconsider the four-year limitation if she came up with a solution that didn't compromise the design. Her mind was a blank slate.

She wasn't qualified for any other job that could support her former lifestyle. She'd moved out of her high-rise condo. She'd sold her Lexus SUV. She'd let go of dreams of greatness in the clouds.

And she couldn't tell anyone why. There was a nondisclosure clause, too.

Clause-clause-clause. Harley wanted to go back to a time when the only clause she knew was Santa. For the girl most likely to change the world, it was humiliating.

Her parents told their neighbors Harley was discovering herself. Privately, they'd counseled her to find a lawyer, not that she or her parents could afford one. Harley's friends thought she'd finally cracked under the pressure of perfectionism. They'd offered platitudes and shoulders to cry on. Harley had rejected them all. Taylor, Harley's older brother, had just shaken his head and told her she should have known buildings always came back to straight lines and right angles. That's how he and their parents approached tile work and life—eyes on the task in front of them—unlike Harley, who was always dreaming.

Without any professional avenues open, Harley had taken a job as a tile installer, a trade her father had taught her growing up. She'd rented a small studio apartment in an almost up-and-coming neighborhood. She kept her head down, away from the clouds. But her eye occasionally drifted toward the architectural elegance of the Houston skyline. And she wondered what she'd do in four years when her non-compete restriction expired. Straightforward lines or curvature that challenged?

In the meantime she lived day-to-day, job-to-job, paycheck-to-paycheck. But the only way she could do that was to have a functioning tile saw.

She stopped at the tool repair shop Vince had mentioned. It was open late because it catered to construction companies. She carried the saw inside.

"Were you in a traffic accident?" Bart, the owner, looked like he'd forsaken years of trips to the barber and opened a running tab at the tattoo parlor next door. He had long brown hair, a haystack beard and line upon line of ink on his arms. "You need to secure your equipment when you drive."

Harley didn't care about Bart's body art, his hair style or his sad attempts at humor. She cared that his hands were nicked and greasy. It meant he was busy making tools go again. "This happened at a job site. Some idiot trashed it." Because some idiot couldn't figure out how to make balconies float like clouds. "Can you fix it?"

"Give me two weeks." Bart stood back, possibly because he'd given customers bad news like this before. Possibly because construction workers could be as volatile as stiffed loan sharks.

Harley fought shoulders that wanted to hunch in defeat and reminded herself that nothing was ever set in stone. There was always another card to play. "How about two days?"

"It'll cost ya." Bart's mouth rolled around before he admitted, "And I might not be able to fix it."

Harley felt sick. Her hand drifted to her waist. "And when would I know that?"

"When I'm done." Bart curled his scarred fingers around the handle of her saw, as if preparing to claim it. "No matter what happens, you'd owe me a hundred dollars just for taking it apart. Fixin' costs extra."

One hundred dollars and days of uncertainty. Her eye caught on a used tile saw in the corner with a six-hundred-dollar price tag. "What if I sold it to you for parts?"

"I'd give you sixty bucks."

That's all? He must have sensed she was desperate.

Harley tried to look like she wasn't. "How about a hundred?"

Bart shook his head. "I can come up as high as seventy. And even then, I don't think I'm gonna get seventy dollars' worth of parts out of it."

A good, new tile saw would cost around a thousand dollars. Seventy wasn't going to get her close. And she hated the idea of taking out more credit. What would she do if the truck broke down again?

Harley thanked Bart for his time and lugged the saw back outside.

Her head was pounding. All she wanted was a cold shower and someone to make her dinner.

She thought of Vince and his talent at the grill, of his invitation to his brother's wedding, of the tenderness of his kiss.

That cold shower. Sadly, it was the only one of her fantasies going to come true tonight.

Tomorrow, however, she might have one more card to play.

VINCE SAT ON a corner of the deck he'd built yesterday and wondered if he could parlay Harley being unable to go to the wedding into him not going to the wedding, too.

It wasn't as if he was a beloved favorite son in Harmony Valley. His return might make it hard on his younger brother Joe, the bridegroom, who'd only just begun to earn acceptance in town. He and his brothers had been hellions as teenagers—cutting class, speeding through streets on deafening motorcycles, wearing black leather jackets instead of the school colors. Vince could use his misspent youth and consideration toward Joe's tentative standing in town as a excuses not to go. But they would only be excuses.

His real motivation for not wanting to go to the wedding? There were things he hadn't told his brothers. Secrets he'd kept for years about their mother leaving. Those secrets. They sat on his chest when he couldn't sleep at night, clambering to be free.

Sleep-deprived, Vince blinked at the blazing sun. He had the case of Jerry's auger motor open and was cleaning the spark plug because the hunk of junk wouldn't start. Pretty soon, Jerry was going to be wondering why Vince wasn't setting fence posts. Soon after that, Vince might lose his patience and tell him his equipment sucked. If Jerry took offense to that Vince might admit why he'd applied for a job with Jerry in the first place. After that revelation, it was a toss-up as to whether he'd quit or be fired.

Secrets. They were dangerous to his family's happiness. Nothing had turned out the way he'd once hoped it would.

He'd left Harmony Valley sixteen years ago, fresh out of high school, determined to find his mother. She'd had a three-year head start, but he recalled she had family somewhere in Texas. He'd needed to know if she was okay and if the decisions he'd made the day she'd left had been the right ones. He'd located her in Sugar Land, Texas, outside of Houston. He'd located her, but he'd never contacted her. Not directly. Though he kept tabs on her all the same…thanks in part to Jerry.

Out front, a truck door creaked and slammed. Harley.

She was trouble. She still saw stars when she gazed at the night sky. She'd earned a degree in architecture, only to give up after what she'd called a colossal failure.

She'd failed once? Boohoo. She needed to learn that life required a strong backbone and the ability to pick yourself up after you got knocked down, no matter how many times it happened.

And yet, looking back, he'd enjoyed his time with her. They'd clicked. After a few weeks of dating, he'd asked her to go to Waco for a weekend. They'd taken the home tour and visited the showrooms of that famous designer. They'd eaten great Tex-Mex. They'd walked along the river and he'd kissed her beneath a rambling oak. And then they'd driven by Baylor University. One conversation thread had led to another and Harley had confessed she'd graduated from Rice in Houston. She was an architect!

She was an architect working as a laborer?

Vince had gotten mad on her behalf. He'd lectured her about how privileged she was to have the opportunity to go to college. He would've liked to have been a mechanical engineer, but his high school grades hadn't been that hot. And Harley had just thrown her chance away? It made no sense.

She'd told Vince he'd never had to stare down the face of ruin, forced to admit defeat. She'd told him to take her home.

And that had been the end of dating Harley O'Hannigan.

Vince shoved the spark plug home. The heat was rising even though it was only midmorning. Digging post holes and setting them in concrete was going to make for a shirt-drenching day. Vince had heard one of the big airlines was hiring aviation techs and mechanics at the airport. Better pay. Better working conditions. But no—

"Vince." Harley appeared as she always did for a job site—jeans, T-shirt, braid. She carried a bucket with her tiling tools and a manual tile cutter. She set everything down near the outdoor kitchen on the deck, frowning at her next project.

He'd been relieved she'd turned him down for the wedding. After the way things had ended between them, he never should've asked her in the first place. "How's that bump?"

She reached up to touch the back of her head. "Better."

He resisted the impulse to see for himself. "And how goes the tile saw repair?"

"Worse." Harley came to sit nearby, a light sheen of sweat on her forehead. "I've been thinking about your brother's wedding."

The humidity in the air pressed in on Vince.

"Is it a formal affair?" she asked.

"It's outdoors and I'll have to wear a suit. Does that qualify as formal?" Whatever the answer was, he hoped she hadn't reconsidered being his date.

"That's not too formal." She smiled the way a woman does just before she says yes to something she isn't exactly thrilled about agreeing to.

Reflexively, Vince smiled back. And then he remembered he'd changed his mind about taking her.

"Since you're in a bind—"

"A bind?" Normally, Vince was slow to anger. Not today. Today anger shot through him like nitrous oxide, making him talk faster, grip the auger harder. "I'm a grown man, not some kid looking for a prom date.

I can walk into a wedding alone." Or, even better, not go at all.

She tucked stray strands of golden hair behind her ears and avoided looking at him. "But you did ask me."

"And you turned me down!" There was no reason that should poke at his pride, but it did, the same as her assuming he was in a dateless bind.

"And now…" Her gaze wound around to meet his and her lips made a slow turn upward. "I want to propose a new deal for us."

The muggy morning air suddenly became too thick to inhale. Vince was a man, after all, and Harley was a beautiful woman proposing something.

"Go on," he rasped when he should have said, "No go."

"I'll… I'll be your plus-one—" Harley couldn't hide the desperation in her voice "—if you fix my tile saw."

Air moved freely in and out of Vince's lungs again. This wasn't a personal proposition. "Couldn't find anyone to fix it?"

"Not for anything less than the price of my firstborn."

She was as boxed in as he was.

A part of Vince was intrigued, the way he

was always captivated by things not working how they should. The saw wouldn't be easy to fix. No telling what kind of damage was inside until he took off the outer casing.

Another part of Vince was reminded that he enjoyed Harley's company, their quick banter, their obvious chemistry. The bargain wasn't completely out of the question.

He ran a hand through his hair, wondering what their relationship would be like today if they'd never talked about higher education and college degrees.

"Well," he said gruffly, "we can't have you selling off your firstborn."

Harley's cheeks pinkened from more than the sun and she looked away. "I'd need the saw before we leave on Saturday."

"That might be a stretch." It was Tuesday. "What if I need to order parts?"

She considered this with the same deliberation with which she ordered from a menu. "Could they arrive while we're gone, so you could fix it first thing when we return?"

Again, the feeling that he shouldn't take her to Joe's wedding gripped him. Vince fiddled with the screw on the auger motor hood, not looking at her. "Can you really afford to miss a week of work?" That seemed unlikely given she couldn't afford to repair or replace her saw.

"Jerry owes me a couple days off and I've lined up some side jobs." She'd put thought into this. She hadn't asked him on a whim.

Unless he had a good reason to retract his offer, he felt honor-bound to take her.

Vince held out his hand for her to shake because he had to keep this on a platonic footing. "I'm paying for transportation, the hotel and food."

"Okay, but..." Harley hesitated, offering a question in those blue eyes, not a handshake. "Why do you want a wedding date?"

He returned his hand to the auger, unwilling to tell her the truth and latching on to the first idea that came to mind. "There's this girl, Sarah, from high school—"

"And you broke her heart." Harley tsked.

He let her assumption stand. "Having a beautiful woman on my arm will keep my visit simple." On so many levels.

Harley leaned back and surveyed him as if he was a blouse she was considering from the bargain rack. "And you'll fix my saw?"

"I'll do my best."

"Fair enough." Harley stood and sealed the deal with a businesslike handshake.

Her going complicated things for him.
He just knew it. So it made no sense that
he felt like smiling.

CHAPTER THREE

VINCE BOUGHT HARLEY a plane ticket.

He packed a bag that included a dark blue suit, matching socks and tie, dress shoes, and an overly starched white shirt.

He took apart Harley's tile saw.

Like his head, it was a mess. Bushings. Armature. Casing. All ruined. He spent a lot of time searching online for parts and thinking about the week ahead.

But a little voice kept whispering that this trip was as disastrous as Harley's tile saw. He didn't just want her to sell the idea that they were dating. He wanted her to sell the idea that they'd been dating for months. And that would require more than a businesslike handshake. That would require more fence-mending between them. That would require answers to questions she hadn't asked and hadn't thought of; ones he didn't want to deal with.

Intending to get her on board with his plan

before they left, Vince picked Harley up at her apartment complex on the east side of Houston. She was waiting out front in a yellow tank top and blue jeans, a small duffel bag and a backpack at her feet. Her hair was in its usual long, blond braid and her blue eyes were covered by sunglasses.

She hopped into the truck with a simple, "Hi," setting her things on the floorboard and making herself comfortable.

He'd expected at least one suitcase, if not two. And maybe a dress or something a bit more feminine for the trip. It was her day off. Usually on her day off or nights out when she had time to change, Harley wore bright colors, interesting patterns, and often skirts and flouncy dresses. They were on their way to a wedding. It was early, but it was already nearly eighty degrees outside and with the humidity, it felt hotter. Why were her legs covered up? And why was she acting as if they were going to a job site?

"Is there a problem?" Harley asked when he didn't immediately drive away.

"I was thinking how weird this is." And he didn't mean his thoughts dwelling on her legs.

"I don't have to go." Her voice was very small and very un-Harley like.

It tugged at him, that voice. She didn't want to go and he didn't want to take her. He should offer to buy her a saw and leave her in Houston. He drew a deep breath. "I should have told you I asked you to go to this thing because of my family, who are—"

"Nuts," she finished for him, shrugging.

Vince's jaw dropped. An image of his dad leapt to mind.

"Isn't that what everyone says?" Harley shrugged again and turned her gaze toward the Houston skyline, visible through the smoggy haze.

"I suppose." Although he never said it. Not even in jest.

"It'll be fine. *I'll* be fine." She said the words forcefully, as if trying to convince herself.

Vince let the truck idle, his plan stuck in neutral. He felt obligated to let her know what she was walking into. "Before we go, I need to tell you something."

"If you want to get back together, I'm going to stay here." She drew herself up and glared at him.

There. That was more like the Harley he knew.

"You've been friend-zoned," she continued. "I don't think about you *that* way anymore."

Ouch. He hadn't expected that statement to sting. Not even if it was a good thing. "I'm not looking for a commitment with you or anyone else."

Down the block, a motorcycle accelerated, winding through the gears quickly, as if there was fun to be had ahead.

Vince held on to the truck's steering wheel with both hands. He hadn't ridden a bike in ages. "In fact, I'm not the marrying kind."

His brother Joe was the Messina intent upon promising "till death do we part."

"Interesting." Harley crossed her arms over her chest, her gaze cutting from Vince to the skyline once more. "Are we going to the airport or not?"

The motorcycle revved, calling all listeners to the freedom of the open road.

Vince couldn't remember a time free of responsibilities, even when he was a kid. "Before we go, I need one thing to be clear. My family will expect us—"

"We're not sleeping together." Harley

moved her hand to the door, as if preparing to jump out.

Ouch. Vince hadn't expected that to hurt, either.

"The friend-zone isn't a deal-breaker, so be it." Her eyes were glued to the skyscrapers downtown, as if she longed to return to her former life as an architect, where everything had been rosy until she'd encountered one bump in the road.

If she thought being an architect was hard, she was learning that construction could be just as demoralizing. There was a price to be paid for every decision you made in life. Best if she learned that now, before she hit thirty.

The motorcycle came into view. One of those colorful Japanese models young guys rode to pop wheelies and do spin-outs and cheat death.

"It's not a deal-breaker. But this might be." Vince waited until Harley met his gaze, waited an extra few moments for the feeling that he shouldn't take her to materialize, but it didn't. "I was expected to bring a plus-one to the wedding."

"You say that as if you told your family

who to expect." Her eyes narrowed. "Who was supposed to go with you?"

He couldn't tell if there was resentment or jealousy in her voice. "They're expecting the woman I've been dating…or, rather the woman who broke up with me last month."

"*I* broke up with you last month." The corner of her mouth twitched up and then just as quickly turned down. "And you never told me you weren't interested in marriage."

"It never came up." And it had never come to mind. They'd had fun together, seemingly without strings. She'd made no mention of settling down. "I like women, but I'm not going to have kids, which means most women either don't want to date me or date me with the hopes of changing my mind. And when they realize my mind's made up, they tend to leave. Promptly."

"It's a moot point now." Her words had an impersonal quality, which gave everything away—her desire for a picket fence, her longing for children, her expectation that he might have shared either dream.

But she didn't get out of the truck.

So far, so good. "Unfortunately my brothers don't agree with my decision to stay single and childless."

"Ah, here's where the nutty part comes in," she surmised.

"There's no nutty. Forget the nutty!" Vince took a deep breath and forced himself to speak calmly. "Over the years, I've told my brothers I was too busy to come home, citing long hours on the job or an intense relationship" To keep them from delving too deeply into why he stayed in Texas and to discourage them from coming to visit. "Each time they press, I fend them off, this time with a relationship."

Her slender brows drew together. "Are you telling me you aren't man enough to confess to your brothers you don't have a girlfriend?"

She made it sound so cowardly.

He rejected cowardice in favor of practicality and shook his head. "I'm telling you…" His tongue slowed and tried to spin her a lie. "I'm telling you…" Usually, he never stumbled over words, or anything, for that matter. This whole trip was like looking under the hood of a foreign, high-end electric car and not recognizing anything. "I'm telling you that I don't want my brothers to know I'm single. Everyone is happy with how things are. Your job is to help me keep it that way."

"You're such a girl, Messina." She grinned and slugged his shoulder.

It took Vince a moment for the meaning of her words to sink in. Even then, he wasn't sure and had to ask, "So you'll go?"

"I'll go." She stretched her legs and put her elbow on the windowsill. "This should be fun."

Fun? Not hardly. This was survival.

Vince put the truck in gear and headed toward the airport and the wedding, which he was now convinced was as disaster-laden as the combustible oil rig he'd once worked on.

HARLEY WANTED TO make sure a week spent with Vince would not be fun.

For one thing, she'd packed clothes that were practical, ones she could dress up or dress down. Today, she wore jeans and a tank top because she wanted to reinforce a boundary with Vince—this was a deal, not a date. She shouldn't have worried. He didn't talk to Harley much on the flight to California.

She took some of the blame for that. She'd had several restless nights leading up to the trip, worried about bills, her career, and Dan. She'd slept nearly the entire plane ride, as if the farther she went from her old boss and her old life, the more relaxed she became. And when they landed, she'd been in awe. She'd never been out of the South. And California wasn't the South. Not by a long shot.

In Houston, the buildings were tall and spaced far enough apart you could appreciate their architecture. In San Francisco, the buildings were crammed together and the roads were narrow. She had to crane her neck to see anything.

In the South, you'd leave the city and see miles of rolling hills, towering pines, scrub oak and wide, muddy rivers. In California, you'd barely leave one city, catch a glimpse of a narrow river, a random sheep pasture, or a field of wild grass, and then reach another city.

There were mountains in California and big rolling hills covered with brown grass or green vineyards. Billboards proclaimed wine tasting at the next exit. And the next. And the next. They could have tasted wine all the way to his hometown.

And they might have if they'd been a real couple. If she hadn't bragged that she had two degrees, they might still be dating. Or not, if Vince had told her he wasn't interested in having kids. Harley would have considered that as much of a red flag as him assuming a lack of maturity on her part for quitting her profession.

They'd separated before their relationship had had a chance to blossom. It'd been a disappointment to let Vince go and it'd been awkward a time or two at work, but her heart hadn't broken.

Unfortunately it hadn't moved on completely, either. This pretense was ridiculous, but it would bring home the fact that she and Vince weren't destined to be together. Their everyday lives would diverge, just as soon as Harley figured out an acceptable fix to delicate balconies or her four-year clause lapsed. Whichever came first.

They reached Cloverdale and stopped to top off the tank before they drove to Harmony Valley, or what Vince kept calling the middle of nowhere.

"I'll be right back." Harley hurried inside the gas station and returned a short time later waving a lottery ticket. "My mother always says you never know when luck is going to find you." She'd scrounged change from beneath the seat of her truck before they'd left Houston for just such a chance at fortune.

Vince looked as if he thought she should have put her spare change in a bank account. "What does your father say to that?"

"That he got lucky when he found Mom." Her father may be balding, but he was a true prince. "Do your parents have any funny sayings?"

"Not that I remember." He steered the rented SUV toward a two-lane road lined with tall eucalyptus. "My dad died when I was in high school."

"I'm so sorry." Why hadn't she known this? The answer lay somewhere between she'd been too busy being flattered that he was interested in her and she hadn't been curious about his past while she was in his arms. "That must have been hard on everyone. How did your mom take it?"

Vince spared her a hooded glance. "My mom left us before that."

"Oh, Vince. That's sad." She couldn't imagine her mom leaving the family. "Did she remarry? Did you ever see her again?"

"I found her a couple of years ago." His voice was flat, as if he was imparting driving directions to the local morgue. "She lives outside Houston. She seems happy."

Harley angled her knees toward him, prepared to hear all the details. "What did she say when you faced her?"

"I didn't pursue it. I just found out where she'd been all those years and that was enough." If Harley had expected him to express hurt or anger with that statement, she'd have been disappointed. There was nothing, not so much as a too rapid eye-blink to indicate his mother's leaving or location or lack of contact bothered him.

"But...weren't you curious about why she left? Or why she never looked back?"

"No." He fell silent, leaving Harley to wonder about his past, his brothers, and what kind of greeting she'd receive as Vince's girlfriend.

"I've been thinking about our relationship," Harley said. At Vince's blank look, she added, "You know, our *pretend* relationship and how we're going to act in front of others. I say, you can hold my hand every once in awhile."

"Whoa, whoa, whoa." Vince took his foot off the gas. "I need more than handholding to throw my brothers a curve ball when they try to get too personal. Besides, no one's going to believe we're a couple if there's no PDA."

"Why do we need public displays of affection?" Harley crossed her arms over her chest, refusing to be distracted by the cumulus clouds above a hundred-year-old, two-story farmhouse in the middle of a vineyard, or the contrast of straight lines and flowing curves. "People who date have personal boundaries."

"We didn't." He blinked at the road and then at her. "We walked with my arm around you. I kissed you when I wanted to."

She practically convulsed with shock. "There will be no kissing!" Because, like everything else, Vince was good at it.

"Nobody's going to believe that we're a couple if I don't kiss you."

"Why?" The butterflies were fluttering in her chest, practically flying in formation to spell Kiss Him. "Butterflies are stupid," she murmured.

"What?"

Harley gave herself a mental head thunk. She'd have to be on her toes with Vince or she'd be right back to Waco. "Do you have a reputation for kissing girlfriends in public or something?"

"No!" He gave the SUV more gas. "Where do you get your ideas?"

"From you and your prepubescent statements about PDAs." She needed to find something else to talk about. "Besides, you said you wanted me to come because of the ex-girlfriend."

"And then I said I needed you because of my brothers."

Butterflies and memories of kisses aside, teasing Vince was kind of fun. She'd never gotten under his skin when they were dating, except when they'd argued over her quitting architecture. "Why do you think they worry about you?"

"They don't worry. They have too much time on their hands," he grumbled, slowing to make a left turn. "They give me grief about every little thing, so I make it a practice to tell them nothing."

"Giving grief is what brothers do," she said smartly. "Take that away and they're like dogs without a bone. Besides, maybe they should worry about you. I bet they didn't travel halfway across the United

States to find a woman and then not make contact with her."

"You want to talk about questionable decisions?" He raised his dark brows. "I'm not the one who got roughed up by a boyfriend who also broke her means of employment."

"If Dan hadn't busted my saw, I wouldn't be here helping you." She needed to correct Vince's assumption about Dan being her boyfriend. "And he—"

"Helping me?" Vince grumbled louder. "That would require kisses."

She bit her lower lip to keep from smiling. "I'll tell you what. I'll kiss your cheek when you fix my saw."

"Lot of good a chaste peck on the cheek will do me when we're back in Texas." He'd turned on a side road and slowed to a crawl. "I ordered the parts. It's a delicate piece of equipment and I might not be able to resuscitate it."

They approached a dead-end street to the right. A sign with an arrow pointed toward the Messina Family Garage, which was a two-story, two service-bay building several hundred feet down the road. It looked to have been built in the fifties: straight lines, no gables, a box turned upside down. Behind it was a small, equally boring ranch home.

Across the road from the repair shop was a field with about a dozen cars half hidden by tall grass. A handful of people were poking around. Beyond that was a mowed strip of grass near a bridge. On it sat an odd cluster of things. A Volkswagen made of stacked stone, a rusted swing set and an old yellow tractor with what appeared to be a mermaid made of metal riding a bicycle behind it.

A woman in the field waved to them.

"Is that your family?"

"Yes." The SUV inched forward as if Vince was having second thoughts. "I could loan you money for the saw in exchange for a well-timed kiss or two."

"You?" A shout of laughter escaped her lips. "Loan me money?"

"What's so funny?" He braked and faced her, scowling.

"You're cheap."

"How can you say that?" His black eyes flashed and he choked the steering wheel. "I took you to Waco. I'm taking you to California. All expenses paid."

"You're cheap." She'd known he was nice, but she hadn't realized his ego could be so easily bruised. She couldn't stop smiling. "The first time we went out, we went to a bar and left when happy hour was over."

"We went after work." His expression darkened, brows dropping thunderously low. "And first dates aren't supposed to last more than a few hours."

"You never brought me flowers. I thought guys your age always brought flowers and wine when a woman cooked for them." She wasn't pulling any punches in defense of her No Kissing policy. "And we went places like the art gallery on free entry day and the farmers market, also free. Plus, in Waco, we stayed in one of those budget motels out by the highway."

"That was the only hotel that had rooms available!" He was practically howling with anger. "And sue me for wanting to go places where we could talk. Maybe that's more important to someone *my age* than paying to have someone sit next to me during a movie without learning anything about them."

"I'm not saying I didn't like going places and talking to you." Her smile threatened to slip, because apparently she'd been yakking about herself the entire time they were together without paying attention to him. "I'm just saying—"

"And I *decided* not to buy you flowers the one time I came to your place for dinner because there was an accident on the interstate and I was running late!" He huffed like a winded bull unsure if he was done seeing red.

She reached over and pressed a hand to his arm, as if to say she understood. They hadn't exchanged enough words between them in the past, at least, not about his past or a vision of his future. "I see where you're coming from now. Thank you for offering to buy me a saw, but I can't accept." She'd get through this rough patch, even if it took her four years of tile work to do so.

All eyes in the field were pointed their way. Thankfully, with the windows rolled up and the air conditioner on, his family probably hadn't heard a word of their conversation.

Vince sighed. "I could turn around and put you on a plane home."

"I'd be willing to bet when we get to the airport you'd hop on the plane with me." Whatever was bothering Vince about coming home, he needed to face it, just as she needed to continue to try to solve the balcony conundrum.

"You picked a bad time to be right." Vince parked in a space at the garage. Three tables and several chairs were set up, as if there'd been a lot of outdoor eating going on. "Since you're a city girl, be prepared for questions about you and about us, and not just from my family."

She'd forgotten she was touching him. Her hand dropped away. "If not your family, then who?"

"Only the entire town." He gave her a stern look. "And don't go telling them I'm cheap."

"You're such a girl, Messina." It needed to be said.

"You won't think it's so funny when reality hits." He glanced over his shoulder toward the field. "They'll want to know everything about you... About us."

"I'll stick to the truth as much as possible." What was he so worried about? Impulsively she stroked his thick, silky hair from crown to neck, the way she used to when they'd been dating. "It'll be okay."

He didn't look so sure.

"Let's have a code word," she said, still

feeling protective. "You know, if things start to get out of control, let's say something like 'It's getting hot in here.' And that's our cue to make our excuses and leave."

"Good idea."

Someone in the field shouted his name.

Harley twisted around. "What are they doing over there?"

"Hauling junkers away, preparing the space for the ceremony. They'll expect us to help."

"It's getting hot in here."

Vince laughed.

She'd missed his laughter. It was deep and hearty and settled stray butterflies.

"Here they come." Vince got out of the SUV, as somber and stoic as if they were going to face a zombie apocalypse.

Harley smiled. For the first time since agreeing to be Vince's date, Harley thought she might actually have fun at this wedding.

CHAPTER FOUR

THE CLOSER VINCE had come to Harmony Valley, the more he'd wanted to turn around.

Harley's joking banter had helped, but she couldn't keep him from falling into the past, not when he stood on the property he'd grown up on.

He'd learned to ride a bike on that driveway, with Mom running beside him. He'd learned to throw a football in that field, with Mom cheering him from the sidelines. And then there'd been the milestones she'd missed. His driver's test. Prom. Graduation.

It'd been worse for Joe, who'd been younger, the baby of the family Mom had doted on. If Joe knew where Mom was, he'd be thrown off-kilter. He might try to contact Mom. Both of them might be hurt. The Messina family was in a safe place. Why rock the boat? Mama drama was the last thing Joe needed just days before his wedding.

"Gosh, the Messina boys are big," Harley said, standing next to Vince.

His brothers sprinted across the field toward Vince, whooping and hollering as if they were in their teens not their thirties.

Gabe slammed into him first, wrapping his arms around Vince and lifting him a couple inches off the ground. He was a mountain of a man with the strength and rigid posture gained from years in the military. But not even the Marines could wipe away the mischievous gleam in his eyes. *"Vince!"* He dropped Vince back on his feet. "How many years has it been?"

"Almost six." That's when they'd gathered for Joe's first wife's funeral in Los Angeles.

Joe hugged Vince with a set of hearty backslaps. He was clearly the runt of the family. He'd never filled out the way Vince and Gabe had. "It's been too long, brother."

"It has been," Vince agreed, feeling some of his misgivings evaporate. He attributed it to the lack of humidity in the air, and two family members happy to see him.

"And who have we here?" Gabe claimed Harley's hand and kissed it.

She laughed and Vince felt a stab of something he didn't recognize in his chest.

He made the introductions, saving Harley's hand from Gabe's because she'd said she didn't like PDA and probably wouldn't like it from his come-on-too-strong brother. "Watch out for Gabe. He used to steal my clothes and my girlfriends."

Harley's cheeks turned a soft shade of pink.

Vince didn't let go of her hand. Totally because of appearances.

A pint-size girl wearing dirt-stained coveralls crashed into Vince's chest next. "Uncle Vince!" His niece Samantha grinned up at him. Her hair was dark brown and just as short as the last time he'd seen her. But instead of looking as if Joe had hacked it with sheep shearers, it was stylishly cut and straightened.

If she was styling her hair, the next step was wearing makeup, talking to boys, and refusing to do oil changes because it wrecked her manicure. "Sam, don't grow anymore."

Samantha shushed him. Her cheeks turned a brighter shade of pink than Harley's. "You're embarrassing me." She glanced furtively at a dark-haired teenage boy, who looked to be about thirteen and was staring at Sam the way Sam had once stared at the stuffed beagle Vince had given her when her mother died.

Vince exchanged a quick what-the-heck glance with Joe, who gave him a subtle calm-down gesture.

"And here's the other love of my life." Joe introduced his fiancée. "Brittany."

Vince's soon-to-be sister-in-law had a thick mane of brown hair with golden highlights, a wide smile that sparkled, and natural makeup. Like Sam, she also wore smudged coveralls. This was no high-maintenance female, even though she ran the town's beauty salon.

Vince liked Brittany immediately. "Welcome to the family." He hugged her warmly.

"Call me Brit." Joe's bride-to-be inched out of Vince's hug. "Joe, why do all your brothers have such gorgeous manes?" She ran her fingers through Vince's hair.

Vince jolted backward until Brit's hands fell away. "It's getting hot in here."

Harley laughed, no help at all.

"Hey, honey, your hands should only be in my hair." But Joe laughed and added, "And that of your paying clients, of course."

Harley was still chuckling, ignoring Vince's

SOS, which he decided to excuse when she reclaimed his hand. "Their hair is unreal, isn't it, Brit?"

"Times three." Brit ignored Joe's warning and ruffled Gabe's hair. "I'm a hairdresser. It's hard not to touch it."

"I don't see what all the fuss is about," Vince said, meaning it. They all had thick, black hair. So what? Joe's hair was a bit too long for a man about to be married and Gabe's was military short. Vince's was somewhere in between.

"Who cares?" Gabe leaned over to give Brit better access to his scalp. "I could get used to this."

"Don't," Joe said firmly, tugging Brit away from his oldest brother. "I draw the line at making Gabe happy. He teased me mercilessly when we were kids."

"Oh, Shaggy Joe." Brit snuggled close to Joe the way Harley had snuggled close to Vince when they were in Waco. "I love your hair best."

Vince glanced down at Harley, which wasn't far considering how tall she was. "I think you should limit your hands to my hair, too." His words came out low and in-

timate. He might just as well have been saying, *You should limit your lips to mine, too.*

Harley got the message. She tried to ease
away, but Vince held on. To her hand. To
her gaze.

"Dear brothers, stop with the googly
eyes." Gabe turned toward the field, looking like he was on duty. "Come on, Sam.
When Brit calls your dad Shaggy Joe, it's
time to vacate the premises."

"Googly eyes are disgusting." Sam pulled
a face.

"Gabe's complaining about googly eyes?"
Vince taunted good-naturedly. "He's lucky
Harley and I don't make out right now."

Harley made a disapproving noise.
"You're impossible."

For show, Vince smiled fondly at Harley.
No kisses? Yeah, he'd make her pay a little
for that.

His wedding date huffed and crossed her
arms over her chest.

"Brad." Gabe shook his finger at the teenage boy. "If I ever catch you looking with
googly eyes at my niece, I'm going to drop
you off that bridge."

Sam gasped and glared at Gabe.

"Why would you say that?" She hissed like an angry cat. "Why?"

"Because I'm your uncle and I love you." Gabe gave her a devilish grin cut from the same cloth as Vince's.

"I will never." Sam raised her hands heavenward. "Look at anyone. Like. That."

Vince had a feeling Sam would eat those words someday.

Still grumbling, Vince's teenage niece took off running. Sam's admirer joined her as she raced past him. Gabe plodded behind them at his own pace.

"Joe, don't give that boy an inch with Sam." Vince nodded toward the young pair. "She's too young to be interested in boys."

"Brad knows what the rules are and respects them, unlike Gabe at that age." Joe grinned and it was like looking in a mirror, except for his eyes. Joe was the only Messina who had their mother's blue eyes. "I hope those are clothes you can get dirty, because we could use an extra pair of hands."

Vince took stock of his blue jeans and polo shirt, as well as Harley's similarly casual attire. "We're good. Are you hooking cars up to the tow truck and taking them somewhere?"

"One at a time?" Joe shook his head. "That would cost a fortune in gas. We found a scrap hauler willing to take the rest away with a double-decker semi-trailer. He comes tomorrow."

"The rest?" Harley shaded her eyes for a better view. "How many cars are there?"

"Joe already got some running and sold them." Brit started walking, beckoning Harley to join her. Next to Brit, Harley looked like a beanpole, as if she lacked curves.

So not true.

Harley's curves were subtle, like her personality.

"We just need to clear the debris between the cars and the road," Brit was saying. "And then tow them into a line them up on the edge of the pavement for the hauler to take them away."

"That sounds easy," Harley said without having any clue how labor intensive it really was.

Vince and Joe fell into step behind the women.

"It would go so much faster if my soon-to-be-wife wouldn't have to look at every piece of debris." Joe wasn't fooling anyone with his complaint. His tone was indulgent.

"I'm an upcycle artist." Brit sniffed and tossed her head. "When I'm not doing hair, junk sculpture is my life."

"You did the mermaids?" Harley pointed to a sculpture of a mermaid on a bicycle above the service bays.

Vince followed the direction of Harley's finger.

Designed in metal and painted bright green, the mermaid rode on a red, white and blue surfboard above the service bay doors. There was another mermaid on the grass near the bridge.

"Yep," Brit said cheerfully. "Mermaids are my thing. You should see the one in my beauty salon. Kiera is my masterpiece."

Vince couldn't stop staring at the repair shop. He couldn't look away. His steps slowed. The sun disappeared behind a cloud.

It should run! It should run! Dad's freaked-out voice. His silhouette seemed to move through the empty service bay, pacing.

It'll be all right. Mom's shadow was close at his heels. *Let's try it again, Vince.*

"The place is different now," Joe said quietly, having stopped beside Vince. "We've made changes. It doesn't feel as if it was ever his."

His. Their father's. A man plagued by voices in his head.

"And there's no trace of her here, either," Joe said resentfully.

Her. Their mother. A woman who'd spent years trying to make peace with her husband's many moods to shelter her children from instability, until she became unstable herself.

Vince acknowledged Joe's comment with a grunt, the only sound he was capable of making.

They moved even with the house. This time it wasn't a gloomy shadow Vince felt but the icy hand of guilt. His actions had left their family without a reliable parent.

"We're remodeling the house." Joe's words rang with pride. "We tore down interior walls, ripped out all the flooring and removed everything in the bathrooms. You wouldn't recognize it."

Oh, Vince bet he would.

He bet he could mark an X on the spot where Dad had his after-work meltdowns. Or stand in the kitchen where Mom would smoke with the window open, hoping Dad didn't notice the tinge of nicotine in the air.

Vince walked faster.

"Sam and I are living in the apartment above the garage until the house is done." Joe stopped Vince with a hand on his arm. "I'm saving to buy you out."

They stood in front of Vince's old bedroom window. There was a reason nothing had ever grown beneath that sill. After dark, he and Gabe had used it as their own personal entrance.

"You don't have to pay me." The three brothers had inherited the property. Vince didn't want anything from Harmony Valley.

"I can't give you top dollar." Joe set his chin the way he had when he was a kid and Vince had told him to go away. "This place was a wreck when we got here. Any value in it is coming directly from my pocket."

"Keep your money. I don't need it."

"Say what you want. There's a check coming your way." Joe walked on, back stiff with all his honorable intentions.

If Joe had gone to Texas, he'd have done things differently. He'd have showed up at their mother's door, introduced himself and told her off.

Vince lingered behind, taking in the property, the small house, the modest business, the cluttered field. Joe might believe things looked different now.

To Vince, things looked exactly the same.

"HOW ARE YOU holding up?" Vince asked Harley hours after they'd started.

He crossed the trampled paths they'd created to get the cars out, looking attractively scruffy.

Harley's butterflies threatened to return.

Vince was eye candy. Not checkout-stand eye candy. Nothing that low quality. No. Vince was like the big Easter eggs Harley's mother bought once a year from the gourmet chocolate shop. When Harley was a kid, she'd thought the fist-size eggs would be filled with more chocolate or thick cream. But, no, they'd been hollow. And so was Vince, carrots aside.

He wanted to project an image that wasn't real to the people he should have been closest to. That was something she shouldn't forget.

"Let's take a break," he said.

Vince stopped in front of Harley and peered at her face the way a doctor once had after she'd gotten a concussion trying to play basketball. That concussion had her sitting the rest of the season. Not that Harley considered that a failure. Being on the team had made her well-rounded on her college applications. She didn't need or want playing time. She'd learned her lesson. Playing was dangerous.

Vince, with his thought-stealing kissing talent, supreme good looks and thought-stealing kissing talent—yes, it needed to be said twice—was dangerous. Harley knew about head-spinning danger. She was staying on the bench.

Vince took Harley's hand and led her toward the garage, dragging her along like a small anchor behind a big boat. "We'll check in."

"I'll go with you." Gabe fell into step next to Harley, as energetic as an over-sugared fifth-grader.

"Gabe, it's five. Harley's tired and she's a guest of ours." It was Vince who sounded tired, no doubt worn out by his emotional homecoming.

Harley had seen how Vince's gaze shadowed sometimes when he looked at his family's garage. "I'm fine, but we can go if you like."

"Harley?" Vince quirked an eyebrow. "You just told me you're tired, didn't you?"

She'd forgotten their scam, having been too busy thinking about his thought-stealing kissing talent. "Yeah. Sure."

"I'm feeling a bit weary, too," Gabe said, still his happy-go-lucky self.

"I just want to spend some time alone with my girlfriend," Vince snapped. "Is that too much to ask?"

"Well, now I feel selfish." Brit stopped inspecting an old car nearby and frowned at them. "I'm a bridezilla without realizing it. There's just so much to do around here for the wedding and the house."

"It's okay," Harley said. "I don't mind helping." That was no lie.

The Messinas were fun to be around. Brad and Sam danced about like puppies who didn't understand exactly why they liked each other. Gabe wielded verbal volleys, taking shots at everyone, including Harley. The bride and groom snuck sweet kisses when they thought no one was looking. And through it all, they treated Harley as if she was one of their own.

"I think you guys should get going," Gabe said unexpectedly. "In fact, I'll make reservations at El Rosal for you. My treat." He tugged a cell phone out of his pocket. "And while you eat, I can make sure your reservation is ready at the B and B."

Vince tried to topple Gabe with a suspicious stare, but his brother didn't fold.

"That's very thoughtful of you." Harley moved into peace-keeping mode.

"Gabe isn't thoughtful," Vince grumbled.

"Maybe I was selfish when I was younger and you outshone me with your huge talent underneath the hood." An angel would have believed Gabe's sincerity. He looked that earnest. "But I'm a changed man today."

Vince scoffed.

"What do you do for a living, Harley?" Again, Gabe's tone was innocuous. His smile that of an angel.

"She's an architect," Vince said before Harley could tell Gabe she was a tile installer. Vince gave Harley a look that telegraphed *Let me handle this*.

"How did you meet an architect working on an oil rig?" Gone was the angel. Gabe looked and sounded more like a hound dog on the trail of a fox.

"Vince doesn't work on an oil rig anymore." Harley pretended she was unable to translate Vince's Morse code. Stick to the truth. Wasn't that what they'd agreed? "I met him on a job site."

They'd reached the parking lot.

"I'm working as a carpenter now," Vince said through stiff lips.

Harley couldn't fathom why he wouldn't want his family to know about his job change or why he hadn't told her his occupation was on a need-to-know basis. This was about his status quo, not hers.

They reached the door to the repair garage's office.

"Brother, why don't you use the shop sink to wash up?" Gabe opened the door and pointed to the stairs. "I'll show Harley the second-floor facilities."

Vince's eyes narrowed.

"Sounds good," Harley said, moving upstairs. Part of her role here was to stop Vince's brothers from pestering him. A little distance between the siblings was called for.

The door at the top of the stairs led to a small, homey apartment with a galley kitchen. The kitchen table and living room furniture weren't stylish retro, they were just old, yet well cared for. Three doors faced her. Two were closed. The open door revealed the bathroom. Harley went in and cleaned up.

When she emerged, Gabe was standing in front of the TV stand that didn't have a TV. Instead family photos graced the top. He set one back down.

"I don't want you to take this wrong." Gabe sounded a lot like Harley's protective older brother Taylor—overly confident and a tad self-important. Both characteristics were softened by Gabe's unabashedly friendly smile. "I like you, but I know you aren't dating my brother."

Harley's shoulders pinched in a near flinch at his assessment. She didn't like lying, but she'd made an agreement with Vince to pretend they were dating. And there was just something about Gabe's accusation that raised her competitive hackles. She'd never liked losing to Taylor, not in checkers and not in verbal chess.

"Really?" Harley forced out a chuckle and crossed the room to study the framed photo Gabe had been looking at. "Present your case, counselor."

Gabe rubbed his hands together, clearly pleased that Harley hadn't taken offense.

"First off, there's your age difference.

How old are you?" Not only did Gabe have no filter, he had no sense of boundaries. If it wasn't for his good-natured demeanor, he would've been annoying. "I'm guessing twenty-four?"

"I'm almost twenty-seven." Harley bent for a closer look. The photo Gabe had set down was of the three teenage Messina boys straddling motorcycles. An older man stood behind them with the same thick, dark hair and lady-killer grin as the boys. Their father? Harley leaned closer, taking in Vince's multicolored striped shirt that seemed too short, blue jeans that seemed too long, and a grin that seemed too wide.

"When I was twenty-three, I dated a girl who said she was eighteen." Gabe watched Harley closely, a spider patiently studying the fly. "Her daddy came after me with a shotgun."

"Well, if we're challenging each other's relationships, I'd like to see the scars on your backside." Harley straightened and laughed, more genuinely this time. "Are you implying I'm too young for Vince?"

"I think I'm spinning it the other way around." He waggled his dark brows.

Harley shook her head. "Nice try, but seven years isn't that big of a deal."

"Sweetheart, it's nearly eight years." Gabe flashed a trouble-making grin. "More in dog years."

"Clearly, it makes no difference to us." Harley rolled her eyes. Gabe could have been cloned from the same genes as her brother.

"Clearly, there's no zing between you two." Gabe's grin didn't dim. "I'm only challenging your claim because we had a rough childhood and I feel responsible for my younger brother. You know, protective."

"Pfft." Gabe was more transparent than a new window in an old house. "You and Joe have a bet."

Gabe's eyes widened and then he began to laugh and nod. "Yep. Joe and I have a bet. Joe says you're legit."

Harley wanted to put Gabe in his place. And the only way she could think of doing it was to mention something personal about Vince, something he'd only tell a girlfriend, not an acquaintance. "Was this photo taken after your mother left for Texas?"

His smile disappearing faster than a cockroach on a midnight raid in the kitchen. "What did you say?"

Too late, Harley realized Vince must not have told his brothers about his mother's location.

Vince opened the door, not looking like a man happy to see his girlfriend. No doubt, his expression would turn thunderous if Gabe asked about their mother.

The smart move would be to smile and make her escape, nose in the air. But then, nothing Harley had done this summer had been smart.

Instead she crossed the room, latched onto the collar of Vince's polo shirt and kissed him hard.

CHAPTER FIVE

"I THOUGHT YOU said you wanted a kiss." Harley's nose was out of joint. She pushed through the door to El Rosal, Harmony Valley's Mexican restaurant, without waiting for Vince to open it. "I gave you one. End of discussion."

Vince followed Harley inside, past a chalkboard posting early bird specials. He glanced over his shoulder to watch Gabe walking across the town square toward the Lambridge Bed and Breakfast. What was his fun-loving, meddlesome brother up to now?

Something had happened between his brother and Harley upstairs. Gabe's good-humored bluster had been deflated. He'd ridden in the back of Vince's rented SUV to the restaurant in near silence. Gabe was never silent. And with his brother's mouth on mute, Vince couldn't fully enjoy Harley's kiss.

She'd claimed him with that kiss, branding his lips in a way that still burned.

Oh, something had happened between Gabe and Harley, all right. And good or bad, Vince had benefitted from it.

Harley had grabbed him, then released him and marched out of the apartment. Vince had followed in the same stilted way a mummy followed its master.

The shock was wearing off. Or maybe it was the loud, bustling atmosphere in El Rosal.

The restaurant's walls, tables and chairs were painted in primary colors: bright reds, yellows, blues and greens. The flat-screen television mounted above the bar was tuned to a muted baseball game. Pop music sung in Spanish filled the air. It wasn't even five-thirty, but the restaurant was packed, primarily with white-haired patrons, many of them having conversations at a volume that indicated their hearing aids might not be switched on.

Over a decade ago, the grain mill in town had exploded and the company subsequently shut down. Being Harmony Valley's primary employer, jobs had dried up and with it businesses had closed their doors. Younger families had moved to find jobs and new opportunities. Older residents had hunkered down and stayed in their homes.

Now there was a new local employer, a small but growing winery. According to Joe, the bulk of the population was still over the age of sixty. And here was the proof. White-haired patrons dining on early bird specials.

A waitress led Harley to a table by the plate-glass window looking out on the town square and its lone oak tree.

She dropped into a yellow chair and hid behind the menu.

Vince sat across from Harley, studying the long, limp hair hooked behind her ears. She hadn't looked this tired when she'd gone upstairs to clean up. "What did Gabe say that upset you? Whatever it was, I'll talk to him." Which was polite brother speak for an exchange of punches.

"Nothing." Her blue eyes flashed over the top of the menu. "I let him get under my skin. The jet lag is catching up to me."

He wasn't sure he believed her, but something, almost like relief, allowed Vince to draw a deep breath, to pick up the menu, to realize he was hungry.

"You'll want the mole chicken tacos." An

elderly woman who could stand-in for Mrs. Claus sat at the next table. She had thick, round glasses and thick, round curls.

She seemed vaguely familiar, but so did over half the restaurant patrons.

Across from her, an elderly Japanese man shook his finger at Vince in a friendly way. "I know you. You're one of the Messina boys."

"Yes. I'm Vince." Vince braced himself for a chilly reception, having left town with a less-than-stellar reputation.

Mrs. Claus gasped and adjusted her glasses, squinting at him. "I should have known from all that black hair." She reached across the aisle and gripped Vince's hand as if she was happy to see him. "I used to admire how you handled a motorcycle."

Vince didn't know what to say. The compliment was unexpected.

"Not me," the old man said, not at all embarrassed to admit it. "Don't you remember how they'd speed through town, Mildred? Motors so loud it hurt your ears."

Mildred tsked. "I suppose you don't remember how I used to speed through town and up Parish Hill, either." Mildred released Vince with a sigh. "The worst thing about getting old has been losing my eyesight and giving up driving. I miss burning rubber coming out of second gear."

"Mildred Parsons?" The name suddenly clicked. She'd been a race car driver in her youth, one of the few adults to earn the respect of the Messina boys.

"Yes." When Mildred smiled, the resemblance to the mythical Mrs. Claus increased. "And this is my beau, Hero Takata."

Vince aimed a good-natured finger back at the man. "Old Man Takata?" The man who used to own the cemetery? The man who'd buried Dad?

"Some still call me by that name." Hero smiled, bringing wrinkles to an otherwise ageless-looking face. "I'm older today than I was when I yelled at kids like you for running across my grass."

Old Man Takata had lived on a corner down the street from the town square, a house located between the school and the ice cream parlor. Of course, kids wanted to cut the corner.

"Is this your wife?" Mildred blinked at Harley, but in a way that created doubt as to whether or not she actually saw her. "Do you have children? A little cousin for Sam to play with?"

"No," Vince blurted. "No on all counts."

Harley slanted a gaze at him that disapproved, folded her menu, and said, "I'm his date for the wedding."

The boundaries that came along with her tone riled something inside Vince, and made him want to refute her statement. Which only went to prove that Harmony Valley was getting under his skin exactly like Gabe had gotten under Harley's.

"Spoken like a woman who doesn't need a man." Mildred did a sort of snuffle-chuckle. "Bravo. What's your name, my dear?"

Harley introduced herself.

The waitress brought Hero's change and Mildred's walker, which she unfolded and set between their two tables.

"Vince," Hero said, dropping his change into his wallet. "Don't take this personally, but I'll report you if I see you speeding."

Joe had mentioned how hard it was to be accepted by the town, but Vince hadn't believed people would be so blatant about it. He felt the beginnings of a headache.

"Hero will only see you if you speed down Main." Mildred stood, staring in the general direction of Vince's face. "I'll see Harley at the bridal shower, and we'll see you two at the Couples Dinner." And then her gaze swiveled toward Harley. "We'll beat you, of course."

Harley smiled in polite confusion. The subtleties of her expression probably went unnoticed by Mildred.

The server was waiting for her order, smiling patiently at her elderly guests as if Hero had given her a good tip.

Hero got to his feet with the aid of a cane. "They'll have the mole chicken tacos, Leti."

The couple moved slowly toward the door.

Leti disappeared into the kitchen.

"I think we're having the mole chicken tacos," Vince said, realizing their menus were gone. "Welcome to Harmony Valley."

"I think we should talk about the Couples Dinner." A grin twitched one corner of Harley's cheek. "It's a competition?"

"We can assume it won't be a dancing one," Vince said, nodding toward the elderly couple moving slowly down the sidewalk.

"Or a mudder." Harley seemed to notice there was chips and salsa on the table, and dove in. "What is a Couples Dinner?"

"This is the first I've heard of it." Vince

managed to insert a chip into the salsa bowl she was hoarding. "The good news is Gabe won't be there, seeing as how he doesn't have a date for the wedding."

"I heard the Messina boys were back in town." An elderly man with shoulders bowed forward leaned on their table with gnarled, age-spotted hands. He wore a wrinkled burgundy-checked flannel shirt, sleeves buttoned at his wrists, and smelled like he could use a shower or his clothes a washing. "Are you right in the head?"

Vince choked on his bite of chip. The rest of it crumpled to the table.

"If not, we don't want you here." The old man pushed off and wobbled backward. "Had enough of that with your father. He jumped me in a bar fight once. No warning. Just *pow*."

Because of the shock, Vince couldn't speak. He couldn't move. He could only watch the old man shuffle away.

"Are you okay?" Harley switched chairs so that she sat next to him. She slid her hand to the nape of his neck. "Breathe in, breath out, remember? What was that about?"

Vince drank half the water in his glass before he attempted to speak. "My dad…"

His voice sounded like sandpaper on metal. "My dad…"

He didn't want to tell her.

"Drink some more." Her hand shifted lower, rubbing across his shoulder blades. "But don't rush it." A minute passed, maybe longer.

He wanted to lean into her touch. He wanted to get up and run away without explaining.

One thought coalesced: it was a mistake to have brought her here.

With every greeting, with every event, his past was catching up to him. And Harley, as witness, was curious and wanting answers.

On some level, he supposed he owed her some.

"My dad had schizophrenia." His words came out drenched in emotion and vulnerability, when he wanted to be detached and strong. He couldn't meet her gaze, but he couldn't stop speaking, either. "And depression. He was diagnosed late in life. That man…" Whoever he was. "He could have been referencing a time before Dad was diagnosed." Or not. There was no magic solution for mental health challenges.

"I'm sorry."

"I don't want your pity." There was the strong, detached tone he'd been looking for. Inappropriate now.

"I wasn't offering pity." Harley's hand dropped away. She moved back into her chair. "I'm sorry your dad had mental health issues. And I'm sorry that man was rude to you."

Harley was compassionate. Genuine. And the first to give the benefit of the doubt.

"That was...rude of me," Vince said, struggling to find words when he was un-accustomed to explaining himself. "I didn't have my guard up and he got to me. I took it out on you. I'm the one who should apologize." And he did.

She stared at him a little too long, not smiling. Earlier in the summer, he would have held her gaze with a hint of a smile and then coaxed a smile out of her. He would have reached for her hand and drawn her close. He'd always felt better when she was near.

"I understand," Harley said.

Vince wasn't sure she did.

THE LAMBRIDGE BED AND BREAKFAST was a large, beautiful, Queen Anne Victorian home painted green with cream colored shutters.

Harley took in the large front porch, dominant Dutch gables, and asymmetrical façade. The kind of straight-lined architecture built to endure generations of family disagreements, brutal storms and intense heat.

Vince had endured much the same. He'd weathered family gales and ill winds from the community. Given his mom had left her family and his father had braved mental illness, was it any wonder he had no interest in getting married and having children?

She hefted her duffel higher on her shoulder, and practically dragged her backpack on the ground as she followed Vince up the stairs to the bed-and-breakfast. It was barely seven o'clock, but the sun was dipping behind the mountain range to the west and Harley's energy dipped with it. Back home it was 9:00 p.m., bedtime for someone who arose before dawn every day.

She couldn't wait to check into a room and be alone. She'd get out her sketchbook and try to solve the playhouse balcony problem.

The door swung open and, for a moment, Harley thought Brit had come to greet them.

"Oops. Those are startled stares." The

woman shared Brit's dark brown hair, her mahogany eyes and her wide smile, but she sounded different, more polished. "I'm Brit's twin, Reggie. I run the B and B. Apologies for the confusion."

Where Brit's demeanor was as comfortable as a set of worn flannel sheets on a soft, familiar bed, Reggie's was more like a bed made with crisp new cotton and military precision. There was nothing rumpled or wrinkled about her—not her hair, not her blue-flowered blouse, not her black pants.

She invited them inside. The foyer was grand and the mood subdued. To the right, a grandfather clock ticked among the antiques in the living room. To the left, a dining table that would fit twelve gleamed as if someone had just polished it.

Reggie smiled and a little of Brit's warmth seeped through. "Are you a party of two? Gabe only made a reservation for one."

Reservation for one. As in only one bed needed.

Harley's shoulders sagged. She'd thought they'd stay at a hotel in separate rooms. She hadn't anticipated Harmony Valley to be so very small.

"That Gabe," Vince said flatly, not looking at Harley. He'd set his suitcase on the floor. His hands fisted, but he said calmly, "What a joker."

"Is there enough room?" Harley asked. "We can drive back to…" Whatever the nearest city had been.

"No need to go anywhere." Reggie bared more teeth. "I have enough beds. It's just that the only room I have left has two singles."

"Perfect," Harley said. "Vince threw out his back." Her cheeks began to heat as she spun a tale. "He's out of commission when it comes to…*you know*."

Vince frowned at Harley.

"And he's cranky about it." In for a penny, in for a pound. Harley forced her lips upward.

Reggie laughed, but it was an awkward sound that echoed in the big, empty space. "Just a little bit of paperwork and then I'll give you the keys."

After Vince registered on a tablet, Reggie led them down a hallway beneath the staircase. "Your room is on the main floor. But you have your own private bathroom. The units upstairs don't."

"Take that Gabe," Vince said, regaining some of his good humor and sibling competitive spirit.

The room was small, just two twin beds. The comforters were a pale green and matched the shade of the thick towels in the tiny bathroom. As soon as Reggie closed the door behind her and it was just Harley and Vince, the room felt as confining as a jail cell.

"You take the bed by the door." Harley plopped her duffel and backpack on the one in the corner. "We need some ground rules. All changing will occur in the bathroom."

"Oops." Vince had ripped off his shirt while her back was turned.

She couldn't un-see that, but Harley covered her eyes anyway in the hope she wouldn't remember when she'd last seen his naked chest. "Put your clothes back on."

"Too late. I'm down to my boxers."

She didn't want to peek. Honest.

But she did. His jeans were still on.

"Made you look." That grin.

He hadn't smiled since they'd stepped foot on his family's property. She hadn't expected to see it after their talk in the restaurant.

The butterflies tried to return. She sucked in a breath and sucked in her stomach, stuffing every reaction to Vince—positive and negative—deep down inside. "What happened to the brooding man I've been with the better part of the day?"

"He came into a bedroom with a beautiful woman and all his cares slipped away." It was a lie. Vince couldn't quite erase the shadows around his eyes. "Or it could be that this is payback for telling Reggie I threw out my back."

He was teasing her.

Maybe that was a good thing. Maybe Vince needed some brevity after the stress of seeing his family for the first time in years.

Harley hit Vince with her pillow, grabbed her duffel and retreated to the bathroom.

It was the size of the closet in her apartment. She contemplated taking a cold shower. But the shower stall was so small, she'd have trouble shaving her legs. She doubted Vince could fit his shoulders in there. She was getting claustrophobic just brushing her teeth. And, boy, was she glad she'd decided to bring a football jersey and boxer shorts to sleep in rather than a nightie. Nothing sexy about a woman wearing a football jersey and boxers that reached to her knees.

"Are you decent?" she called through the door once she'd changed.

"You used to think so."

The impulse to submit to his charm was strong. Harley gritted her teeth and returned to the bedroom.

Vince sat up in bed, on top of the coverlet. Still no shirt on.

Harley's jaw popped. This was going to be a test of wills. Mostly a test of her will.

"What are you wearing?" Vince looked aghast. He reached over and drew the window shade down.

She could feel frumpy from his reaction or triumph. She chose triumph. "Clearly, this is an Atlanta Falcons jersey."

"But..." He pointed at her. "You live in Houston. We have two perfectly good football teams in Texas to choose from. You didn't have to defect to Atlanta."

"I didn't defect. I'm loyal to my roots." Still feeling out of sorts from the stuffy bathroom, she climbed into bed and pulled her sketchpad out of her duffel. For years, she'd come up with her most creative ideas at night, transferring the intriguing ones to fresh sketchpads so she could refine her work. "Don't tell me you're not loyal to a California football team."

"It was always the Cowboys in our household."

His mother's team, she bet.

Vince got out of bed and took his shaving kit into the bathroom. He closed the door, but she could still hear him say, "Look at the size of this shower. Gabe did this on purpose. He's a dead man."

CHAPTER SIX

HARLEY WAS STILL asleep when Vince got out of the cramped shower the next morning.

The pajama wars with Harley last night had been amusing. And after spending time with his family, he'd needed something to smile about. Truthfully, it wasn't so much the family that had bothered him as their buildings and the memories contained within.

Vince sat on the bed and tied his tennis shoes, glancing at the mass of blond hair on Harley's pillow. He'd never told her how much he was drawn to her thick, blond hair or the honesty in her clear blue eyes. He was fairly certain he'd never look at her without remembering the softness of her lips beneath his or the richness of her laughter.

Regardless, that wasn't enough to entice him to break his rule about relationships never being permanent. His goals today were to keep up the dating façade without leading Harley on and to contain the memories of the past.

To do so, he needed caffeine. Vince went in search of coffee. He found his brother instead.

"This is my dream breakfast, Reggie." Like Vince, Gabe was wearing basketball shorts and a T-shirt. His short, dark hair was rumpled, as if he didn't own a comb or had left it back in the barracks. "I may just have to marry you."

"Let's not get carried away." Reggie wore a skirt, a soft pink blouse, and heels better suited to downtown Houston than Harmony Valley. She caught Vince's eye and pointed at Gabe's plate. "I've never seen anyone top pancakes with blueberries, powdered sugar *and* syrup."

Vince scrutinized Gabe's breakfast. "My brother has always lived for carbs."

"Hey, I need the energy." Gabe loaded his fork with dripping blueberries and pancake. "I ran up Parish Hill this morning while you were getting your beauty rest." He stuffed the large bite in his mouth and talked around his food. "This is my reward."

"Your *heavenly* reward? Because eating like that will send you to an early grave."

Vince inventoried the sideboard and selected two hard-boiled eggs and a large apple. Before he sat next to Gabe, he poured a tall mug of black coffee.

Reggie disappeared into the kitchen, leaving the two brothers alone.

"Speaking of heaven..." Gabe swallowed and reached for a glass of orange juice. "Where is your angel?"

Vince's shoulders tensed. "Harley's sleeping. I'll bring her something when I'm done."

"You'll be regretting not having carbs when we're working on the house this morning." Gabe poured more syrup on his pancakes. "In addition to installing the flooring, I hear Brit found a deal on new doors. She's nearly as good as I am when it comes to bargaining."

Be inside the house? Vince's stomach churned. "I didn't bring my tools."

"Not to worry. I borrowed everything we'll need." Gabe loaded his fork once more. "Nail gun, compressor, level, crowbar." He always had been one to make things appear out of thin air, which was why he was so good at managing supplies for his Marine unit. "We're only working through the morning. Brit's got a shower this afternoon, leaving us some down time." His hand stilled midway to his mouth. "It's weird, isn't it? Being back in town after all these years?" He lowered his fork. "Without Dad. Without Uncle Turo."

Their uncle had raised them after their dad committed suicide.

"It's weird without Mom," Vince added. She'd tried to keep things normal for more than a decade.

"Mom?" Gabe rolled his eyes and jammed the fork in his mouth. "She deserted us."

She hadn't. "Like Dad didn't abandon us when he overdosed on pills?" Vince lost his appetite. He pushed his plate away. Two shelled eggs and one apple untouched.

"That was different." Gabe's fork drowned in a sea of syrup. "Dad carried the burden of chaos inside his head, and not by choice." Gabe's voice was too loud, too hard, too full of conviction. He'd never see anything but his own view of the world. "Mom gave up on her wedding vows, by choice. She left her kids, by choice."

By choice? Vince felt sick.

"And don't tell me there's ever an excuse for that," Gabe railed. "It's like going AWOL on the battlefield. You don't put yourself above the good of your unit."

Vince leaned back in his chair, needing a steadying force. He stared across the hall at the antique couch with its carved wood trim. It looked about as comfortable as the short bed he'd slept in last night, and as painful as this conversation.

He had a sudden urge to see Harley, to exchange a good-natured barb. Anything but this attack on their mother, when it had been Vince's fault that she'd left.

"Do you ever see Mom?"

Gabe's question wiped Harley's smile out of Vince's head. "No."

"Harley let slip something about her being in Texas." Gabe would have made a good interrogator. He continued to devour the sugar-laden pancakes on his plate as if this talk wasn't vital to the stability of their worlds.

Vince pressed his lips together. He should have told Harley his brothers didn't know he'd found their mother. "You know Mom has family in Texas. I don't see her or her relatives."

"Seems funny you'd stay away from Mom since you're always sticking up for her." Gabe tapped his fork on his plate. "When she left, we made a pact. We vowed not to mention her anymore, not to see her, not to look for her."

"That came from Dad."

He'd wanted them to pretend she was dead. Except there'd been no body, no funeral, no eulogy. Vince hadn't had any closure. Truth was, he didn't have any now, either. But he had peace and predictability. That was worth more.

"I know how you think, Vince. You believe everybody needs a helping hand, including our cold-blooded mother." Gabe stared at Vince as if he was a misbehaving puppy. "You need a head-clearing session with Dr. Gabe."

"There's the pot offering to sandblast the kettle." Nothing Gabe could say would clear Vince's head.

"What did you tell our *sainted* mother when you first saw her?" Gabe's demand came fast, made assumptions, accused.

Back when they were kids, Vince had fallen for Gabe's quick, bulldog inquisitions once too often. When in a sparring match with Gabe, he'd learned to remain calm or he'd give everything away.

Gabe waited for Vince's answer with a

casual look that was anything but casual. He shouldn't have become a supply chief. He should have gone into interrogation. It was unfair to blame Harley for her slip about Mom being in Texas, but Vince couldn't not fault her, either.

Vince tried to give his reply finality. "I told you, I haven't seen her. End of a non-story."

Needing to get away, Vince moved to the sideboard and filled a plate for Harley, nearly dumping a hard-boiled egg onto the wood floor. He hadn't drunk near enough coffee to be feeling so jittery. His fumbling fingers were a result of his irritation at Gabe, his annoyance at Harley, his anger with himself for telling Harley about his mother in the first place.

Gabe was uncharacteristically silent, not even offering a parting shot as Vince left him, coffee in one hand, Harley's plate and utensils in the other. The build-up of anxious energy continued with each step down the hall. Vince needed to vent. Slamming their bedroom door and letting Harley know what she'd done was a good place to start.

Harley pried her eyes open when Vince opened the door. She stretched and then sank back beneath the blankets, nothing but a blond halo visible on her pillow.

Now this is how a man should wake up in the morning.

Tension drained from Vince's body like a fast-receding tide. He closed the door softly instead of slamming it the way he'd planned just seconds prior.

"What time is it?" Harley asked in a muffled voice.

"Seven thirty." He came over to sit on the single bed across from hers. Bitterness pressed on the verbal gas at the back of his tongue. Words spewed out, fast and low. "Don't ask me how I slept. You snore. And you blab, although, not in your sleep."

"Shoot. Gabe." Harley bolted upright, thick, blond hair a tumbled mess that his fingers wanted to straighten. "I meant to tell you last night. I meant to apologize. Gabe and Joe have a bet about whether we're a couple or not."

Vince didn't have to ask to know which brother was betting he and Harley were faking.

"Gabe pushes buttons like a kid playing video games, over and over, until you can't take it any more. And then I... It was just..."

She lifted those big blue eyes to him, making it hard to stay angry. "He's as frustrating as my own brother, challenging everything I say simply because I don't agree with him."

How right she was. "That was why you kissed me?" Because of Gabe? The tide of tension began to flow back in, flexing his fingers, working his jaw.

Harley nodded. "He didn't ask about your mother specifically. I just felt as if he needed some kind of proof that we were a couple. And since he probably knows about the scar on your bicep from that bar fight, and since you don't have a beauty mark only a lover would know about, it was all I had."

"You kissed me to…protect me?"

"That sounds so honorable." Harley's cheeks pinkened. She threw off the covers and swung her feet to the floor near his. Her toenails were painted a soft shade of blue. "I did it for purely selfish reasons."

"I like where this is going." Vince couldn't contain his smile. It felt as if it spread from his lips to Houston.

"I kissed you to put Gabe in his place." Harley straightened the offending football jersey and stood, staring down her delicate nose at him, her hair in a tangled cloud about her face. "I didn't enjoy it."

Oh, what a lie. "It didn't feel that way to me."

Cheeks reddening, she stomped into the bathroom and slammed the door. And then she shrieked. "Why didn't you tell me my hair looked like this?"

"Because it's karma." Vince went to the door so he wouldn't have to shout and potentially be heard by the entire bed-and-breakfast. "That's karma coming around to get you for telling Gabe about my mother and telling me you didn't enjoy that kiss."

Sometimes the smallest victories were the most enjoyable.

THE CLOSE QUARTERS of the bathroom made Harley nauseous.

Her upset stomach was more discouraging than her bed-head reflection and realizing she'd been talking to her ex-boyfriend while looking like the Bride of Frankenstein.

She sniffed when she got out of the cramped shower, trying to uncover a smell that turned her stomach. She sniffed as she dressed in a pair of black capris and a gray-striped sleeveless blouse. She sucked in air through her nose like a bloodhound as she tamed her hair into a single braid down her back, but still, she couldn't identify anything amiss.

She'd dreamed of Dan chasing her through a shadowy playhouse last night and being unable to escape him because there were no balconies to run to. Maybe her stomach trouble was a product of stress, not environment.

"Hey, let's get moving." Vince knocked on the door. He was a morning person, always the first one to the job site, but he had a point. Brit and Joe probably had a ton of things to do for the wedding and needed their help. "You should eat something before we leave."

She opened the door. Vince stood holding a small plate of food.

Ugh. Neither the hard-boiled egg nor the bagel and cream cheese he'd brought appealed to Harley. "I'd like tea, thanks."

"And I'd like a new deal." Vince's smile was lukewarm. "Given Gabe doesn't believe we're the real thing, he's not going to let Joe win the bet without a fight."

"Don't get overly dramatic." Harley grabbed her cell phone and a five-dollar bill, shoving both in her pants' pocket, wanting to get some tea in her stomach as soon as possible.

"He's not going to give either one of us any peace."

Vince looked serious and seemed seriously annoyed, as if he'd been tearing out his Disney prince-like hair.

Harley crossed her arms and thought about peppermint and apples, anything that might calm her stomach. There had to be something funky in the bathroom, something that made her feel queasy. Was Reggie using an odd brand of bathroom cleaner? A cheap brand of shower caulking? "And what do you propose to do to convince Gabe?"

"Another kiss." Vince said it straight-faced, standing in front of the door like a palace guard. "This time in front of both my brothers. So that Gabe will have to concede. Joe will make him concede."

"No." Her suspicion meter pinged a warning. "I might consider it if you were a frog prince and my kingdom rested on this kiss."

"Ribbit." He didn't crack a smile. "Your Highness."

"There's nothing in your proposition for me," she said, putting her royal nose in the air.

What a flimsy statement. A kiss from Vince wasn't a hardship.

Vince knew it, too. He quirked a brow.

Her gaze went from that brow to his mouth to the floor, which made her dizzy.

What was going on here? She drew a deep breath in, willing herself to feel better. She couldn't handle Vince when she wasn't on top of her game.

Harley raised her gaze to his once more. "Cut to the chase. What are you willing to offer?"

His smile was sly. "I could clean your engine when we get back to Houston."

She waved that bargaining chip aside. "Offer me something you can deliver here. Like the truth. About anything."

He made a derisive noise and glanced away.

Harley reached up and cupped his smooth-shaved chin, forcing his gaze back on her. "Tell me something…" She wanted to know more about the man she'd once given her body to. "Tell me why you're not a mechanic. Gabe mentioned you were talented with engines. He was surprised you were no longer on an oil rig. Why?"

Vince seemed taken aback. His brows

converged. His dark eyes narrowed. "It's… complicated."

Diversion. Denial. She was over it. "I need fresh air and tea." To settle her stomach so she could handle these negotiations to her utmost advantage. She reached for the door-knob.

He pressed the flat of his hand against the door, holding it closed. "And for this, you'll agree to stage the kiss?"

The room shrank from the size of a jail cell to a cardboard box. Even the shower seemed larger than the space they currently occupied.

Every inch of Harley's body pleaded for caution.

"Yes," she said, throwing caution to the wind.

Vince took a deep breath, as if what he was about to disclose was going to be pain-ful. And then he said, "My mother is dat-ing Jerry."

What did that have to do with Vince not being a mechanic?

"That's it. End of truth telling?" And then a thought struck her, so hard she forgot about upset stomachs, fresh air and tea. She grabbed his white T-shirt. "Did you know this before you came to work for Jerry?"

He nodded.

Harley's mind raced. "And you were on an oil rig…"

His gaze darted sideways. "My mom dated an oil company mechanic."

"There were…other men? Other jobs?"

He nodded, standing still, telegraphing that this conversation was too close to his soft emotional center.

"You realize that's creepy, right?" Her stomach came back on line, agreeing.

Vince washed a hand over his face. The same hand that had held the door closed.

Harley made no move to go.

"It didn't start out like that. I wanted to make sure she was okay and not making the same mistake, choosing a guy who couldn't make her happy."

"You wanted to make sure she wasn't dating someone like your father," Harley said slowly. "You mentioned your father had mental health issues. Did your mother care for him? Support him? Nurture him?"

"Yes." The relief in his voice was palpable. "They say people have a romantic type."

Crikey. Her type was probably him. Tall, dark and emotionally unavailable.

"You were worried about your mother getting into another co-dependent relationship." Harley digested his nod, his past, her reaction. "You were…trying to watch out for her." She gaped at this caring, complex man. When she'd dreamed of her Prince Charming, she'd imagined him to have come from a happy home, without emotional baggage or misdirected good intentions. To be fair, she supposed men wouldn't be attracted to a woman who was thousands of dollars in debt and a professional failure.

"You don't approve," he said.

She stared into Vince's eyes, those black eyes that could express so much warmth, so much humor, and so much pain. "It's not the way I would've gone about it." Understatement. "And when your mom finds out, she's going to be upset."

His eyes widened. "She's never going to know."

"Or maybe she knows already." The sickening feeling of claustrophobia returned. Harley couldn't wait any longer for fresh air and green tea. She opened the door and hurried down the hall. "All it would take is one of her boyfriends to mention your name."

Vince made a sound that was half groan, half sound of disgust. "No one's ever said a word about me."

"Meaning no police officer ever came to your door with a restraining order."

Harley greeted Reggie in the dining room and asked about tea.

"I just dumped the hot water." Reggie apologized. "You can get tea at Martin's on Main Street. It's on your way to the garage. I'll see you there in thirty minutes."

"So we're good?" Vince asked Harley when they'd stepped onto the broad front porch.

"Honestly? I don't endorse you stalking your mom, but I understand why you did it." Harley tried to smile, but between the stomach upset and the choices he'd made, it felt more like a grimace. "And you have delivered on your end of the deal."

"Yes," he said firmly.

"Well…" Harley licked her lips. She was in big trouble here. Should she set a time limit on the upcoming kiss? She had a tendency to lose track of time when his arms came around her. "As long as you agree our performance is no longer than ten seconds, we're good." There. That ought to do it. Nothing bad could happen in ten seconds. Harley scurried down the porch stairs before she could dwell on the bargain she'd made. "Did you smell something strange in our bathroom?"

"No."

Harley widened her stride, breathing deeply, trying to clear out whatever was making her feel out of sorts. "Does your head feel heavy or your stomach odd?"

"No. And since when do kisses have time limits?" The Vince she'd dated was back. His tone invited her to play on the flirtatious playground.

"They do." Harley couldn't resist a ride on the merry-go-round. "Gratuitous kisses always have time limits. Hadn't you heard?"

He laughed, making her heart beat faster. "Where do you come up with this stuff?"

"I have a folder with all my silly ideas to make you cross-eyed." Actually, it was a sketchpad and made architects like Dan cross-eyed. "I keep a scorecard."

He laughed. His laughter filled the street. It filled her chest. It made regrets about obligatory kisses fade.

The temperature was brisk, quite a change from hot, muggy Houston mornings. Wisps of fog still lingered on the broad expanse of grass at the town square. Floating, the way Harley's balconies couldn't.

"We don't have oaks like that in Texas." Harley slowed to appreciate the lone tree in the town square. Its branches spread at least twenty feet on either side of the trunk like sturdy bird balconies. "They could put ten more benches under there. Why is there only one?"

"Because that's the bench where folks in Harmony Valley propose."

And presumably kiss afterward. Granted, she was becoming a bit obsessed about kissing.

She'd missed his wit. She'd missed his laugh. She was afraid to admit she'd missed his kiss.

Harley turned her feet in the other direction, not thinking about kisses or sons who kept tabs on their wayward mothers. She stayed a step ahead of Vince, having remembered where Martin's was from their drive to the bed-and-breakfast last night, a few doors down from El Rosal.

They turned onto Main Street. The sidewalks were brick with gas streetlights every thirty or forty feet. El Rosal was doing a brisk breakfast business, one that spilled out onto a patio ringed by a black wrought-iron fence.

A few elderly patrons pointed and whispered as they passed.

Mildred was among them, standing out with her thick, round glasses and thick, round, white curls. She didn't whisper. She called out a greeting when she realized who they were.

"They're talking about you and your Rapunzel-like hair," Vince teased.

"Vince, Vince, Vince. They're talking about you and the infamous Messina hair," Harley shot back. "With hair like that, you've got to be *somebody*." This last she put in air quotes.

"They already know who I am." He said it as if it was a bad thing to be a Messina in Harmony Valley.

She'd witnessed both a positive reception and a negative one, and refused to validate Vince's fears.

She couldn't let his gloomy mood set the tone of the day. "They may know your name, but they don't know you." Heck, she hadn't really known him until this trip.

The architecture on Main Street was from the Gold Rush era. Lots of brick. Lots of square lines. Not exactly Harley's preference, but the style was charming in its authenticity.

Beyond a few more storefronts, they reached Martin's Bakery.

"We used to get doughnuts here on the first day of school." Vince paused outside the door. "Gabe would order a bear claw and Joe liked sprinkles."

"What did you order?"

Vince opened the door for her. "Whatever was in the day-old section."

Harley's heart panged. She touched his arm as she passed. "You don't have to do that today."

He gave her a small smile.

The bakery was filled with mismatched wooden tables and chairs. True to the Gold Rush style, the ceiling was high and plain. One wall was cluttered with old yellowed photographs of what looked to be previous bakers. Her father had a similar wall at the tile store, but it only went back one generation, not one century.

The bakery case was L-shaped, broken up by a counter with a cash register near the middle. The case was filled with cookies, doughnuts, scones and all kinds of flaky confections. The scent of warm chocolate and fresh coffee filled the air.

Harley's stomach shimmied, overwhelmed by too many smells.

Nearly every table was taken. The customers were mostly gray-haired, except for the salesclerk and two toddler boys who played with blocks in front of the window seat. All conversation ground to a halt when Vince and Harley entered. Even the toddlers looked up.

And then the commentary came as fast as popping corn.

"Is that one of the Messina boys?"

"'Course it is. Those boys always did have a preference for blondes."

"Except Joe. He got himself a brunette."

There was a smattering of laughter.

"Okay, okay. You've had your fun. Don't scare away my customers or I'll raise my prices." A pregnant woman with dark hair and a soft smile stood behind the counter. Her brown apron had Jessica embroidered across the breast pocket in block letters.

"Welcome to Martin's. What can I get for you?"

Her customer service didn't halt the crowd's observations.

"It's the middle boy. He's back for the wedding."

"Is he the one who dated all those girls?"

"No. He's the one who barely graduated high school."

This last remark slid between Harley's shoulder blades with a sharp edge that made her suck in a breath.

Vince pretended he was hard of hearing, standing erect as if he were in the military. They'd shut up if he glared at them or laughed it off.

Harley opened her mouth to defend him but Vince laid a hand on her shoulder. "Don't bother." And then his hand drifted to her nape, where he gave her a gentle squeeze, as if loosening her tense muscles.

Her tense muscles? His must be locked in place.

Their gossip made her wonder. What would people back home in Birmingham be saying about her?

"I told Harley her ideas were too bubbly

and cartoony." That's what her brother Taylor would say.

"Some people do and other people teach." That would be her high school principal, Mr. Ethridge, hoping she'd decide to return to her alma mater as a teacher.

"It's better to be a big fish in a small pond than a little fish in a big ocean." That's what her mother had said just last week when she'd asked Harley to come home.

Harley sighed, demoralized by her train of thought. She could really use a hug right now, something to validate the bad feelings and let her know someone cared.

Vince sidled closer, giving Jessica his coffee order.

Or she could use a kiss. Kisses rated right up there with hugs in terms of emotional therapy credits. With the right guy.

She couldn't stop staring at her wedding date.

I am so in trouble.

"And what do you need this morning?" Jessica asked.

Harley yanked her gaze from Vince. "Hot green tea to go." She pulled the five out of her pocket and pushed Vince's wallet out of the way when he tried to pay for her order as well as his coffee.

A tablet propped on top of the bakery case had a message scrolling across the screen. "Horseradish chocolate cake?" Harley's stomach twisted.

"Horseradish grows wild here." Jessica smiled over her shoulder as she filled a large paper cup with hot water. "I blog about modernizing old recipes, but I fear I'm becoming the Horseradish Queen. I keep finding ancient recipes that include it."

"There's nothing wrong with that," said an old woman with short purplish-gray hair. She wore a lime-green track suit. A set of black reading glasses perched atop her bangs. "Eating horseradish leads to a long life."

"As does being ornery." Jessica was still smiling when she unwrapped a tea bag and dropped it in a cup.

"Classic Harmony Valley," Vince whispered in Harley's ear, his lips close enough to kiss her cheek. "Wait for it."

If she turned her head, Harley wouldn't have to wait for anything, including that kiss.

She stood as still as Vince.

"You could live a long life if you ate your greens." Jessica kept the ball rolling. "If you walked. Or sang. Or just spoke your mind without a filter."

"Is that a dig at me?" The purple-haired woman raised her voice primly. "Duffy told me the other day he thought I talked too much."

"I think Jessica was referring to me," an old woman with jet-black hair and a widow's peak said. "I always speak my mind."

"There are no digs. This is a dig-free zone." Jessica moved from behind the counter to hug her concerned customers and then she leaned down to kiss one of the toddlers. "Now, who's up for horserad-ish chocolate cake?"

Several patrons raised their hands.

The way she was feeling, Harley wasn't brave enough to try it, but something else caught her eye. "What pretty mermaid cook-ies. They look just like Brittany's sculptures."

"We're partnering with her." Jessica se-lected a mermaid with purple frosting hair and gave it to Harley. "A free sample with the hope you'll come back for more."

That started a whole new line of banter.

"Is that Messina boy staying after the wedding?"

"If so, I hope he's single. My granddaughter can't hold on to a man."

"There's no ring on that girl's finger, Vince." Someone tsked.

This last comment seemed like Harley's cue to leave. Vince had his coffee.

"Um…" Harley's tea steeped on the back counter, out of reach. She caught Jessica's eye.

Jessica dunked the tea bag a few times. "Almost done."

"Vince!" A woman about Vince's age stood in the doorway. She had short, streaky, teased blond hair and the kind of curves that made Harley blush, mostly because there wasn't enough material in her blouse to cover them. The woman ran forward, flung her arms around Vince and squeezed.

"Hey, Sarah." Vince pried himself free with a jolt and draped an arm over Harley's shoulders. "I heard you were back in town. This is Harley."

If the bakery had been quiet before, the patrons held their collective breath this time while Sarah processed Vince being unavailable.

Moving his hand to Harley's waist, Vince snuggled her body next to his, which made Harley momentarily forget her stomach woes, personal boundaries and the appropriateness of kissing one's ex. Her heart beat faster. Her lips curled upward. And she angled her face up to his. All conditioned responses from weeks spent dating him.

But, hey, this was part of what she was here for, wasn't it?

Instead of planting a big one on Harley or looking at her with googly eyes, Vince flashed Sarah a friendly smile, warm without being too warm, like the ones he'd given Harley after their breakup. "It's always good to reconnect with school friends, isn't it?"

He'd managed to put both his ex-girlfriends in their places without elevating either one.

Annoyance tangoed with jealousy in Harley's stomach. Or maybe the smell of all that sugar was turning her belly in a different way. She wanted to grab hold of Vince and give a little PDA to brand him as taken. But what she was going to do was take her tea and high-tail it out of there.

"Almost done," Jessica said, reading Harley's mind.

Sarah stared at Harley as if trying to place a once-familiar face, perhaps having taken Vince's comment about reconnecting and assuming it included Harley.

"Um…" Harley took pity on his ex. Sarah wasn't going to recognize her. "I'm not from—"

"Sarah?" Vince interrupted, pointing to the sidewalk and an old woman moving slowly with the aid of a walker. "Is that your grandmother?"

"No." Sarah glanced over her shoulder and then back at Vince, unconcerned. "She's my client. I work for Becca Harris as a caregiver. That's Mrs. Edelman. She used to teach third grade."

"She was one of my favorite teachers." Vince hurried to the front, angling his head as if to tell Harley to follow him out the door. He stepped outside and greeted his former teacher.

The bakery customers jumped into the void.

"Did he dump the blonde?"

"Which blonde? They're both blondes."

"He left them both for Carly Edelman."

"He's got good taste."

Laughter filled the room, bouncing off those high ceilings.

Harley's cheeks felt warm.

By contrast, Sarah seemed oblivious, either because she was hard of hearing or she'd become immune to the long-living blurting residents in Harmony Valley.

"Ignore the peanut gallery," Jessica advised, finally handing Harley her tea. "Not much happens around here, which means every little thing is a big deal."

"Vince is just the nicest guy, isn't he?" Sarah sighed. She gave Harley a competitive woman's once-over.

Harley tried to look unthreatened.

"Well…" Sarah pouted. "Let me know if you cut him loose. I was a fool to let Gabe turn my head." She went to find her client a chair, waving to catch Mrs. Edelman's attention when Vince held the door for her.

"For what it's worth, they talked worse about Joe when he first came back." Jessica nodded, smiling. "They'd all defend Joe now."

That didn't mean their words didn't hurt Joe's pride or Vince's, for that matter.

Harley carried her tea and cookie, and

joined Vince outside. She tried to make light of his reception. "You must have broken Sarah's heart. She latched onto you like a bride at a wedding dress clearance sale."

"She's scary." Vince took Harley's arm and led her down the sidewalk, adding in a lowered voice, "She pinched my butt."

"You lie." Harley stopped, completely taken aback. "She wouldn't do that in front of a roomful of people."

"Oh, yes, she did." With a furtive glance over his shoulder—possibly to see if Sarah was following them—Vince tugged Harley back into motion. "Didn't you see me jump?"

Harley chuckled. She had.

"Don't laugh. You're supposed to protect me from her."

How she wished someone could have protected her from failure with Dan. "You should have bargained for a kiss in front of Sarah." She knew the words were a mistake as soon as they left her mouth.

"I still could." Vince's gaze fell to her lips, his steps down-shifted to slow-mo and his expression turned serious.

Harley's breath caught in her throat. Against her better judgment. Against all experience to the contrary. Harley wanted to be held by Vince.

Not for show. Not to fulfill her end of a bargain. But because she liked him and because, when he kissed her, when his arms came around her, she felt that all her mistakes didn't matter.

All her mistakes…

Pride had led her to accept a job with Dan. Pride had made her show her sketches to him. Pride had made her quit.

"You were wrong the other day about men needing pride," Harley stated. "Pride steals your footing. It makes you doubt. It brings you down." To a place where you needed someone to lift you up.

She wanted that someone to be Vince. But that would go against the pep talks she gave herself about being resilient, not to mention, Vince didn't want to be her rock.

"You don't need another kiss." Her voice was a thready whisper.

He cocked a brow. "I don't?"

She hadn't been talking to him. She'd been talking to herself, talking herself down from the kissing ledge. "No. You need this." She didn't kiss him. She hugged him. She hugged him tight.

And, for just a moment, she didn't worry about balconies in the clouds, dreams lost or hearts that might be broken.

CHAPTER SEVEN

WHEN VINCE DATED a woman, he held her hand, he slung his arm over her shoulder, he looked a woman in the eyes when she talked and listened to the subtext of what she was saying.

He tried to be in the moment, to be authentic and intimate. But he tried to do it without being the guy a woman classified as "the One."

To do that, he had certain rules. He was always honest about where he saw himself five years from now—a common dating question. His answer? Pretty much the same as his life was now.

He was always honest when the inevitable question arose about marriage—a question many women his age posed. His answer? "I don't see myself getting married. And I'm not interested in having kids."

And he'd found that certain behaviors made sure a woman got the subliminal message that things just weren't going to work out. He didn't call or text every day. He didn't take women to fancy restaurants or away for fancy weekends. And he didn't hug.

Holding a woman for emotional support implied a connection, which implied a relationship, which implied there'd be a future.

Harley had said he needed a hug. But how she held on to him wasn't possessive. It wasn't suggestive. It was truly an offer of support. Two shoulders to lean on, as if she suspected he could use an outlet from the stress of being home.

Vince drew her closer. He hadn't realized how much he needed those two shoulders, those two arms, that she could read him so well.

"That did the trick, I bet." Harley released him and immediately focused on straightening her blouse.

Which didn't need straightening.

He blinked. Disoriented. The woman in his arms was gone. Walking away from him. A swing to her step.

"Hang on." He jogged to Harley's side. "What just happened there?"

It suddenly dawned on him that he'd managed to break every one of his rules with Harley.

He should send her home on the next plane.

"You looked like you could use some TLC," Harley said. She reached the crosswalk and checked both ways, more careful crossing the road than she was with her affections. "Did you know a twenty-second hug has been proven to reduce stress?"

"It had the opposite effect on me." Vince was tied up in knots. He wanted to kiss her. He wanted her to want the same things he did.

"It was just a hug." She sounded exasperated. "If it bothers you that much, pretend that hug happened weeks ago." She walked faster than he'd ever seen her go. In no time, she'd nearly reached Snarky Sam's, which was half antique store, half pawn shop. "Pretend we stepped into a time machine and that hug occurred in Waco just before I shared my greatest triumph and biggest failure, and you decided I wasn't worthy."

"I never said you were unworthy or a failure."

She huffed.

Snarky Sam had filled the sidewalk in

front of his store with items for sale. A three-wheeled adult bicycle with a large basket behind the seat. A potbellied stove. A fireplace grate and a matching set of tools.

Harley slowed down to drink some tea before they reached the sidewalk obstacle course.

"Since we're in your time machine…" Vince studied her features, trying to isolate the motives behind her impulsive hug. "I was being honest when I said you should be out conquering the world of architecture, not the curvature of someone's luxury spa."

"And I told you I couldn't do it. Not for four years. Don't you remember?"

"Yes, but… You didn't tell me why it'll take four years." He recognized that tone she used. Harley was in the you-can't-win-this-argument zone.

Vince caught her arm, slowing her to a stop next to the three-wheeler. He noticed the veterinary office down the road, to the left. The parking lot was filled with cars. A mile ahead and they'd be out of Harmony Valley.

Oddly, Vince wasn't pining to escape town. He was more interested in straightening the record with his ex.

Best to remember the *ex* part.

"I told you to try architecture again," he said in his most rational voice. "Being knocked down once doesn't mean you're out forever."

"And I told you I couldn't." She tugged her arm, barely, as if she didn't really want him to let go. "In my entire life, I've never faced a problem I couldn't work out. Until…" Her features bunched and she looked away. "Never mind."

"Tell me." He stopped abruptly, wanting to show he understood she was stressed. "Or I'll give you a twenty-second hug."

Her gaze found the rooftops of the brick buildings lining Main Street and the clouds drifting high above them. "As a kid, I used to imagine grand structures. Domes that tilted and swirled crookedly. Buildings that had curved walls. Second stories that seemed to float on air." Her words came to a halt and her gaze came crashing back to Vince. "My family thought I didn't understand how a conventional building happens. Tiles need flat surfaces to adhere, you know. So I kept my ideas in a sketchbook. And then I took years of math and science and art, all the while hoping to learn how to bring my impossible ideas to life." Unsuccessfully if her quitting was any indication. "I studied the work of Zaha Hadid. She was a pioneer in liberating architectural geometry."

Vince was lost, period. And a bit lost in the passion he saw in her eyes.

Harley blinked. "I'm boring you."

"Not in the slightest." He paused, figuring the best means to get to the bottom of this was a direct question. "Did you think you'd be a pioneer in the field, too?" Did she honestly believe it would only take a few years?

Her mouth worked. Her nose wrinkled. Her eyes rounded with watery disappointment. "Yes. I thought I could blaze new trails in architecture. Does that sound conceited?"

"No. It sounds like a really great goal." Lacking one himself, he was envious she had one.

"A goal." She blew out a breath and shook her head. "More like a pipe dream."

The glass door to Snarky Sam's swung outward. A small, spritely old man wearing a red-flannel shirt and a deep scowl pinned them with a glance. "Are you buyin' or sellin'?"

"Neither." Vince held up his hands.

"No loitering allowed." The old man

pointed to a sign in his window that said as much. "Loitering decreases my sales. You get me?"

"Gotcha." Vince tugged Harley across the street.

"Is your stomach all right?" Harley passed a hand side-to-side over her waist. "I must have eaten something yesterday that didn't agree with me."

"I'm fine." Other than being confused about his feelings for Harley, twenty-second hugs and the unaccountable loss of pipe dreams.

FIFTEEN MINUTES LATER voices drifted from inside the house Vince had grown up in.

Carefree laughter. Indistinct words spoken with happy tones.

And yet Vince heard the sounds of the past.

His mother's voice, so clear. Her words roughened by too many cigarettes and too many cares.

I can't do it anymore.

Vince's steps slowed. Stopped. Guilt pressed at his temples. He should have reacted differently all those years ago, been stronger, thought about what his brothers needed instead of himself.

Harley kept walking without realizing he wasn't next to her. They hadn't talked since Snarky Sam's. She'd been lost in her thoughts, and, for once, he'd been wondering about his future, only to find he was still anchored by the past.

"What's wrong?" Harley stood in front of him. Real and solid, and not falling apart like the people in his past.

Vince didn't budge. "I haven't been in that house since I left."

"They said they gutted it." Harley studied his face. "But you can stay outside if you want to." Her gaze moved to the house with a flicker of interest. She wanted to go in.

I can't do it anymore.

Twenty years had passed and he couldn't shake his mother's words. He'd thought Mom had meant she couldn't handle their father any longer. He hadn't thought she'd meant she couldn't handle her sons, as well. Up until then, he'd been her fixer, but he couldn't fix her.

Gabe stood in the doorway, crowbar in hand. "Here come the professionals just in time to criticize all my hard work on the doors."

"He hasn't put in any doors yet, but come

see." Joe appeared at Gabe's shoulder, looking joyful to be remodeling the house they'd grown up in. "My friends and I laid laminate all through the night."

"I can tell you don't want to go in." Harley moved between Vince and the house. "Let's take a walk over to the bridge. Your brothers are watching and you can…you can…kiss me." She said this as if she were telling a nurse she was ready for a tetanus shot.

"Now you're letting me choose when I get a kiss?" Vince managed to keep his voice low but failed to smile reassuringly, or at all. There was nothing reassuring about his memories or his guilt. "Where were you when Sarah goosed me?"

"I'm a little slow on the uptake." Harley stared at his Adam's apple. "It won't happen again. Now, how about we put on a show for your brothers." She tilted her face upward, still not looking at him.

"Too late. They went back inside."

Harley turned to face the house. The wheels were spinning in her head, all right. She was regretting that impulsive hug outside the bakery and was probably disappointed she'd been unable to clear the air between them.

"Go inside." Vince needed to sort through his emotions, including ones toward Harley. He'd meant for her to be a distraction for his family, not a distraction for him. "Go on. I can tell you want to poke around."

Harley gave him a sideways glance. "If you're sure…"

"Really. I can handle it alone out here."

"You're lying." But Harley left him nonetheless.

Vince lingered near the front walk. From his position, he could see through what had once been the living room and kitchen to newly installed French doors on the back side of the house.

Mom would've hated those doors.

There'd be no window to crack to extend her cigarette outside.

And Vince? He didn't like change. Who knew if Joe's redesign would make the house any better?

"Uncle Vince." Sam put her hands and feet on either side of the front door frame and climbed up. She wore blue jeans and a neon-orange tank top. "Come see my room." She deftly dropped to her feet and then began to climb again. "*Please.* Dad says it used to be your room." This time when she dropped, she ran out to Vince and took his hand.

Vince followed her. His steps were hesitant. His gaze fixed forward. His ears muffled everything but his niece's voice.

"It was nasty in here when we started." Sam dug in her soles to keep Vince moving forward. "I told Dad we should just tear it all down."

Vince wished they would have. There was so much guilt here. What he'd done to his family… And there was sadness, looking at his beautiful niece, feeling his heart swell with love for her, and realizing he'd never have a child of his own.

Sam looked behind her so he could see her smile. "But you know how Brit is about recycling. She never throws anything away."

Suddenly he was stepping over the threshold. There was no furniture, no kitchen cabinets or sink, no walls with nicotine-stained framed pictures of roses. His mother used to love roses, which made no sense. Nothing about their life had been rosy.

I can't do it anymore. Mom had taken a big drag off an unfiltered cigarette and then tapped the ashes into the grass. *He's getting worse.*

"Over here." Sam led Vince past a stack of flooring material and doors to the hallway.

Manageable. The memories were manageable if he stared at Sam's short, bouncy hair. Vince followed Sam to the room he used to share with Gabe.

"I'm going to paint one wall purple and one wall green." Sam released his hand and turned around, a hopeful expression on her face.

Vince smiled at her innocent ability to dream. He'd let go of his dreams when he'd realized his high school grades weren't good enough for college.

Gabe appeared in the doorway. "Remember when you used to fly off the top bunk, little brother?"

"I remember you pushing me," Vince joked. Their banter had a familiar feel to it.

Separated by a year, they'd been competitive kids, but it was the good kind of competition. He and Gabe had raced to the top of Parish Hill on motorcycles and then sat staring down on Harmony Valley, marveling at how small it looked. They'd swum across the Harmony Valley River. The loser had

had to swim back to get the sodas and then they'd lain on the grassy bank on the other side, talking aimlessly.

In his years away, Vince had forgotten how close they'd been. When they'd shared this room, he'd known how many girls Gabe had dated and the one that broke his heart. He'd known the things Gabe considered before choosing the military. He'd known that Gabe was looking for a more stable "family" and that he'd found it with his fellow Marines.

Joe called for Gabe from somewhere in the house. Gabe disappeared.

Sam smiled and spun some more. "Did you wear a cape when you flew off the top bunk?"

"I did." Vince had forgotten about that, too. "My cape was a blue pillowcase my mom pinned around my neck."

His mother had always been creative when it came to playing. One year, she'd made a fort in the garage from a refrigerator box.

"Dad made me a pink cape like that." Sam rushed forward and grabbed Vince's hands, using them as ballast as she twirled around, just like when she was six. "Capes must be a family tradition. Like fixing cars. I *love* fixing cars."

He had, too. "You don't have to fix cars. You can learn how to fix space shuttles or airplanes." She could go to college and become an engineer and learn how to build things people had yet to dream of.

That had been Vince's dream.

"Nope. They don't make space shuttles in Harmony Valley." Sam released him and stood near the window. "I'm going to put my bed right here so I can see the stars at night." She snuck him a sly grin. "And that way, Dad won't see the light of my laptop if I'm on it."

Vince ruffled her hair. "Your dad may not catch you, but Brit will." She was one sharp cookie.

"Hey." Sam smoothed her bangs back in place. "I'm not a kid anymore."

Vince snorted. Sam was still a kid. She danced around and climbed the walls.

"If you're going for classic…" Harley's voice drifted to Vince. "You can't go wrong with white subway tile."

Vince stepped into the hallway. Joe, Brit, Gabe and Harley were scrunched in the nearby bathroom, which had nothing but plumbing, a tub and concrete floors.

"I know a guy," Gabe was saying. "I can get you tile. Cheap."

"If you get tile this week, I can set it for you." Harley blinked, as if she couldn't believe she'd offered.

"Wait. Just…wait." Vince joined them. "Harley's on vacation." Not to mention, she needed paying jobs.

"I've already offered." Harley's gaze sharpened, warning of boundaries being crossed.

Her sidewalk hug and drive-by kiss had created a humongous hole in the borders defining their ex-relationship.

"We don't accept barter." Joe frowned.

He was a stickler about that and had been ever since he'd worked as a mechanic for their uncle in Beverly Hills. Uncle Turo had bartered into trouble with the law by accepting stolen goods in trade. Joe had been oblivious to their uncle's shady dealings, but had almost been guilty by association.

Harley shrugged, no longer meeting Vince's gaze. "Consider it my wedding gift."

Wedding gift? Vince felt a moment of panic. He had yet to buy one.

Brit squeaked, trying to contain her excitement.

Vince shook his head. "Harley…" She needed money. She didn't need to grout over Vince's past.

"It's okay, Vince. It's subway tile." Harley ran a hand over the new drywall above the tub. "That stuff goes up within hours."

"With or without a tile saw?" Vince finally found an argument to sway her.

Her brow furrowed.

"I'm sure I can find you one of those." Gabe again, annoying in his confidence.

"Great." Harley brightened, as if her stomach was no longer upset.

Brit gave Joe a pleading look. "Surely we can accept wedding gifts like this."

Joe heaved a sigh that predicted capitulation. "How many bathrooms have you tiled, Harley?"

"More than I can count."

"I thought you were an architect." Nothing got by Gabe.

"It's getting hot in here." Vince tried to catch Harley's eye.

She ignored him. "My parents own a tile store." There was a hint of color in Harley's cheeks as she navigated the fine line between truth and fabrication. "I grew up on job sites."

Which explained why she was so comfortable on them now.

"Could you teach me how to do it?" Brit was in hopeful mode, gushing. "That way, I could do the shower in the master bathroom."

"If it's not too much trouble to teach her," Joe said with an apologetic glance at Vince. "Because it is your vacation."

Vince blew out a breath. "Finally, someone else remembers."

"Vince doesn't have a say in how I spend my time off." Harley's voice was firm and her blue eyes dared him to protest.

Brit squealed and hugged Harley. "I'm that much closer to having a finished house!"

"That's it, then." Gabe prodded Vince's ribs. "Are you ready to get to work?"

Joe tugged on a pair of protective leather gloves. "We're putting in doors wherever we have new floors."

Vince hesitated. How could he explain that doing anything to make this house livable felt wrong?

"Are you shirking work?" Gabe studied Vince. "You never were one to stick to anything. Like school."

Yes, Vince loved his brother. Yes, he might just have to punch him.

A flash of golden hair signaled Harley was moving toward Vince. Here came another drive-by kiss.

This one's for you, Gabe.

Vince smiled like he knew his brother was going to regret prodding him.

Or not.

"Vince and I will put the doors on for the two smaller bedrooms." Without a meeting of lips, Harley spun Vince around and guided him toward the doors stored in the living room. "And we'll finish before Joe and Gabe have the master bedroom and bathroom doors on."

"Only a girlfriend could manage a bit of tricky negotiation like that." Joe smirked at Gabe.

Harley removed her hands from Vince's shoulders. She'd gotten what she'd wanted, he realized. By taking on the tile project, she could keep her distance from him without making it seem as if they weren't a couple.

"Yep, Vince is her man," Brit said enthusiastically from behind them, sounding as if she was totally convinced they were dating.

"I certainly am." Vince turned and caught

Harley's hand, dragging her next to him because, like it or not, they were in this together. "Maybe next time I'll prove it with a kiss."

Harley's gaze shuttered, but not before Vince saw a flicker of longing.

One that matched his own.

One they both knew they shouldn't give in to.

CHAPTER EIGHT

"IF YOU BREAK one more ribbon, you're going to have six children!"

Peals of feminine laughter filled Martin's Bakery Sunday afternoon. The room was crowded with women of all ages for Brit's bridal shower. Since Harley had been there this morning, pink and white streamers had been hung on the walls and a banner proclaiming "Joe and Brittany Forever" was fixed in the window.

"You'll be next." Mildred stared up at Harley in that unfocused way of hers. Something behind Harley caught the old woman's attention. "Unless it's Reggie." She lowered her voice. "That is Brit's sister Reggie serving cake behind you, isn't it?"

Harley glanced over her shoulder. "Yes."

The bride had invited Harley to the shower after a morning spent working on the happy couple's house. Reggie, Brit's twin, had seen Harley's discomfort when she'd arrived and had asked her to help with the event. Harley was grateful, because helping made her feel less of an outsider.

Several silly games later and the presents were being opened.

Harley refilled Mildred's punch glass while Brit pulled apart the wrapping on her next shower gift with the utmost care. The bride-to-be didn't look as if she'd spent the morning at a job site. Her hair was straight and combed, her makeup flawless, and her dress a lilac flowered print that brought out the pink in her cheeks.

Harley envied Brit's energy. She still had a jet lag hangover.

Joe's teenage daughter, Sam, sat next to Brit, wearing a blue sundress and a sunny smile. She was making a bouquet from the bows and ribbons from Brit's shower gifts.

"Where did you meet Vince?" Mildred asked, keeping Harley from moving to refill the punch glasses at the next table. "Was it at a racetrack?"

"No." Harley set the heavy glass pitcher on the table. "It was—"

"Oh, I bet it was through an online dating service." A diminutive woman with white hair barely longer than Gabe's military cut edged into the conversation from her seat next to Mildred. "You can get anything on the internet nowadays."

"My money's on a matchmaker." A thin woman with elegant features and a tight white bun at the nape of her neck grinned. "So many young people don't have time to date."

Three pairs of eyes stared at Harley, waiting for her to answer.

"I'm afraid it's not as exciting or buzz-worthy or romantic as any of your guesses," Harley said, feeling flustered.

"Never mind the inquisition." Jessica appeared at Harley's side, smelling of sugar. She carried cupcakes with white frosting and flower rosettes, which the baker distributed from a tray. "Don't you remember what I told you this morning? Not much happens here, so any news is big news."

"I'm not news," Harley insisted, suddenly concerned that they'd wheedle the balcony failure from her just as easily as Gabe had discovered the location of Vince's mother. "I also have no news. In fact, I'm not interesting in any way. Did you hear the mother of the bride got stuck in traffic and couldn't make the shower?"

The elderly women leaned closer, gossip predators smelling blood.

"I'd tell them where you met Vince," Jessica advised. She finished doling out cupcakes and repositioned her tray, pausing to stare at each white-haired woman in turn. "Sometimes you ladies come on too strong."

"Who? Us?" The petite woman with the pixie cut sat back.

"I think I'm offended." The slender woman with the ballerina bun sat back.

"I think Jessica knows us too well." Mildred sat back and grinned.

Harley picked up the pitcher and poured punch into the next empty glass. "It's all very boring. We met at work. He's a carpenter and—"

"She's an architect," Reggie interrupted, although Harley didn't remember telling her. "Ladies, I'm collecting your bingo cards. Make sure your names are on them."

"An architect." The woman with the bun handed over her card, sounding impressed.

"Dating a carpenter." The diminutive woman gave Reggie her card and Mildred's. "Common interests lead to lifelong partnerships."

"A match made in heaven," said Mildred. "She dreams it. He builds it."

Harley moved on with the punch. "If only it was that easy."

"DID YOU GET a wedding gift for the happy couple?" Gabe stood at the corner of the town square.

The afternoon sun was warm but not Houston brutal. The sky was a cloudless blue, like Harley's eyes.

The brothers had just finished watching a baseball game at El Rosal while Brit had her bridal shower. Joe was inside, having stopped to talk to the sheriff.

"I haven't bought anything yet." Vince had been too worried about showing up at the wedding. "Any ideas?"

Gabe rubbed his hands together. "I've got a sweet lead on a motorcycle. It needs a little work, but—"

"Seriously?" Vince poked Gabe's solid bicep. "Joe's first wife died in a motorcycle crash."

Gabe swatted Vince's hand away. "Hey, Sam works on cars. You think she won't appreciate a motorcycle for a little rebellion?"

"Ah, the truth comes out." Vince shook

his head. "You're trying to make sure our niece carries on the Messina family tradition and terrorizes the town on two wheels."

Gabe shrugged. "Admit it. The idea appeals to you, too."

"It doesn't." Well, Vince wouldn't mind taking to the saddle once more, just for old time's sake.

"It does." Gabe read his thoughts and grinned.

"It might," Vince allowed. "But to be clear, it holds no appeal for me as a gift, either for Joe or for Sam. If you're looking for a big-ticket item, they could use a riding mower. There must be three acres of grass to mow on that property."

"We'll talk motorcycle getaways later." Gabe nodded toward El Rosal, where Joe was exiting the restaurant. "I know a guy who can hook us up with a deal on a mower, I think."

"Someone in town or—"

"Of course, someone in town." Gabe rolled his eyes. "I know people everywhere."

And as if to prove it, a truck drove slowly past. The driver honked and waved. "Hey, Gabe!"

"How...?" This was nothing like the reception Vince had received. Or Joe, for that matter. "You've been here…what? A week?" And already Gabe knew someone who could hook them up with a deal on a riding mower?

"People like me, brother." He gave Vince a love tap to the shoulder.

"Sorry for the wait." Joe joined them and they headed toward the river, where there was a shortcut back to the garage. "What were we talking about?"

"Inside El Rosal?" Gabe chuckled. "Who can remember? But what we need to discuss is your bachelor party. Do you want to go into the city? Do you want to do something wild? Do you want me to find a strip club?"

"This is my second wedding." Joe waved his hands in the negative. "I want to keep it low-key or do nothing at all."

They passed by small Craftsman homes, many of which had well-kept yards or fresh coats of paint. The town was experiencing a rebirth.

Vince snapped off a leaf from a shade tree as they walked beneath it. "Gabe wouldn't know low-key if it jumped out at him from that tree."

"If low key jumped out at me, at the very

least, I'd introduce myself." Gabe strolled backward in front of them. "Seriously, we need to do something to mark this occasion."

"Well…" Joe hesitated.

"There is something you want to do," Gabe crowed.

"I wouldn't mind having a bachelor party with some of my friends here in town." Joe spoke tentatively, as if he expected Gabe to make fun of the idea.

"Sure, sure." Gabe continued to walk backward. "We'll invite Will. He's your best man. And the sheriff. I could still arrange for a woman to come out of the cake."

"No women. No cakes." Vince's little brother was all grown up, ordering Gabe around.

Which was great, considering Gabe had never grown up.

"Beer and nachos then," Vince suggested. "We can hold it at the garage. Pick a day and invite whoever you want."

"You might be surprised as to who I invite," Joe said somewhat cagily.

"But it's your day, so who cares?" Vince silenced Gabe with a glance.

They reached a stretch of undeveloped land by the river and took a path that led to the bridge near the garage. A few minutes later, they'd returned.

"I'm gonna make some phone calls." Gabe settled at a picnic table, giving Vince a look that said he was going to contact a guy about a riding mower.

"Vince, I want to show you something." Joe unlocked the door to the office and led him into the service bays.

Vince had gone into the garage yesterday to wash up and he'd done so quickly, trying to avoid the memories with some success.

A whiff of motor oil as he stepped in and he was cannonballed back in time.

I can't touch it. Dad sat huddled in the corner of the garage with Mom next to him. *It's booby trapped.*

Vince knows all about traps. Mom had her arm around Dad's shoulders. *Just tell him what the timing is for a '57 Chevy.* She kissed Dad's forehead and then looked up at Vince encouragingly. *You can do that, can't you?*

Vince wasn't sure if Mom was asking him or Dad. He'd been eight or nine. Mom had discovered his talent for taking things apart and putting them back together. She'd been pulling Vince away from play time more frequently to cover in the garage. But this was the first time Vince remembered watching his father and wondering why he was acting so strangely.

"You comin'?" Joe called out to him, impatience threading his voice.

Vince walked slowly across the service bays.

There was a shiny red-metal tool chest on the back wall. A bulletin board with photos of Brit and Sam hung nearby. A calendar with a heart drawn around Saturday's wedding date above the workbench. Comforting sights. Comforting because they hadn't been around when he'd grown up.

"Over here." Joe stood by a cupboard hung on the wall in the far corner.

Cheap plywood. Never painted. Hung slightly off level. Vince wanted to straighten it.

Fix it. The story of my life.

But the cabinet… It was where Vince used to store things when he was called home from school. He couldn't remember what he might have left in there.

Joe opened the door and removed a stack of books, setting them on the small counter-top. "Sam found this stuff after we moved in. I figured I'd leave it for you to go through."

The stack was organized from thinnest to thickest. A car magazine. A slim, black, photo album. Vince's freshman yearbook. An algebra book.

Vince didn't touch any of it. "This is all trash."

"Sam will be disappointed." Joe smiled at Vince as if they were the closest of brothers with no secrets between them. "She's read every signature in your yearbook. She's asked about every photo in this." He held up the photo album and flipped it open. "Do you remember this picture?"

Vince bent forward to see.

Mom was standing behind the three Messina boys. Joe looked as neat as a staged living room in one of those mansions Vince worked on in Texas. Pressed trousers and a blue-checked, short-sleeved button-down. It'd been his fifth birthday. He beamed at the camera.

Gabe's red-and-white-striped shirt was streaked with dirt. He'd been frogging down by the river and had been upset to be called back, even if it was for cake. He wore a black motorcycle helmet with the visor up.

Vince's hands were stuffed in the pockets of his grease-stained blue coveralls. The legs and sleeves were cuffed, because they were Dad's. He was grinning, probably because he was on a cake-induced sugar high.

Mom had her hands on Vince's shoulders and Gabe's. Her soft brown hair curled around her face, accenting an easygoing smile. She loved birthdays. Anyone's birthday. She'd sing "Happy Birthday" from breakfast until bedtime, making the birthday boy feel special.

Vince leaned back, swallowing thickly. "That was a good day."

"Look at the captions." Joe read them, perhaps sensing Vince needed distance and wouldn't. "'Gabe, the jokester. Vince, the fixer. Joe, my favorite.'" Joe lifted his blue-eyed gaze to Vince's.

There was so much of their mother in his eyes. In the cheekbones. In his smile sometimes.

"Don't feel like you have to apologize," Vince said gruffly. "Gabe and I knew you were her favorite."

Joe shrugged, closing the album. "Didn't keep her from leaving me." There was hurt in his voice, even after all this time.

Vince stared at the pile of books. Should he take them?

"Sam found these in your algebra book." Joe held up a small stack of hall passes. "All signed by Mom. Never used. You had carte blanche to take a hike whenever you wanted to. And here I thought I was her favorite."

"You were. It says so on the photo." It hurt to argue the fact since Vince had been the one she'd relied on.

Joe picked up the books and handed them to Vince. "You should have these."

Vince hesitated before taking them. His curiosity won out.

Outside, car doors slammed. Gabe said something. Harley laughed. That laugh. It called to him. Vince started walking.

Joe stepped in front of Vince as he moved toward the door. "Do you know why Gabe and I worry about you? Why we pester you to get on the phone and talk, and ask about your relationships?"

Vince had told Harley he'd thought they had nothing better to do than pester him, but now that he was with them, he knew that wasn't true.

When Vince didn't answer, Joe said, "Because you'd never tell us if something was wrong."

How right they were.

"But if you had someone, someone you loved and who loved you back..." Joe's gaze drifted to the office and the females who were filling it up. "They'd be there when you wouldn't let us be."

"You mean if I'm diagnosed with depression or schizophrenia, like Dad, that I'd have someone to rely on." His worst fear. The words tumbled off Vince's tongue like bitter pills. "Someone who'd stick with me, for better or worse. Like Mom." Like Mom would have done if Vince hadn't told her to get out.

"No." Joe drew back. His face was chiseled in confusion. "I meant we worry about you being alone and not having a family."

"I'm not alone." Anger tunneled into his chest, a big emotion in a small cavity. "I have... I have..." He couldn't think of who he had—not Harley or his mother—but he wasn't pathetic, the way Joe's words made him feel. He'd built his life to avoid a repeat of his childhood.

"Hey, settle down." Joe put his palm on Vince's shoulder. "I mean, of course, you're not alone. You have Harley now, who seems great. Why wouldn't you want to marry her?"

The books felt heavy in Vince's arms. "Just because you found someone to marry you, doesn't mean I need someone. Marrying Harley would be a huge mistake."

A door latched.

Harley stood a foot away from them, staring at Vince as if he needed a hug and she wasn't going to give him one.

CHAPTER NINE

HARLEY'S CHEEKS WERE PALE. "Excuse me." She slipped out the door.

Vince was moving before he realized he was going after her.

"Shaggy Joe." Brit appeared in the doorway, slowing Vince's pace. She held a bouquet of ribbons as if it were a bouquet of flowers. "I received four Crock-Pots at my shower. I'm not sure people in Harmony Valley know what a bridal registry is."

"She also got two nighties. Eeww." Sam stood behind her. She had a pink curly bow in her hair above one ear, the kind that went on presents. "Those gifts should have come with a warning label—not for the eyes of children."

Vince edged around them and hurried outside.

"Dude—" Gabe held his phone away from his ear "—you better hurry and catch

Harley. I've seen friendlier faces across the North-South Korean border."

Harley was nearly to the bridge. She'd changed for the bridal shower. The hem of her yellow dress flirted with her knees.

Vince called to her, jogging to catch up when she didn't stop.

The late-afternoon light made the river look a refreshing, deep green. A cool breeze came over the mountain range to the west, the one separating Harmony Valley from the ocean. Vince didn't feel cool or refreshed.

Harley set foot on the bridge. He could feel her slipping away the same way he could feel the humidity rise in Houston. He lengthened his stride, running awkwardly with the books in his arm.

"Harley, wait!"

She did, finally, turning to face him, her thick, blond braid swinging, her cheeks flushed with color, her eyes flashing with hurt.

"I thought I could do this. I thought I'd feel a twinge of guilt for misleading your family about our relationship, but I thought I could do it anyway." She wrapped her arms around her waist, tightly, the way you did when you didn't trust the person you were speaking with. "I didn't sign up to be humiliated in front of your them." She nodded toward the garage.

He looked back and winced. They had an audience. Joe, Brit, Sam, Gabe.

"I thought when we were dating that you were comfortable in your own skin." Harley straightened, her arms still snug around her waist. "In Houston, I'm comfortable being who I am. But in Harmony Valley, I don't know who I am, who you are, or who you want me to be. Why am I here?"

"Because you want your tile saw fixed." He knew it was the wrong thing to say, but he couldn't seem to stop himself.

She huffed. "Were you this sarcastic when we were dating?"

"I was." *Well, maybe not to this extreme.* Harmony Valley seemed to amplify all his flaws. He set his mementos from the past on the bridge.

Her gaze drifted toward the river. "I must have missed that somehow." Her words were heavy with disappointment.

His chest felt as if the tow chains they'd been using yesterday to haul cars had been wrapped around him and were cutting off his air supply.

Vince liked Harley too much to let her think what they'd had was a sham. "You didn't... You weren't..." How to say he'd been happy around her without making her think there was still a chance for a future together. He couldn't come up with a thing. "I'm sorry."

She laid her palm on his cheek. "Your family is awesome. I'm going to give them my regrets. And then I'm looking into flights home tomorrow." She dropped her hand and took a step back.

Their audience was still riveted. It was amazing Gabe wasn't walking over to hear what they were saying.

"Hold on." Vince bit off the words and swallowed the urge to tell Harley no saw would be fixed if she abandoned him. He caught her arm. "I'm falling apart here. Joe said something and I... I overreacted." That, at least, was the truth. "I'm sorry. Don't go."

She screwed up her nose as if he'd offered her smelly sushi. "No."

Her refusal meant he'd be facing his siblings alone the rest of the week. "I could pay you." Not much, but still...

Her blue eyes sparked with anger. "My wanting to leave isn't about money or my saw. It's about you and me, and who we were when we were together. I thought I kind of got us, but it seems I was wrong. Which means you charmed me into bed, like some Casanova—"

"Casanova…" Vince's self-image plummeted. "That's not the way it was." Now his chest ached for a different reason. He didn't want her to think their time together was about him trying to seduce her. "I have a lot of respect for you."

She tugged her arm free. "I suppose that's better than you saying you worshipped my body."

"I… Wow… It wasn't like that." He ran a hand through his hair. "What can I do to convince you to stay?"

"You can be honest and explain what's going on, and why this place throws you off your game."

"Okay."

Her gaze softened. "I understand family baggage. My brother thinks I wasted time and money getting a degree." Her voice trembled. "Taylor and my parents don't understand why it's important to me that walls curve or rooms intersect in unusual ways. Their world is flat-surfaced. Right-angled.

Tile-ready. My family would've been happier had I gotten a business degree and come home to work in the family store." Harley shifted from one foot to the other. "I've talked too much. I didn't give you a chance to speak. I seem to do that a lot around you."

"I like listening to you." Too much.

"Listening goes both ways." She clasped his hands. "Tell me. Start with something small." Her voice was as warm as melted chocolate. Her hands as smooth as a ribbon of caramel. A gentle breeze lifted the wisps of golden hair she'd tried to tame around her face.

Another man wouldn't let go of this awesome creature.

Vince didn't want to break the moment by speaking. He glanced at their joined hands and then back at the garage where their audience was applauding. They liked the show. But Vince didn't want an audience just then.

"My mother…"

Harley squeezed his hands gently when he faltered. "None of the tension around here is caused by your mother."

How wrong she was.

Vince stared at Harley's blue sandals, covered in a layer of fine dust. At her long legs and the hem of her yellow skirt. At her hands, gripping his. Finally he stared into her clear blue eyes. He'd missed her touch, her smile, her curiosity, her cut-to-the-chase attitude. But when he'd been with her, he hadn't been honest. He'd diverted her personal questions with kisses, despite the ever-growing need to tell her things he hadn't told anyone else. It'd been a relief to find she was afraid of something, that she'd failed, that she was human. It had given him an out from the feelings he'd felt blossoming for her.

Except, he didn't want Harley to be fearful, or to fail, or to be less than perfect. Because she was pretty darn close to his ideal, if he'd wanted to get married and deserved someone like her. If Vince couldn't have her, he wanted her to have the best. Which wasn't Vince Messina. Not by any stretch.

"Quit making googly eyes at each other and kiss her!" Gabe called.

Harley gave up on Vince and made to pull away.

"If you hold my hand while we walk across this bridge…" Vince held on, an idea taking shape. A really bad idea. "I'll tell you everything."

She stopped struggling. "I don't want to barter with you. I want you to trust me."

A surprisingly strong ache of longing filled his chest. "Why?"

THE BUTTERFLIES WERE BACK.

Why *did* Harley want Vince to trust her?

Because she wanted her tile saw fixed for free.

Sometimes the biggest lies are the ones you tell yourself.

Harley's mouth went dry. She didn't still feel about Vince *that* way. After watching him with his brothers, she'd been curious, that's all. She should have known that with Vince curiosity led to vulnerability. Hers. She didn't like being put on the spot. She avoided it. The same way she'd avoided turning in late papers when she'd been a student, because being less than perfect wasn't how she rolled. Nor was making mistakes.

But here she was, blundering through things with Vince.

She never used to make mistakes.

Ah, for the golden days of my childhood.

Vince was staring at her, waiting.

Mistake. Mistake. Mistake.

And now she'd backed herself into a corner without any defense other than the truth about why she wanted Vince to trust her. "Why? Because we were close once. And I still care about you."

His eyes widened. He dropped her hands.

Could she jump over the bridge railing and float away without Vince jumping in after her and making her feel like a bigger fool?

"Let me rephrase." She infused her voice with a business-like quality. "If any of my friends asked me to pretend to be something I'm not, I'd do it if they gave me a good reason, because I care about them."

The panic vanished from his eyes.

If that was regret spiraling in her stomach, she pretended not to notice. "You talk. I'll listen." She picked up the books he'd been carrying and handed them to him. And then she claimed his free hand in hers.

A wrinkle appeared on his brow.

She squeezed his hand and then released it. She wanted to tell him not to bother divulging his mysterious background. After all, she had to work with this man. If the past was so terrible, she'd never be able to look at him the same way.

But there was the gentleness in how he'd

held her hands just a moment ago and the pain in his eyes that she instinctively wanted to soothe. And then, miracle of miracles, he started to speak.

"My dad was diagnosed with schizophrenia after Joe was born." His words came out as slow and deliberate as the sun moving lower on the horizon. "He'd never taken as much as an aspirin before his diagnosis. Afterward...well, Dad had a slew of pills he was supposed to have every day."

She could see where this was going. A sense of doom pressed upon her, stifling butterflies and internal voices that whispered about pitfalls and blunders.

"There were times Dad couldn't remember how to fix a car. Or he could remember, but he couldn't bring himself to do it. My mom worked when she could, and quit to stay at home when Dad was taking a nosedive."

"Did your father have other employees? Someone to help pick up the slack when he couldn't perform the duties that kept food on the table?"

Vince shook his head.

"Who did your father rely on when he couldn't function?"

"Me," he said softly.

"But…you were a boy."

He nodded, gaze fixed on his family.

"They don't know it was you." Harley gestured to their audience, tried to wrap her head around that. "Joe and Gabe don't know you helped at the garage. How could that be?"

Vince's black eyes came back to rest on her. He didn't fidget or shrug. He contained all the bad memories and all the messy emotions behind a mask. Only his eyes hinted at the extent of his pain. "I'd show up late to school, waiting to see what cars would come in and what mood Dad was in that day. I'd ride my bike home at lunch…"

"And sometimes you wouldn't go back," she finished for him.

He nodded. "Which didn't go over well with my teachers."

"And gave you quite the reputation." As a slacker. Just this morning someone in the bakery had mentioned he'd barely graduated.

"The school thought I went home sick a lot. When I was in high school, Mom got me a flip phone. She'd text me when she needed me." His gaze was back on his family. "I liked school."

He'd mentioned in Waco that his grades weren't good. He'd sacrificed a chance at a future to protect his family. No wonder he'd been upset that she'd seemingly thrown her career away. She'd never done anything with a higher purpose. Every move she had ever made had been for her own future.

On the day Dan broke her saw, Vince had said there were only two things a man needed—honor and pride. Standing next to him, Harley felt as if she had neither. At least, not in the amounts Vince had.

"Growing up in a house like ours..." Despite being a mere foot away, Vince's voice sounded distant. His eyes saw something other than Harley. "Never knowing what the day would bring..." His dark gaze returned to her and she almost wished it hadn't. The emotion there was too raw. The pain evident in every tense line on his face. "I'm thirty-three. A year older than my dad was when he was diagnosed."

The gentle breeze that had felt refreshing moments before felt as cold as the Arctic.

"It's why you don't want to get married." Harley rubbed her bare arms. She couldn't imagine thinking about her future and not having the vague impression of a child at her feet and a man at her side. What an adolescent she was. With silly dreams. "In case it happens to you."

His eyes filled with regret. He knew the personal loss his choice would cause. He mourned. And he mourned alone.

"You should tell them what you sacrificed. How you held the family together."

His mouth hardened into a firm line.

"They'd understand. There'd be no need for fake girlfriends." No need for her. Anguish traced a fragile line around her heart.

Meanwhile, that hard line of Vince's wasn't budging.

Which could only mean one thing. Vince hadn't told her everything. Her heart clenched.

Why would he bare his soul? She was nothing to him but a pretend wedding date.

Vince held out his hand.

He'd fulfilled his part of her request. He'd told her a secret. He'd put this trip in context. But he didn't claim her hand per their bargain. He was giving Harley a choice. Stay with him and endure the past at his side. Or go.

Harley feared the elusive riddle of floating balconies. It kept her awake at night.

But after hearing Vince, balconies seemed inconsequential.

She'd gotten what she'd wanted. He'd opened up to her.

Why wasn't she satisfied?

"TALLY HO!" A GOLF CART with three elderly men turned onto the road in front of the garage.

Had Harley been about to take his hand? She didn't touch him now.

Vince bent to pick up his books. "Let's find you a flight home." The defenses he'd erected around his past had crumbled like a disintegrating engine gasket. He didn't want to say anything else in front of his brothers that might hurt her.

"Tally ho! Tally ho!" Whoever was driving that cart was in a better mood than Vince.

"Let's not." Harley placed both hands on his chest and halted him in his tracks. "What you've done for your brothers is honorable. You have nothing to be ashamed of. You need to tell them."

He should tell her about the last day his mother spent in Harmony Valley. The harsh words. The limit he'd reached when he'd told his mother to go and never come back. Harley wouldn't look at him so kindly then. And if he told his brothers that, they wouldn't look on him kindly, either. "The chance of me telling them is less than the chance of me getting married." And if she'd been listening, she knew how slim matrimony was for him.

"Pizza's here!" Sam shouted, pointing to the approaching cart, which was zipping toward the garage. "Come on, Uncle Vince!"

"Let's go eat." Harley turned him back the way they'd come, grabbed his free hand and tugged him home. "Everything looks better after pepperoni."

"You won't look better," he blurted, still in the numb zone of oversharing. "You look beautiful all the time."

She scoffed, cheeks blossoming with soft color. "After seeing my reflection in the mirror this morning, I'd have to disagree with that statement."

The golf cart parked near Vince's SUV. Sam ran around to the back where an old man rode next to a small stack of pizza boxes.

"Finally, the original bad boys of Harmony Valley are back together." The front-seat golf-cart passenger, a slight man with a belly that hung over the belt holding up his blue-plaid shorts, raised his hands as if praising the Lord. "Just look at them. Most men would be quivering in their boots. And most women—"

"Watch yourself, Irwin." Gabe laughed and went to greet the elderly men with handshakes.

Vince groaned. "Just what we needed. Groupies."

Harley chuckled. "It's exactly what you need."

The driver swiveled his sizeable girth sideways, the better to take in Vince. He wore a baggy Hawaiian shirt over yellow-and-pink-checked golf shorts. "That looks like the middle Messina, all right."

"I hadn't realized when we were dating that you were a celebrity," Harley teased.

"Only within Harmony Valley." Had her hand not been in his, Vince would have retreated to the bed-and-breakfast.

The gangly-limbed man in the back of the golf cart got to his feet, swaying as if he might fall. "You two are idiots."

"Grandpa Phil." Brit had been approaching the golf cart. She rushed to his side to steady him.

"I'm fine." The old man sounded annoyed but didn't shrug her off. "Just getting my sea legs after the wild ride Rex gave us."

Gabe admired the golf cart. "How fast does this thing go, Rex?"

"She'll go twenty," the big man said with a booming voice. "Thanks to Joe's fine-tuning."

"Thanks for nothing, Joe." Brit's grandfather spotted a chair in the driveway and tottered toward it.

"Do you know them?" Harley asked.

"I think Brit's grandfather used to be the town barber," Vince replied. "He's giving her away, but I have no idea who the other two are."

They didn't have to wait long to find out. The old man who'd ridden shotgun was beelining right for them.

"I'm Irwin." He planted his feet in front of Vince and hitched up his blue-plaid shorts. "We have something in common."

"Really?" Vince glanced at Joe for some clue, but his little brother was busy rearranging tables in the parking lot.

"We're both bad-ass bike riders," Irwin

announced with brass. He waited for Vince's response.

"Irwin named his motorcycle Barbara." The corners of Gabe's lips twitched as he hefted a cooler from the golf cart. "Because all bad-ass bikes need a name."

"What was your motorcycle's name?" Irwin stared at Vince the way children gazed at actors who played superheroes.

"Mother." Gabe snorted derisively.

Vince nearly choked when what he really wanted to do was choke Gabe.

Harley smoothed the conversation gap. "Gabe means Vince named his motorbike after their mother."

"Gwen," Irwin breathed. "That is so cool."

"Brit is bringing salad and fruit from the apartment," Joe announced. "Let's eat."

Irwin didn't need to be asked twice. He hurried to join them.

Vince didn't budge. Or look at Harley. "I have never named a motorcycle in my life." Talk about being unmanned. Worse, he stood holding his schoolbooks.

"What does it hurt that an old man thinks you have?" Harley tried to slip her hand free.

Vince held on tight, although he had no

right to. Her dreams were so different from his. "A man needs two things."

"Yes," she nodded. "Honor and pride. I'm on record disagreeing with pride."

Honor and pride. It was what his father used to say when he was in his right mind and lamenting drifting to the edge of elsewhere. "Honor and pride. Without them, a man is nothing."

"I think a man needs more than two things." She tried to lighten his mood. "What about food? A man needs food." A woman does, too, apparently. Her stomach rumbled.

Despite a belief that he had no right to make this woman any promises, Vince gazed at her with a smile. "A man does get hungry." His gaze dropped to her lips.

A motorcycle named Gwen. That stomped on his pride. What he wouldn't give to get Gabe back.

He could use a kiss. Or at the very least, a twenty-second hug.

"Even a hungry man goes on a diet," Harley said with a smile that quickly disappeared. "Because not every food is good for him."

He laughed.

She took advantage of him loosening up to draw her hand free, marching toward the food.

He wasn't laughing a few minutes later as he tried to get some pizza.

"This is exciting. The bad boys of Harmony Valley together again." Irwin followed Vince around the garage parking lot like a lost dog waiting for a scrap of food to drop. Except Irwin had a plate full of food. Presumably, he was following Vince around so he could sit next to him while they ate.

The old man treated Vince's brothers like the backup band, which might have given Vince some satisfaction if not for the way he treated Vince—as if he were the lead singer.

"Do you eat breakfast?" Irwin elbowed Vince. "What am I thinking? Of course, you eat breakfast. I mean…heh, heh, heh…would you like to have doughnuts with me in the morning?"

At the picnic table, Joe bent his head, trying poorly to hide a smile. Gabe choked on a bite of pizza. Even Harley was biting her lip.

"I don't eat doughnuts for breakfast," Vince managed to say without bug-slapping irritation. He scooped watermelon onto his plate next to two slices of meat-laden pizza.

"I should have known you were a protein man." Irwin leaned around Vince's shoulder, watching him select a bottle of water from the cooler on the table. "Doesn't matter. We'll hook up eventually. With the three of you back, there could even be bar fights again." He said these last words gleefully, as if there'd be advance warning and seats sold.

Bar fights? Vince hadn't yet eaten, but it felt as if pizza grease was congealing in his stomach.

"There could be bar fights," Rex, the golf cart driver, said speculatively. "If we had a real bar in town. El Rosal doesn't count. It's more restaurant than bar."

"There will be no bar fights," Joe said sternly.

Irwin sighed dreamily. "And motorcycle races up Parish Hill."

"If any of us had motorcycles," Gabe pointed out with a significant glance at Vince.

"And we're going to be part of everything this time," Irwin finished breathlessly, clearly hanging on Vince's every word.

"Idiots," Phil mumbled.

Vince agreed.

Harley sat on the end of an otherwise

empty picnic bench. Across from her, Joe and his family sat together. The only person vying for a seat near Vince was Irwin.

Vince came to stand beside Harley. "Shove over." He didn't wait for her answer. He sat on the few free inches of wood on the end and nudged Harley to the left with his hip. He frowned across the table at Sam. "Who does Irwin belong to?"

"Us." Sam grinned as if she'd been taking lessons from Gabe.

"It's good to be loved." Irwin sat on the opposite end of the bench, spreading out like an overly watered oak tree. His fork and napkin were placed to the far right, along with his soda can.

Brit smiled at Irwin as if he was no trouble at all. "Irwin and Rex adopted Sam and Joe when they arrived in Harmony Valley."

"We've had trouble getting rid of them ever since," Joe admitted, but he was smiling, too.

"We're family now." Rex had already cleaned his plate. He eyed the pizza boxes. "I'll be here for the Messinas as long as it doesn't interfere with *Jeopardy.*"

"Or a Game Show Network marathon," Irwin agreed.

"Imagine how your life would change if you knew how to record shows." Gabe's comment seemed to be directed to Irwin and Rex, but he looked at Joe when he said it, devilment sparkling in his eyes.

"My grandkids tell me it's possible." Rex handed his plate to Sam and nodded toward the pizza boxes. "But going to the moon is also possible and I don't do that, either."

Sam got up and filled Rex's plate with pepperoni pizza, just the way she might have done for a favorite grandfather.

The breeze rustled eucalyptus leaves. Shadows seemed to shift inside the service bays. The smell of spicy pizza and inane commentary was a balm to Vince's conversation with Harley on the bridge. He took a bite of pizza and could almost pretend his confession had never happened.

Beside Vince, Harley shivered in her sleeveless dress. Vince spread out, planting his feet more than hip distance apart. He set his elbows on the redwood table. His left arm and leg touched Harley's, offering her some warmth.

The planks in the table were cracked but had been filled and stained a traditional redwood color.

Vince leaned back and tried to get a good look at it. "Is this our old picnic table? The one we used to have in the backyard."

Joe nodded. "Took a sander to it and re-finished it."

"Why add to the landfill?" Brit patted the surface. "The wood is still good."

They'd often retreated outside when Dad's emotions got the better of him. Vince would sit on the table and watch Mom try to talk Dad down from paranoia, wishing she'd let him inside to help her, but little Joe had needed a responsible babysitter, which Gabe had never been. Now this... This, Mom would like. That Joe had kept a part of his childhood instead of gutting it and throwing it in a Dumpster. "I suppose that swing set over by Brit's art display was once ours, too."

"It is." Brit looked proud.

Vince knelt sideways and looked underneath the table where he found a carved heart and a set of initials. "You didn't sand off Gabe's graffiti."

"Graffiti? Those are works of art," Gabe said, smiling. "Do you know how hard it is to carve a heart with a pocketknife? Much less a girl's initials? I'm lucky I have all my fingers."

"I bet some of those girls wished you'd taken off a digit when you dumped them." Vince couldn't resist poking fun at his Casanova brother. "Like Frances Edwards."

Some of the exuberance drained from Gabe's face. Franny was the one girl in Harmony Valley to break his heart. "I didn't carve that many hearts."

"That's not true." Sam laughed. "Brad and I find Gabe's hearts all over town. He's a legend."

Gabe scowled. He so rarely wore any expression other than a big smile that it was as if a cloud had cast its shadow over them. But mostly over happy-go-lucky Gabe.

"I wonder where Franny is today," Vince said, because he rather liked the idea of Gabe suffering.

"I'm tired of hearing about Messina romances that don't feature me." Brit seemed intent upon turning the conversation to safer waters. She caught Harley's eye. "Tomorrow is a big day. Reggie is throwing me a bachelorette party."

"Ha!" Gabe laughed and gave Vince a meaningful look.

"And tomorrow night is the Couples Dinner."

"Ha," Vince said with less gusto than Gabe had used. "I guess Gabe will be eating leftover pizza."

"Ha," Gabe said again. "Nice try. I'm the master of ceremonies."

"Anyway…" Brit waited to make sure everyone was listening to her. "I wanted to make sure Harley knew she was invited to both events."

Harley thanked Brit. "Are you sure you want me along for the bachelorette party?"

"It's not really a party," Sam explained. "Reggie's hosting a lunch, but Brit wants to go salvage something she saw upriver first with Dad and me."

"When you get married, you can do anything you want for your bachelorette party," Brit said kindly.

"I will." Sam pulled apart two pizza slices. "I'll make everyone go to a car race and we'll pay extra to be in the infield."

"Over my dead body," Joe muttered.

"I got your back on that," Gabe seconded.

Maybe Irwin was right. Maybe the bad boys of Harmony Valley were back together, because Vince agreed, too. You didn't have to be a Messina to know the racetrack infield was where the wildest parties were held.

A sense of well-being descended over Vince, of belonging. He was having a good time with family. He had a beautiful woman next to him. "Your dad doesn't approve, Sam. Or either one of your uncles. And it's safe to say your grandmother Gwen wouldn't approve, either."

"Speak of the devil," Gabe said with a sly look in his eye. "Vince knows where Grandma Gwen is."

There wasn't enough time to regret Vince's slip or whisper, *It's getting hot in here*, to Harley.

"I guess now's as good a time as any to announce…" Harley got to her feet and dragged Vince to his. She smiled and waved at Gabe. "Vince asked me to marry him. And I said yes."

CHAPTER TEN

As A KID, when Harley had imagined becoming engaged, she'd imagined a man who was sure he loved her to the clouds and back, and that he'd get down on one knee.

She hadn't imagined blurting out an engagement to a man who she knew didn't love her and who seemed dead-set against marriage and fatherhood. And if she would've imagined it, she would've also imagined he'd refute her statement.

Other than raising an eyebrow, Vince refuted nothing.

Which made the butterflies ecstatic.

"I can't believe it." Brit had rushed around the picnic table to hug them.

"I can't, either," Gabe mumbled, handing over a twenty-dollar bill to Joe. "I guess you win the bet, brother." He came around to hug them both, as did Joe.

"This is depressing." Irwin pushed his plate away. "First Joe comes back and I learn he's not in a gang. And now the baddest Messina is getting married. Pitiful." He shook his head.

"I take offense to that remark." Gabe's chin jutted. "I happen to be the oldest and the baddest Messina around."

"Well, at least you're single," Irwin begrudgingly admitted.

Sam hugged Harley. "I want to be a bridesmaid. I like being a bridesmaid, even if the bachelorette party doesn't have dancing cowboys."

"What did you say?" Joe stuffed Gabe's twenty in his wallet. "Who told you that nonsense?"

"Brad." Sam stuck her little nose in the air and walked back to her seat. "His older sister got married last year."

"What did I tell you about Brad?" Vince demanded of Joe.

"I'm gonna throw that kid in the river," Gabe said.

"Stop." Brit rapped her knuckles on the table. "Everyone just stop. This is supposed to be a joyous time for Harley and Vince. And I'm so full of questions, I don't know where to start." And then she disproved that last statement by rushing on. "How did he propose? I bet he had some romantic things to say. Did he ask you when he put his books down? Did you pick a date? Are you going to get married here? Or in Texas?"

"It's getting hot in here," Harley murmured, feeling exactly the opposite. The evening breeze was kicking up and she didn't have a sweater.

Vince draped his arm over her shoulders and pulled her close, rubbing her bare arm. "We haven't made any decisions yet. We'll let you know as soon as we do."

"And kids," Brit piped up. "Have you talked about kids?"

Vince stiffened beside her.

"Lord love a duck." Brit's grandfather stood. "I'm done. I managed to stay out of most wedding discussions this week, I don't need to listen to all this romantic drivel. I'd like to go home and I'd like someone other than Rex to drive me."

Vince jumped up. "We can take you. Harley doesn't have a sweater and it's getting chilly."

And in a moment Gabe was going to realize Harley's announcement had derailed his conversation about their mother.

Harley got up. There was another round of

hugs and congratulations. This time, Harley began to feel guilty. These were good people and she was deceiving them to act as a buffer for Vince.

Brit helped her grandfather into the backseat of the SUV and then hugged Harley a third time. "I thought there were just a few couples who might win the Couples Dinner, but now I have to add you to the list."

"What is the Couples Dinner?" Vince asked from behind the wheel.

"It's like that *Newlywed Game* they used to have on TV," Phil said from the backseat. "It was Irwin's idea, but apparently it's a thing."

"It's a more coveted invite than to our wedding," Brit agreed. "Rex and Irwin have said they're offering prizes."

"Idiot prizes," Phil said none too softly.

Brit glanced over her shoulder at Joe and Gabe. "Can you believe those two? They're betting on who'll win Couples Dinner—you two or Joe and me."

"Game on," Harley said automatically, being a competitive perfectionist.

"Game on," Vince mumbled when she'd closed her door and buckled in.

During the short drive into town, Phil dozed, snoring in the backseat.

"I don't snore like Phil, do I?" Harley asked, searching for any conversation now that the bombshell had been dropped in their lives. By her, no less.

"It's more like heavy breathing." Vince drove down Main Street at a very sedate pace, perhaps worried that Mildred's boyfriend Hero would alert the sheriff to him speeding. "At least when you snore, I know you're alive."

"Sorry...about before. First, I let the thing about your mom slip, and now this."

"And we still have six more days to go." Vince stopped at the town square and then turned right. His tone may have been calm but his features were carved out of ice.

Phil choked for a second and then uttered a sleepy admonishment about Vince not speeding up to stop signs.

"He didn't," Harley said.

Vince gave her the evil eye. "I think you've spoken up in my defense enough for one day."

Harley pressed her lips together, which is what she should have done when the engagement thought flew into her head earlier.

Thankfully, Phil's house wasn't far off the town square. They escorted Brit's grandfather to the door and then returned to the SUV. And then they were alone.

"Two days." Vince's voice was chilly. "Imagine how far our relationship can progress by next weekend."

"You're mad at me. I don't blame you." Harley was mad at herself.

Vince wasn't listening. "We could announce your pregnancy tomorrow. Maybe an adoption by Wednesday. Oh, and by Friday we could skip Joe's wedding completely and tell them we're going to elope."

"It was just a little slip."

"Slips seem to happen around you."

There was something sharp in his tone that prodded her humility. "It's not like you haven't had pretend girlfriends before. So now you have a pretend engagement. And next week you can have a pretend breakup."

His jaw clamped together and he barely moved his arms as he steered through the turn that led to the bed-and-breakfast.

"I was just trying to protect—"

"Protect me. Yes, I know. That seems to be a theme of yours." Vince pulled into the bed-and-breakfast's driveway. "Stop doing that."

"I will. Of course, I will."

He held up a finger as if he'd just made an important discovery. "You know…" The hard planes of his face were shadowed by the large tree they'd parked under and the gathering twilight. "This means there will be kisses." His voice sounded almost…triumphant.

"Oh, boy," Harley huffed in disgust and practically threw herself out of the SUV in indignation.

But a tiny voice in her head whispered, *Oh, boy*, with a much different tone.

I'M ENGAGED TO HARLEY.

That statement engendered equal parts annoyance, dread and excitement.

Harley returned to their room alone while Vince sat in the dark dining room of the Lambridge B and B. He placed the books he'd taken from the garage on the table in front of him.

I'm engaged to Harley.

A fake engagement was something he'd expect of Gabe.

Or was that a shotgun wedding?

He'd known Harley was impulsive. He'd

attributed it to her youth. He hadn't expected her to be a watchdog. It made him smile to admit she had his back. Not that her announcement had done more than delay the inevitable discussion with his brothers about their mother.

I'm engaged to Harley.

The engagement was just a farce, of course. He wasn't going to buy her a ring. He wasn't going to worry that she'd have expectations when they returned to Texas. But it did give him carte blanche to put his arm around her, to keep her close, purely for pretend purposes—who knew what she'd say next?—and perhaps to steal that kiss they were both longing for.

The door to the bed-and-breakfast opened. Two men walked in.

"You waited up." Gabe came to rest across the table from Vince, leaning on the formal chair back. "And here I am in before curfew."

"I figured you'd want to talk." Vince settled into his chair, looking at Joe, not Gabe.

"Mom's in Texas." Joe scowled. "You're in Texas."

"I told Gabe," Vince said evenly, "we don't talk."

"No," Joe said, visibly struggling to keep

his voice down. "We don't talk." He gestured back and forth, Vince to Joe. "What good could possibly come from you having a relationship with Mom? She left us."

"I told you, I don't talk to her. And I didn't tell you where she was because I knew you'd get upset."

Joe came forward and sat in a chair at the head of the table. He pushed Vince's books away. "Mom signed hall passes for you."

"I…" This wasn't the direction he thought the conversation would go.

"Don't look at me." Gabe pulled out a chair and sat. "She didn't give me hall passes."

"And she was gone before I wanted to get hall passes," Joe added sharply.

"That's because neither one of you worked in the garage." How Vince wished Harley were here to hear that statement.

"I worked in the garage plenty." Joe bristled.

Vince reached for his yearbook, flipping to a section in the middle for school activities. "You played sports." He jabbed his finger at a picture of the football team.

Joe's jaw jutted. "Your grades weren't good enough for you to play."

Gabe leaned forward. "Because he didn't go to class enough. Why didn't you go to class, brother?"

"You know why." Vince's throat was raw and that rawness came through in his tone. "Someone had to cover for Dad and fix cars."

"Dad asked you to cover for him?" Joe scoffed. "I don't believe that. When he needed help, he wouldn't think to ask."

"Dad didn't ask me." Vince reached for a hall pass, sliding it over the polished wood to Joe so he could see the authorizing signature. "Mom did."

Joe shook his head. "Why would she do that? Why only you?"

"Because Vince could fix anything, don't you remember?" Gabe picked up the hall pass and stared at it. "And I was too interested in girls to help, unless they made me."

"And you only wanted to play sports." Vince didn't mean for it to sound like an accusation, but it did nonetheless.

"Also, I was her favorite," Joe said hoarsely. He got up and left. To his credit, he didn't slam the door.

"We should talk more often." Gabe spun the pass back to Vince.

"And by 'more often,' do you mean not at all?" Vince held his breath. He hadn't realized until Joe walked out how important his brothers were to him.

Gabe stood, his face in shadow. "You're so naive." He turned, heading toward the stairs. "You should marry Harley. Women like her don't come along every day."

Vince blew out a shaky breath and centered his things in front of him on the table. Slowly, his head came down to rest on top of the photo album. He wanted to believe the worst of it was over, but it wasn't. He hadn't told them why Mom left…

Vince sat on the redwood table in the backyard. *I want to go back to school.* He had an algebra test that afternoon.

Your father needs you at the shop. Mom took a deep drag on her cigarette and picked at her cuticles. She'd torn the skin around her nails until they bled. *Eat your sandwich and forget about school.*

No. Vince threw his baloney sandwich on the ground. He liked school. He liked math.

As if on cue, Dad started shouting. Something wasn't going right in the garage.

I can't do it anymore. Mom started to cry.

Something wasn't going right at home, either. Vince's stomach roiled.

He's getting worse. She stared at Vince with hollow eyes. *You'll have to quit school.*

Vince lifted his head. He'd been selfish. He should have dropped out of school.

Back at the B and B, he picked up his books and with leaden feet drifted down the hall. Harley had left the door unlocked. She was far too trusting. And too impulsive. And too generous. She needed someone to watch out for her.

I'm engaged to Harley.

He stood with his back against the door a long time before he went to bed.

CHAPTER ELEVEN

HARLEY WOKE TO Vince sitting on his bed, looking as if he hadn't slept.

"If this is what being engaged does to you…" she said, pushing herself up and finger-combing her hair. Her stomach was in the neutral zone, neither friendly nor ready to make war on her equilibrium. "I say we call the whole thing off. I kept you awake all night with my snoring, didn't I?"

He shook his head. "I've been wondering why a smart woman like you ended up in a situation like this." There were dark circles under his eyes and stubble on his chin. "An architect working as a tiler."

Harley considered his words as carefully as she considered him. "Why does it matter? You needed a wingman and I was available."

"You distract me." He was wearing the same T-shirt and basketball shorts he'd had on yesterday. They were rumpled. He hadn't changed. "You didn't used to."

"I didn't used to come to your rescue, either."

"No." He stood and reached over to brush Harley's hair into what she hoped was some semblance of order. His fingers traced the path Harley used when she brushed her hair, over the ears, toward the crown, down the back.

It was intimate. It was loving. It made butterflies swoon. And if they'd been in Waco, Harley would have been his.

But they weren't in Waco. They weren't engaged. They weren't even dating.

Vince didn't retreat when he was done. He continued to stay next to her, staring at her as if she was a set of steps he had to build using a non-standard angle. "Why did you quit being an architect? Tell me straight."

The question caught her by complete surprise.

At her hesitation, he hinted at bridal-couple indulgence, "Pretend you're telling your fiancé."

Pretend? She'd never be able to pretend again.

"Okay," Harley said, feeling as if her entire body was blushing.

Close. He was too close. Butterflies trembled with anticipation.

She gulped, cautioning butterflies and hearts to be realistic. "I told you, I draw buildings." Harley reached beneath her pillow for her sketchbook. She flipped a few pages open quickly, embarrassed by all the characteristics her brother Taylor had associated with her drawings. They were loopy and unclear in form. They were cartoonish and had no basis in reality. They couldn't be built.

"They're unique." Vince sat on the bed next to her. "But I wouldn't go so far as to say they can't be built. Think of all the impossible structures out there. The pyramids. The Taj Mahal. That ball in Epcot Center."

Had she really whined out loud? She closed the book and dropped it in her lap. That's where her gaze landed, too.

"And the problem that led to your quitting happened…?" he prompted softly.

Harley twisted the hair he'd combed, bringing her gaze up to his. "Architecture is stuffy for a reason. There are two branches. In the first are those who build things, anything from basic houses to tall, gloriously twisted skyscrapers."

"And in the second?"

"Those in the second branch live in the truly creative side, the completely impractical side." She tapped her sketchbook, warming to the topic. "They refine designs and enter them in competitions—not to be built, but to be admired for their vision, for the impossibility, for the future."

His gaze was sincere and accepting.

Harley drew a deep breath. "When I first began drawing buildings, I didn't realize there were two branches. I saw movies and cartoons where characters lived and worked in impossible structures."

"The sky's the limit." He took her hand and it seemed right, sharing a room, sharing a confidence.

"Exactly. And when I went to work, I'd already won some awards. I'd gotten a lot of job offers out of college and I was a bit high on myself."

"Ah, pride goeth before a fall. No wonder you rejected my honor and pride rule."

"Indeedy." She opened the sketchbook to a page. The Page. Her stomach gave an early indication that it wasn't back to normal. "The City of Houston requested submissions for a playhouse. I went to my boss and showed this to him, knowing the balconies couldn't be built, but hopeful that he'd respect my design and build upon it in his submission."

"He stole your design." Vince let go of her hand.

"No. Kind of." She was tap-dancing, trying to protect her pride, when she shouldn't. Not with him. "I mean, I was employed by him and had gone to him with it, so he had every right to use what I'd created." Her voice weakened as she talked, until it became a whisper. "I just didn't expect him to use it as it is. Every impossible curve."

Vince studied her drawing, leaning his dark head of hair closer. And then he leaned back. "I'm not sure how he plans to build those balconies."

Harley gave a nervous chuckle and closed the sketchbook. "Me, either. It's a purely creative drawing. Meant to be entered in a competition to build my name and my company's reputation."

"But if you only enter competitions, when do you get to build something?"

"That's just it. The most well-respected architects win awards with designs that cross the limits of modern building capabilities into no man's land. And then reel their designs back to what's possible and then sell and build real structures, to make a career." She hugged the sketchbook to her chest. "This design isn't pulled back enough and my boss is convinced someone can come up with an idea that will make it viable, still retaining this look. My career...well, if more people knew I was attached to this mess, my career would officially be over." In four years, it would all come to light before a company hired her, during that time when they did their due diligence and checked into her background and references.

Vince's brow wrinkled. "To make balconies like that float on air, you use cantilevers."

"These aren't that kind of balcony." She moved her hand back and forth, as if tracing a path up a switch-backed road. "They weave in and out, and up and down, like the swirled layers in clouds. There aren't rows. There are clusters of seats in bends in the structure."

He touched her cheek. "Someone will come up with a compromise."

"Maybe. Hopefully. But it won't be me. Because..." She cleared her throat. "Well... what if I wasn't cut out for architecture in the first place?" She looked into Vince's eyes, searching for reassurance.

He put his hands on her upper arms and gave her a gentle smile. "What if you're destined to dream on the creative side and leave a trail of breadcrumbs for future generations of architects? Never crossing over to mundane realities like ranch homes and four-story office buildings."

No butterflies fluttered.

Instead there was just a feeling in her chest that she was right to have defended this man. And that she'd defend him for the rest of her days, even after he broke off their fake engagement and their fake relationship. Even if she fell in love with him and he broke her heart.

CHAPTER TWELVE

VINCE LET HARLEY sleep a little longer while he showered.

When it was her turn in the bathroom, Vince sat on the floor of their room, his back against his bed. He brought out his photo album and stared at the picture of his mother. How hurt she'd be to learn Joe and Gabe wanted nothing to do with her. Or maybe he was reading her all wrong. Maybe she never thought about her sons, never longed to pick up the phone and call or to take a trip to California to visit.

Vince tucked the photo album in his suitcase and stared at the rose-patterned wallpaper on the wall behind Harley's bed. He missed the job site. He missed being bone-tired at the end of the day and falling asleep almost as soon as his body went horizontal.

The corner of Harley's sketchbook was visible beneath her pillow. Her sketch of the playhouse had been unlike anything he'd seen before, much less anything he'd tried to build. He wouldn't mind looking at it again.

Vince stayed put on the floor.

The shower water was still on.

Vince checked the time on his phone. Nearly eight. He checked for messages. None. And then when he was done checking, he reached for Harley's sketchbook.

She'd flipped through it so fast, he hadn't gotten a good look at it. The first few pages shocked him. Structures that looked like lopsided, flattened muffins. An apartment complex that looked like a swirling soft-serve ice-cream cone. And then her visions took on a more sophisticated feel. The muffin looked healthier. The ice cream like gracefully sculpted snow. He landed on a sketch of her theater, covering a two-page spread. The orchestra was hidden beneath the stage. The walls undulated toward the back in vertical waves. And the balconies ebbed and flowed like a ribbon of water, sometimes pooling in a deep bend and offering ten seats together, sometimes straightening for only two seats across. The heights were different, too. Some sections higher, some lower.

It wasn't the best use of space. You'd get more seats in a traditional design. But it was fascinating. She'd created curved theater boxes instead of a usual down-sloping balcony. And nothing seemed to hold it up.

A turn of the page revealed a house with a roofline like the big hill on a roller coaster. A gentle climb up and a dramatic drop down. It was simultaneously sophisticated and fun. Whoever lived in that house would need to be confident in their own skin, because people would either love it or hate it.

Vince came down on the side of love, if only because it would be so much fun to make.

The shower had stopped.

He returned Harley's book beneath her pillow and searched the internet with his phone for any information on the architect who'd inspired Harley. They both had the same loathing of right angles. And then he searched for information on the companies that built those designs.

Before Vince had a chance to find any companies in the US, there was a soft knock on the door.

"Vince." It was Gabe.

Vince stepped into the hallway to talk to his brother, who was grinning like he'd just been promoted. "You're talking to me?"

"I'm never going to stop talking to my brother." Gabe's grin turned into a half frown. "But, hey—" that grin went back on high beam "—I found the perfect gift for the bride and groom." Without waiting to see if Vince was interested, Gabe headed toward the lobby.

Before they got there, an old woman in a blue dress stepped into their path. She had gunmetal-gray hair swept behind her neck and a severe expression reminiscent of their former high school principal. Her bony hands were gripped in front of her as if she needed that grip to hold herself together. "Well, if it isn't the Messina boys."

Gabe halted in his tracks. "Mrs. Lambridge?"

If this was Mrs. Lambridge, she was Brit and Reggie's grandmother, and the sourpuss who'd looked down her nose at the Messinas since the dawn of time.

"I know how you boys like to joyride." She may have been old, but she still knew how to put people in their place. "I told Reggie to lock up my car keys."

Gabe held up his hands as if the old woman had a gun. "Little Joe took your car, ma'am. And Vince here dared him to do it." Gabe flashed a sly glance at Vince. He still knew how to throw his brother under the bus.

"In all fairness, Mrs. Lambridge…" It was a struggle to keep any amount of civility in Vince's tone. "You used to leave your keys in the ignition and you walked everywhere. That car practically begged to be taken out for a ride, just to clean out the carburetor. Joe was doing you a favor."

"That's what your uncle said." Mrs. Lambridge didn't sound as if she believed it, then or now.

Since Uncle Turo was currently in the big house, the two Messina men kept silent.

"Turo's argument wasn't what swayed me not to press charges." She went on in a triumphant voice the way villains did as they spilled all their dastardly plans. "It was the idea that sitting behind bars for an afternoon was punishment enough for a boy. I believe Joseph learned a lesson."

"He did." Gabe nodded. "Look at him today. About to marry your granddaughter."

"But you seemed not to have learned anything." Her snooty words echoed in the foyer. She raised a bony hand and pointed to the door. "There's a motorcycle on my front walk."

Vince frowned at his brother. Gabe definitely could *not* be taught.

"That's ours," Gabe said with pride. "It's a wedding present for Joe and Brit."

"I suggest you look at her bridal registry. They still need a cake plate." She walked toward the dining room with the careful steps of the aged, pausing in the arch. "I don't want to see that motorbike on my property again. Understood?"

"Yes, ma'am," they both said smartly.

Her footsteps echoed on the hardwood and then became muffled when she went into the kitchen.

Gabe shuddered, and beelined to the door. Vince gladly followed, relieved until he saw what had upset Mrs. Lambridge.

Shades of Easy Rider.

A bright red chopper with ape hanger handlebars stood on the walk. It was the kind of motorcycle people rode for show, not comfort. The handlebars stretched more than two feet above the gas tank, leaving the grips and controls at head height.

"Ta-da." Gabe stared at the bike as if it was his first love, Franny.

Vince stopped on the bottom step, unwilling to stoop to Gabe's level. "What is this?"

"It's called free and I couldn't resist." Gabe rubbed the teardrop gas tank as if it was Aladdin's lamp. "It doesn't run, but you're going to work your magic to make it run, and then we'll give it to the happy couple. They can use it to tour up and down the coast."

"This isn't a motorcycle for touring farther than down the block." Vince could feel a scowl etching itself into his face. "We talked about this. We decided to get Joe and Brit a riding mower, not a motorcycle."

"But…" Gabe held out his arms to encompass the bike as if it was a desired prize to be won. "It was free."

"It wasn't free. You traded something for it," Vince guessed. It was a skill Gabe had learned from Uncle Turo, otherwise known as Prisoner 05045-123 in the federal penitentiary.

"So what if I did?" Gabe scoffed. It took more than a poke at his technique to rile him. "The other day I noticed Grandpa Phil was having a yard sale. He had a riding mower—"

Anger snarled its way up Vince's throat.

"I went back today and he *gave me* that mower for free."

Vince refrained from rolling his eyes. He knew better than to expect Gabe to stop at one trade. "And then…"

"I took the mower back to the garage and put it on the battery charger, in case it was merely a dead battery."

Vince came down the last step. "And this thing?"

"While the mower was charging, I drove by a house a couple of blocks over where I'd seen this beauty sitting in the side yard. The old woman who answered the door said she'd give me the bike—*free!*—if I mowed her yards. You fix that mower to give to the bride and groom, and we'll own this cycle."

Vince had to admire his brother's skill, even if he didn't always use his powers for good. "Do the Marines appreciate your talent?"

"No, sir." Gabe rolled his shoulders back into military attention. "I'm on permanent report, although, not that it matters when my guys show up with what the troops need."

Vince took in the sleek lines of the gas tank, noted the rust on the mufflers and the grime on the carburetor. It wouldn't take much to make the bike shine brighter than a new nickel. The inner workings might present a challenge, but to ride all that power, to experience all that freedom…

It was irresponsible. He would not be sucked into one of Gabe's schemes. "We need to take the motorcycle back."

Gabe's grin fell.

"We can give Joe and Brit the riding mower as a wedding gift." Vince stopped dreaming of the open road and started thinking of his younger brother. "This chopper… it'll upset Joe."

A small motorcycle that was one step above a moped turned onto their street. The rider wore tight, red, riding leathers, the kind professional racers favored. He brought his bike to a wobbly stop near the curb and removed his helmet. It was Irwin. "Saw Gabe pushing that motorcycle over here. I'm ready to ride with your posse."

Vince and Gabe exchanged glances.

Harley joined them. She wore a blue-velvet skirt, a gauzy blue blouse and a hesitant smile that said she either regretted telling him of her failure or she regretted the fact that they—the recently engaged couple—had an audience. It was a toss-up as to whether she'd go back inside or come forward and kiss him to put on a show for Gabe.

She yawned and came forward, resting her hand briefly on Vince's shoulder before taking in the monstrosity Gabe had succumbed to.

"What in the world is that thing?" Harley's gaze landed on Gabe's chopper, but Irwin misunderstood which bike she referred to.

"This is Barbara." Irwin got off his bike and took a step toward them. His motorcycle almost fell over since the old man had neglected to put the stand down. He caught it just in time. "She kicks gear. But she's nothing like that hog." He pointed to Gabe's find. "That thing is a monster. A classic. Aged to perfection. Like me." He yanked up his too tight leather pants.

Harley squeaked.

Vince kept his eyes on Irwin's face, sucking back a smile. "How long have you been riding?"

"Just a few months. Before my wife died…" Irwin paused, fighting the face-crumple of grief. "She didn't let me do anything dangerous. And I didn't want to make her worry." This last was spoken softly, without the bravado Irwin normally exuded.

"You loved your wife enough to stop doing something you loved." Vince spoke to Irwin, but he made sure Gabe was listening. "Joe's made a lot of changes to his lifestyle for Sam."

"Joe is boring." Irwin hitched up one knee and tried to sit on the chopper. His red leather pants were so tight, he couldn't get his leg over without Gabe's assistance. When he was settled on the seat, he flashed a grin decorated with silver crowns. "Joe isn't like us. We're men of action. Men who take risks and live life on the edge." He had to stand on his toes to reach the hand grips.

Gabe gestured to Vince, as if daring him to destroy the Messina image by refusing a free motorcycle.

"Living on the edge is tiring." Vince wasn't perpetuating any image, edgy or otherwise. "Gabe just brought this bike over for me to admire. It's not ours." And the look he gave Gabe said as much.

"That's a shame," Harley said. "I bet Brit could use it to make a mermaid for her art display."

"Ahh," both Messinas said at the same time, having found common ground.

Vince looked at Harley and mouthed, *Thank you.*

"This hog is a lady magnet, not art." Irwin released the handlebars and sat back down. "Don't destroy this road-worthy beauty by making it into a mermaid."

"Not even one with red riding-leather flippers?" Harley teased.

"Not even." Irwin was having none of it.

A red Thunderbird convertible zipped around the corner. A very thin woman with a very tight white bun waved as she passed.

"Did you see that? Rose waved at me," Irwin said breathlessly. "I have to have this bike. Rose would go out with me if I had a chopper like this."

The motorcycle was too big for the small man. He'd kill himself before he ever rolled out of the driveway.

"You know what might be better than this bike to win Rose?" Gabe had that look in his eye, the one that said he was onto something.

"What?" Irwin was all ears.

"Pointers from the ultimate chick magnet." Gabe tapped his chest.

"You?" Irwin stood and gripped the handlebars again. "You'd help me?"

"I'm out." Harley skipped past the chopper and reached the sidewalk, turning toward the town square.

Vince didn't want to wait to hear what cockamamie scheme Gabe had hatched, but his brother caught his arm. "I know you think I run through life without considering the consequences, and that might be mostly true." He glanced over his shoulder at Vince's fake fiancée. "But consider the consequences of your actions with her before you take this farce any farther."

"I have." In addition to fixing her tile saw, Vince was going to help Harley return to architecture. He just had to figure out how. He hurried after Harley and, when he reached her, he said the first thing that came to mind.

"Hey, you ran off before I could kiss you goodbye."

"ALL RIGHT. KISS ME like you can't live without me, honey," Harley said with forced cheer for their audience. And here she'd thought a simple touch in front of Gabe would suffice.

Harley moved closer to Vince to face the

music of the engagement she'd created, smiling when Vince's face came into view, so familiar, so handsome, so sad that he'd never be hers. At least, not outside of Harmony Valley.

Vince's head jerked back. His body didn't tilt toward hers and the offered kiss.

Did he have a case of stage fright?

She checked. Two houses back, Gabe was paying no attention to them as he talked animatedly to Irwin, probably imparting those love tips he'd promised. Two houses ahead, a toddler with dark brown hair shrieked happily as he ran through a fountain sprinkler with a small golden dog. And in front of her, Vince stood as if waiting for his cue. It was the perfect time to convince Gabe they loved each other despite their differences, that they cared, and yada-yada.

She'd expected Vince's eyes to shine with humor or his lips to turn upward impishly. Instead his eyes regarded her apologetically and his lips formed a firm straight line.

There were no butterflies. No rapid heartbeat. No feeling of connection like they'd had while discussing her wreck of a career.

Literally, she'd never faced a man and seen him be less interested in her affection.

How had she fallen from homecoming queen and the girl most likely to succeed to a woman living on the edge of ruin obligated to bestow an unwanted kiss?

Oh, she knew how. She could start that hypothesis with, *Well, I envisioned floating balconies...*

"Let's get this over with," she mumbled, leaning toward Vince.

"Stop." He placed his hands on her shoulders.

The sky was a clear, deep blue. Blooming wildflowers bordered the sidewalk at her feet. Irwin's laughter mingled with the joyous squeals of the toddler. It was the picture-perfect setting for a kiss, all within sight of Gabe.

And yet Vince had called a halt. Vince, who excelled at kissing and hadn't complained about her surprise kiss this weekend. Vince, who wanted his brothers to believe he was in a relationship so he could continue to avoid talking about their mother.

"Why?" she asked him in a voice barely above a whisper.

Vince didn't say anything, but she saw the answer in his face. She felt it in his tender touch.

"You're trying to protect me," she said. The shock of it chilled her skin.

His expression didn't change.

Protect me?

From what?

From Gabe's jests? From prying eyes? No.

From hurt. From heartbreak. From him.

"Vince." Harley covered his hands with her own, intent on reassuring him she wasn't falling in love. "The one thing I need—" a solution to her playhouse design "—you can't provide."

His brow furrowed. Not in anger. More like regret.

The last thing she wanted from him was regret. She wanted… She'd like… She…

And then it hit her. It hit her harder than the need to rise to his defense. She had feelings for this man. Deep feelings. Possibly… love.

She loved Vince.

In her head, the words felt right.

I love Vince.

She loved his strength. She loved how humble he was. She loved his willingness to sacrifice for others and his courage to go it alone. She loved how he looked at her sometimes as if he could look at her all day, all night, and forever.

Her father would look twice at him because of their difference in age and education. Her mother would be charmed by Vince's manners and fall for Vince's hair.

I love Vince.

In her head, the words felt authentic. Loving Vince seemed possible. But then again, in her head the vision of swirling balconies felt achievable. Who was she kidding? Harley was setting herself up for one whopping disappointment because Vince had vowed not to marry.

Standing there on the sidewalk, not kissing her, Vince was trying to protect her heart.

Too little, too late.

It seemed to be cracking. There was certainly a deep pain in her chest.

Gabe's hearty guffaws echoed down the street. A window slid open behind her. A car backed out of a driveway.

Funny how Harley felt she and Vince were alone, isolated from it all. If they had been, they might be able to come to some sort of compromise.

Vince leaned in, almost as if he'd reconsidered.

She hoped he'd reconsidered.

But he merely touched his forehead to hers.

"Why aren't you kissing me?" Her words dropped below a whisper. They were more like a sigh.

"Besides the fact that Gabe went inside?" Vince gave her a wry smile and pulled away. "We're in the friend zone, remember?" He started walking away.

Harley couldn't move, perhaps afraid to trip on the pieces of her heart littering the sidewalk. "I'm confused," she said in a strained voice. There was still a kiss on the table and, of course, her tile saw. Was all that debt being forgiven?

"The jig's up. Gabe knows it's a fake engagement." Vince smiled at her without devilment or agenda. "Let's see if Martin's is still open. I can get a coffee. You can get a tea. And then we'll head over to Joe's place in time for that bachelorette luncheon."

CHAPTER THIRTEEN

"VINCE MESSINA." AN OLD MAN with a gray ponytail and a purple tie-dyed T-shirt came to stand outside El Rosal. He stuffed a cell phone into the back pocket of his cargo shorts. "Welcome home."

"I'm just visiting, Mayor Larry." Vince slowed, stopping, hand extended, because his mother had instilled Vince with some manners, even if he didn't want to talk to the guy.

While Vince had been walking, he'd been thinking about the rest of his life. Without commitment. Without love. Without Harley.

She'd told him to kiss her as if he couldn't live without her and Vince had been struck with the sudden need to do just that.

Oh, he knew she was only kidding. But on some level, a passionate embrace seemed wrong, like cutting a corner on a marathon race or eyeballing a window opening instead of using a level.

They were falling back into the place they'd been pre-Waco, except this time they were talking about things that meant something. He didn't want Harley to look at him as more than a friend. He couldn't give her what she needed.

"Think twice about leaving town, son." Mayor Larry was a two-handed shaker. He'd been the town leader for as long as Vince had known Harmony Valley had a mayor. Back in the day, he'd talked to Tony Messina several times about encouraging his three sons to be better citizens. And now he wanted Vince to stay?

The mayor's statement almost sounded like an ultimatum issued by a sheriff in a B Western. Except the sheriff never wore purple tie-dye and usually told the bad hombres to get out of town, not hang around. Vince tested the mayor's words for sincerity while simultaneously looking to see if the mayor was tipsy.

El Rosal had a bar, after all. And the mayor could probably get a Bloody Mary with his breakfast.

"Harmony Valley is thriving." Mayor Larry pumped Vince's hand, smiling at Harley. "It warms my heart to see so many of your friends and family returning, getting married, having babies. Speaking of families, introduce me to this charming fiancée of yours?"

Vince made the introductions.

And then Mayor Larry worked Harley's hand with that same shake-and-cover, two-handed enthusiastic technique. "Young lady, I hear you're an architect."

Vince's guard went up. He drew Harley free of the mayor's clutches. "She's an architect, all right." Or she should be.

"Ah, here's the town council. Just in time." The mayor nodded toward a dated green Buick parking in one of the few open spaces nearby. "When I called they were just around the corner."

"Sorry. We're on our way to get Harley a cup of tea." Vince tried to tow Harley toward Martin's. In his experience, any time the town leaders wanted to meet with him, the news was bad.

"Just in time for what?" Harley was too polite, digging in her heels when she should have been taking Vince's cue and finding a bunker to hide in.

"We wanted to set up a meeting with you, Madame Architect."

"Oh, I…" Harley's panicked gaze went to Vince. She tried to move on, but three elderly women were invading, cutting off their retreat.

Although Vince wanted Harley to return to her chosen field, he didn't like the vulnerability on her face. He pulled her closer.

"I'm so glad we caught you." Rose, the thin, elegant woman who'd been the object of Irwin's affection earlier, approached them with graceful steps. She wore a long, full, blue skirt and a pink blouse with ribbons on the sleeves. Her severe white bun contradicted the subtle breeze-induced dance of her skirt and ribbons.

"Vince and Harley were heading to Martin's for tea." Mayor Larry looked pleased with himself, rocking back on his Birkenstocks. "We can talk there."

"Talk about…architecture?" Harley gripped Vince's hand as if he held her dangling from a ledge.

"Yes. That sounds lovely." Rose introduced herself and the ladies exiting the car. "You know Mildred. That's her with the walker. And that's Agnes."

"I don't get a qualifier?" Agnes had hair as gray as Harley's saw, but it was shorter than Gabe's. She'd been slighted in the height department, too, but not in confidence. "My granddaughter would say I need a qualifier people would respect, like Great-Grandma Overlord." Spoken like a woman who'd been slighted.

"You need to get over Christine mentioning you were too bossy with her nanny." Mildred lifted her walker over the curb and followed it up with careful steps. "Is that Vince?"

"That's me," Vince said warily.

"Rose saw you with a motorcycle." Mildred stared in Vince's general direction through her thick lenses. "Are you going to take your fiancée for a ride later?"

"Actually…" Vince met Harley's gaze. He should end this now and come clean about the pretend engagement with everyone. "She's not—"

"Running," Harley finished for him. "The bike. Gwen Two Point Oh."

Vince leaned down to whisper, "It's getting hot in here."

"I like this topic better than architecture," she whispered back.

"I could have used you on my racing team, Vince." Mildred's wandering gaze was only disconcerting if she faced Vince head-on. "You could fix anything, including my Volkswagen."

"German engineering." Vince couldn't keep the reverence out of his voice. Fixing it was an art form.

"Yes, yes." Mayor Larry positioned himself to lead them to Martin's. "You can catch up all you want at the bakery." He set off at a good clip.

Vince and Harley followed. The three town council ladies brought up the rear at Mildred's slower pace.

"We could make a run for it." Vince spoke only loud enough for Harley to hear. He didn't like not knowing what the town council wanted from her. "They'd never catch us."

The mayor disappeared inside the bakery. Now was the time to make a move.

"Much as I want to go, it's good Messina public relations to listen." Harley smiled at Vince for the first time since he'd refused to kiss her, but it was as polite as her plan. "Besides, I think Mildred has a crush on you. You shouldn't disappoint her."

Mildred wasn't who Vince wanted to avoid letting down. It was Harley.

Resolved to stay on his toes with the town council, Vince held the bakery door open for them.

"Welcome. Come in and keep me company." A blond woman waved from behind the counter. The bakery was nearly empty and her apron free of stains. "It's a light crowd today because there's a breakfast and lecture at the winery."

Harley ordered tea and a black coffee for Vince.

"I met Harley at the shower. I'm Tracy, a bridesmaid." The blonde waved. "You might remember me, Vince. I'm Will's kid sister. He's Joe's best man," she said for Harley's benefit. "Am I bringing the rest of you the usual?" she asked the town council.

There was a hearty chorus of the affirmative.

"Two coffees black, two lattes, two hot green teas and three scones." Tracy made tea for Harley and Agnes first, and then rushed to grind beans and prepare a large, fresh pot of coffee.

The mayor directed Vince to push two rectangular tables together and once they'd all taken their seats, he called the meeting to order by slapping his palm on the table. "Our town needs an architect."

"Why?" Harley cradled a mug of tea between her hands. "I see plenty of empty storefronts."

"All small." Agnes unfolded a sheet of paper with a map of the downtown area drafted in pencil. She smoothed it on top of the table. "And some of the interiors are crumbling."

"We need to knock down walls." Mayor Larry flicked his age-spotted hand over Agnes's map.

"Get rid of rodents," Rose added with a dramatic shiver.

Mildred adjusted her thick glasses on her nose and squinted at the drawing. "I'd appreciate more businesses being handicap accessible."

Despite worrying about the stress the conversation was giving Harley, Vince was intrigued.

"That doesn't sound as if you need an architect," Harley said gently, if with a note of relief. She had the confidence of Agnes, the regal posture of Rose and the warmth of Mildred. "You can do all that with a structural engineer and a good contractor."

"It's much more than that." Mayor Larry's wrinkles cascaded from his smile. "I'm considering opening a retail outlet for my business. I need something unique that will speak to people, appeal to them and their wallets."

Vince couldn't remember what business the mayor was in, but this was just the kind of boost in confidence Harley needed to get back in the game.

"Something unique…" Harley stared into her green tea like a fake fortune teller in a traveling circus.

"And I want to build a very small theater," Rose said. "For plays and musical performances. A small, yet grand stage. Rich acoustics. Beautiful balconies."

"Balconies…" Harley sat back, leaning as far away from Rose as she could without falling out of her chair. Balconies were her Achilles' heel.

The town council was waiting for Harley to say something, but it was clear she'd been knocked into a personal zone that didn't include the rest of them. Her mouth gaped and her gaze was distant.

Vince came to her rescue. "There doesn't seem to be a large enough population in Harmony Valley for a theater or a large retail store." He gestured to the sidewalk, which was empty.

Tracy delivered their drinks and several scones, more than they'd ordered. She set a plate in front of Vince, along with a white paper napkin. "You look like you could use some carbs."

Three Italian wedding cookies sat on his plate, dusted in powdered sugar. His mother used to make them every Christmas. He couldn't remember the last time he'd had some.

Mayor Larry checked his watch as if Vince hadn't spoken. In fact, they could have cared less about Vince. And not just because he was a Messina, but because he was unnecessary to this project.

I'm unnecessary.

His ears buzzed, drowning out everything else.

He'd made himself superfluous to his brothers through physical and emotional distance. Harley wouldn't need him to fix her saw if she embraced architecture again. And his mother? She'd never needed him once she'd left California.

That was what he'd wanted, wasn't it? To be superfluous to those he loved so their lives wouldn't be hamstrung if Vince developed schizophrenia.

Harley swiped one of his wedding cookies, sniffed it and then returned it to his plate, wiping the residual powdered sugar on his napkin.

He could love Harley, Vince realized. She wasn't hard to look at. She wasn't shallow. She wasn't high maintenance. That left a lot in between to love.

If love was what he was looking for.

Which he wasn't.

A pink shuttle bus stopped outside the bakery. The lettering across the side said Harmony Valley Sightseeing. The double doors opened and about two dozen people spilled out onto the sidewalk. They were smiling and laughing, and carried oblong cardboard wine boxes imprinted with a black horse on a weathervane. About half of the bus riders entered Martin's. The other half headed for their cars or up the walk, presumably to El Rosal.

"Perfect timing," Mayor Larry said. "Here come some tourists who went to the winery breakfast."

The driver waved to his passengers. It was Rex, the heavy-set older owner of the golf cart last night. He closed the doors and drove off.

"Tourists go to the winery. They eat. They drink. They take the bus ride to the top of Parish Hill to enjoy the view. And then they come down and spend a little more at Martin's, El Rosal or the boutique across the road."

Agnes finished the last of her tea. "We need more things for people to do in town."

"Yes, to capture more of their dollars." Rose daintily dabbed her lips with a napkin.

"And their hearts." Scone crumbs ringed Mildred's latte like a dusting of snow. "We don't want anyone to regret coming to Harmony Valley."

Vince took in Harley's delicate profile. He had to be careful or she'd regret what wonderful times they'd had.

"Finish your tea," the mayor said to Harley. "We want to show you around Main Street."

HARLEY HAD SEEN Main Street.

It had the bones of the century-old Gold Rush architecture: narrow brick buildings, tall, interior ceilings, ironwork porch railings. But many buildings had also been modernized with swinging glass doors, plate-glass windows and stucco fronts. Everything was straight-lined, basic construction, put in place quickly to serve the swell of fortune seekers who'd come to California.

Harley wasn't seeking her fortune or a job in Harmony Valley. And if she had been, she'd be looking for tile work, not architectural projects. So it didn't make sense that she let herself be swept out the door of Martin's and along the sidewalk. Except that Rose had mentioned a theater balcony and Harley wanted to see the space.

To torture myself.

Harley's mother used to say *Inspiration never comes when it's convenient.*

For the last few months Harley had edited Mom's statement to *Inspiration never comes.*

"We can't stay long," Vince was saying. "Brit's bachelorette luncheon is today."

Harley wasn't hungry. At least, not for food. She was hungry for solutions to architectural riddles. No one had a special recipe for that.

"I'm so looking forward to the wedding." Rose glided ahead of her. "Phil promised to make me a redhead while Brit was on her honeymoon." She glanced over her shoulder at Harley. "He's the colorist at Brit's beauty shop."

"You always chicken out on coloring your hair." Mildred was winded, keeping up with her walker.

Harley slowed down. She was in love with an emotionally unavailable man and she'd failed at the one thing she wanted in life. Why rush?

"Are you okay?" Vince asked her in a low voice.

She nodded, knotting her fingers. If they'd been engaged for real, he'd have held her hand.

Mayor Larry led them to the corner, his long, gray ponytail swaying behind him. "This location would be ideal for Fit to be Tie-Dyed. Tourists will see my store as they enter the town proper."

The town council was congratulating the mayor on his clever store name, while Harley was biding her time, waiting to see this building before the one they thought was good for a theater.

The mayor unlocked the door to a small, empty, retail space. "This used to be the locksmith shop. I'd like to have some display space here by the windows and a counter-top in the middle." He pointed here, there and everywhere. "And a row of sinks along the back wall where people can make their own tie-dye."

"You don't need an architect for this." Harley finally found her voice. "You need someone like Vince. He builds things."

She'd expected Vince to frown, but he surveyed the space with a critical eye.

"We have a local contractor." The mayor's smile never wavered as he rejected Vince.

Vince's frown came and went so fast, Harley might have missed it if she hadn't been staring at him.

"We didn't know an architect." Agnes beamed at Harley. "Until you."

"Let me finish telling you my vision." The mayor regained the floor. "I wanted to knock out this wall into the empty space next door and build dressing rooms, plus have additional retail space and storage. I want it to be more like a loft you'd see in downtown San Francisco."

"But with more pizzazz." Rose raised her hands and lowered them like a jazz-fingered rainbow. "You young people want to shop the internet. Larry is talking about building an experience, not just a T-shirt store."

Mayor Larry nodded emphatically. "Folks are always looking for something else to do in town."

"Let's not forget it's my granddaughter's wine that brings people here," Agnes said with pride, as if making sure the mayor knew the pecking order of Harmony Valley attractions.

"I still say we could charge for go-kart trips up and down Parish Hill." Mildred sat on her walker, staring out the window. "How fun would that be?"

"Great fun," Vince seconded enthusiastically.

"Until someone crashes on one of those hairpin turns." Rose slapped her hands together.

"Not everyone is as good a driver as you were, Mildred," Vince said, earning him smiles from Agnes and Rose.

"There is that, I suppose," Mildred said morosely.

Harley was intrigued enough to walk the space. "You've got good bones here, except it's brick, which isn't always stable when you remove it to create new doorways and

windows. At least, not when it's this old."
A century, if not longer.

"But it can be done?" the mayor half
asked, half stated.

"Anything can be done with the right vision," Harley said before catching herself.
That had been a phrase she'd often heard
from one of her favorite college professors.

"That's the spirit," Vince murmured.

"Let's look at my project." Rose did a little shuffle toward the door. "It's across the
street."

She led them toward a mid-century, flat-
topped building with floor-to-ceiling windows and a sign on top in red letters that said
Groceries. Agnes had a key and took them
inside. The metal shelves still created aisles,
blocked by cobweb girders. A miniature train
track ran along the outer walls about seven
feet up. The track was held up by suspension wires.

"I see this as the lobby and the entry to
the main seats."

Mildred sat on her walker near the door.
"It's rather large for a lobby."

Rose peered down an aisle. "Perhaps
we could have dressing rooms in the back
there."

"Where do you see the stage?" Harley had to ask. The building was just a flat box. Any stage would be at floor level and hard to see.

"Next door." Rose led them outside and into a two-story building with tall ceilings. "The stage would be small—maybe thirty by twenty." She turned and raised her slender arms to the ceiling. "There'd be small balconies above us."

The building wasn't ideal for a theater. It was built like a long, narrow box. It felt better suited for a tattoo parlor than a playhouse.

"I can see the balconies." Vince was staring up at the wrong end of the building for balconies. There wasn't enough support on the long wall.

Rose twirled to his side. "Can you see a ceiling painted with a scene from Greek mythology? And walls painted with other balconies, as if Renaissance lords and ladies watched the performance?"

"You said you wanted a couple to be kissing," Mildred pointed out.

"Or whispering secrets and pointing to a handsome man in the crowd," Agnes added.

"Well, *I* can see it." Somewhere between the bakery and the theater, Vince had switched allegiances. He quirked a brow at Harley, as if daring her to see the old woman's vision.

"Can it be done?" Rose clasped her hands to her chest, eyes widening hopefully.

Disappointing her would be like disappointing her own grandmother. "Anything can be done with the right vision," Harley allowed carefully, adding a qualifier. "If you have enough money."

"No problem." This from the mayor whose shorts were worn at the seams and whose Birkenstock sandals had deep, dark, toe imprints from years of wear.

"I'm going to borrow from my grandson-in-law." Rose said emphatically. "For which I'll pay him back with interest."

Mildred sighed. "Here's hoping you live long enough to pay him back."

"Mildred," Agnes scolded.

The mayor drifted toward the door, as if keen to avoid town council drama.

"I'm not saying she shouldn't have dreams." Mildred's gaze landed on Vince, perhaps seeking an ally. "I'm just saying a traditional bank would laugh her out the door for having dreams at this age."

"Pah!" Rose's willowy white brows came

down as hard as her foot on the scuffed linoleum. "You should never stop dreaming, no matter the cost."

"Dreams aside, we need a plan to move this forward." Despite his tie-dye and long ponytail, the mayor was more of a pragmatist. "Could you draw up plans for us?"

"Certainly, she could," Vince said. "Harley is a dream believer."

Harley frowned at Vince. "Unfortunately, I'm not licensed to practice in California." Not to mention she hadn't completed her internship with Dan.

"We wouldn't want to tax you professionally," Agnes said, speaking when the mayor and Rose seemed too crushed to do more than pout. "But if you could sketch your ideas so we could bring them to someone else, that would be most helpful."

"Someone else will have a different vision." A more executable vision. Harley refused to look above their heads to balcony height.

"What we're saying is, we lack imagination ourselves," Mildred said flatly, the true pragmatist among them. "We need a boost on the swing before we can swing alone."

When Harley didn't immediately answer, she added, "We would pay you, of course."

"Done." Vince clapped a hand on Harley's shoulder.

Harley mumbled something noncommittal and waited until they'd left Main Street to turn on Vince. "You had no right to tell them I could do that."

"You're just like them." Vince shrugged. "You need a little push to get you back on track professionally."

"I'm right where I need to be." But how it turned her stomach to say that.

"There's no future as a laborer in construction, Harley."

She frowned. "Says the man who's a laborer in construction."

CHAPTER FOURTEEN

NEWS IN HARMONY VALLEY never traveled at a snail's pace.

By the time Vince and Harley reached the garage, his family was aware Harley had been presented with a job opportunity.

"You're moving here!" Sam cried, skipping around them on the driveway. She wore a sophisticated white-and-orange-striped sheath. Her orange flip-flops snapped with every skip.

"What?" Vince couldn't contain his horror.

"Dad said the mayor hired Harley." Sam skipped back toward the shop. "You can't let Harley move here without you, Uncle Vince, because you love her and you're going to marry her."

The L-word stuck in Vince's throat, preventing him from saying anything.

Love.

Love had brought his mother to Harmony Valley. It'd given her three children and years of happiness. At least, until things went south. Had love been worth the pain to her? The answer had to be no. Didn't it?

He looked at Harley. She had everything a man wanted in a woman. Everything Vince wanted in a woman. But was love worth the risk? Could he stand to hurt her if he developed any of the mental health issues his father had?

The answer twisted his insides uncomfortably. The answer was no.

Thankfully, Harley was just as upset at the prospect of living in Harmony Valley as Vince was. She filled the void left by his silence. "There is no job. I'm not moving here. It's a misunderstanding."

Gabe and Joe lingered in the open service bay, watching.

"Oh." Sam pouted. "You'll miss me." She flashed the trademark Messina grin and Vince's insides twisted some more.

Vince would miss her. He'd miss them all. Joe's steady presence. Brit's infectious enthusiasm. Even Gabe's endless and troublesome stream of ideas.

"That's too bad because I'm sure Harley could whip up plans for a house here in no time." Gabe dangled a set of keys in his hands, presumably for the mower he claimed was inside. Apparently it wasn't a surprise wedding gift. "You guys could get married and build a house right in that field."

Harley removed herself from the conversation, drifting away to the mowed area by the bridge where some of Brit's upcycle art was on display.

Joe didn't comment.

"If you moved here, Vince," Gabe went on cheerfully, "Joe wouldn't have to buy you out."

Joe still said nothing.

Gabe came over to Vince and gave him the keys. "Maybe I'll move into the apartment above the garage when I retire."

"Uncle Vince could work at the garage, Dad." Sam tapped her feet, as if she'd taken dance lessons from Rose.

"No, he can't," Joe said emphatically, with a hard glance that swung Vince's way but stopped somewhere near his feet. "There's not enough business to support two mechanics."

"Three." Sam pointed her thumb at herself. "You're forgetting me."

"How could I forget you?" Joe slung his

arm around his daughter and drew her in for a hug. "It's you and me in that garage, kid."

Sam beamed at her dad, and Vince felt a pang of something foreign in his chest, something like envy. Which was ridiculous. He didn't want to have kids.

"I'm not moving here," Vince said firmly, heading toward the Messina-free zone that was Harley.

"But Harley might be." Gabe chortled. "Hey, tell her I found some tile for the shower today. And the tools she needs."

"When did you have time?" Vince asked.

"A hardworking man has enough time to get everything on his list done and then some." Gabe shot Vince with his finger gun. "And who said I found it this morning?"

"Where did you get the tile?" It was rare for Joe to get annoyed with Gabe, but there was that no-barter rule of his sharpening his words.

"Mayor Larry is renovating his house." Gabe toned his usual exuberance down a notch, but it was a very small notch. "He special-ordered tile that he doesn't like and can't return."

"And you bought it from him?" Joe demanded. "Tell me you paid him cash money."

Gabe momentarily lost hold of his smile. "Okay. I'll tell you. I'll tell you whatever you want to hear."

"Gabe," Joe warned, unhappy with his oldest brother's tendency to weave an entire story around a single thread of truth.

"Hey." Gabe held up his hands. "I picked up a job driving the Harmony Valley Sightseeing shuttle for the mayor for a couple of days this week, starting tomorrow, because Rex is going in for a procedure. And I told Mayor Larry whatever he was going to pay me could go toward compensating him for that tile."

"You'll get a paycheck," Joe demanded. "You'll cash it and give the mayor money. No barter."

"But there are so many more hoops to go through your way." Gabe looked to Sam and Vince for support, but the two of them were wise enough to stay out of it.

"You'll leave a paper trail." Joe retreated into the service bay, but he wasn't done talking. "Promise me. I'm not joking about this. That tile is for *my* house."

"Okay, okay." Gabe finally looked serious. "I'm going to drive the ladies to their bachelorette lunch. Vince, can I take your SUV?"

Vince tossed him the keys and then crossed the field toward Harley, who was sitting on one of the old swings. There was a set of slick racing tires arranged in a circle across from the swing she was on. He'd bought them the summer he'd tried building a dragster.

"Does Joe know I lied about our engagement?" Harley stared at the sky. Her hands clutched the rusted, slender chains.

"I'm not sure." He sat on a nearby tire. "We were too busy dickering to talk about you."

"All families argue." Harley lowered her gaze to him. "Don't think your mother left because you and your brothers fought."

"I know it wasn't because of that." Vince didn't want to talk about his mother or moving to Harmony Valley. He wanted to get to the bottom of what was bothering Harley. "Did you come out here to contemplate the mayor's offer?"

"No." She twisted side-to-side on the swing. Not smiling. Stress was evident around her eyes. "Do you remember building houses with Lincoln Logs when you were a kid?"

"Sure." They'd had a set. Secondhand and missing a lot of smaller logs. He and Gabe had used the longer logs to stage sword fights. Vince could still feel the sting of wood on his knuckles.

"Did you ever try to make houses with porches or balconies?" Harley's voice was too casual. She was leading up to something important.

"That went beyond my skill." Vince was reminded of her theater sketch. "I made rectangular cabins, mostly without windows."

"I used to make elaborate log cabins. There were room additions and decks. And then I discovered Legos." The tense lines on her face smoothed. "You can create beautiful castles with Legos."

"With the right tools, anything's possible."

She gave him a half smile. "When I was twelve, my grandmother gave me a sketchpad. That's when the world of architecture became unlimited to me." The smile fell. "I've been drawing impossible structures ever since."

"Impossible is nothing but a puzzle yet

to be solved." He'd probably seen that on a poster in a bar somewhere.

She winced. "Impossible is a career killer."

Laughter from the garage invited them to lighten up. They ignored the invitation.

"When I was a kid, just learning how to change the oil on a car, my dad didn't expect me to be able to change a transmission." Vince moved to stand before Harley. He knelt and put his hands on her bare knees.

Love.

The word came unbidden, pressing Pause on his train of thought, because when he looked at Harley, the L-word seemed to fit.

He didn't want it to.

He removed his hands from her knees and pulled his gaze away. "What I'm saying is you can't judge your potential when you haven't mastered the simpler things."

"You think I should apprentice myself to an architect who specializes in housing developments?" Her words shook with anger, which was good, considering that meant she'd found her backbone. "You think I should spend my days drawing straight lines for cookie-cutter homes?"

"You spent years studying your craft from

top to bottom with your eyes on the clouds." She was always looking up. "Yes, I think you should cut yourself some slack and go back to basics."

She straightened her legs, pushing back on the swing and away from him.

He stood, moving aside. "I've never seen you give up on a tile job. No matter how high the moon Jerry promises, you always deliver somehow. And I'm sure that's because your dad trained you in his craft. Find an architect you respect to hitch your wagon to. One who has the answers you need." If anyone had an answer for ribboned balconies, that is.

Brit called to Harley. They were driving into Santa Rosa to have lunch at some fancy restaurant.

Vince forced himself to smile at Harley. "The answer will come to you when you least expect it." Probably when he was long gone from her life.

The chains on the swing rattled as she stood. "I'd rather the answer had come to me when I needed it most."

THE COUPLES DINNER was shaping up to be the social event of the year.

Cars lined the road leading up to the Messina Family Garage. Cars were parked around the corner and along the street leading to the highway. The mayor's tourist party bus had been put into use. Gabe kept picking people up and dropping them off at the garage.

Harley took one look at the long line of tables set across the garage's parking lot with name cards set in front of every pair of chairs and turned to Vince. "We shouldn't play." The game involved answering personal questions about your spouse or significant other. She feared they'd fail miserably.

"We can always back out." He stared down at her with an unreadable expression. The breeze ruffled his black hair. "But don't you want to know how well we know each other?"

"Yes," she admitted, somewhat exasperated, having spent the better part of the day with women who were overjoyed that she was who Vince had asked to be his bride. She was growing weary of the ruse. "But why?"

"Why play any game other than to win?" He surveyed the crowd. "Do you remember the night we played darts in that pub?"

Harley nodded. They'd found a hole-in-the-wall bar to watch a baseball game. "I was so upset when we didn't win, mostly because you let that lady have a do-over."

"Everybody needs a do-over sometimes." Vince ran the backs of his fingers over her cheek. "You, of all people, should agree with that."

True.

"And sometimes you have to live in the moment." Vince escorted her to a table for the contestants. They were assigned a spot between Mildred and Hero, and Jessica, the bakery owner, and her husband Duffy.

There were white folding chairs set up facing the contestants' tables and it seemed every one of them was filled. There must have been at least sixty people in the audience.

"Ladies and gentlemen." Gabe had a small microphone attached to a karaoke machine. "Welcome to Joe and Brit's Couples Dinner. You've all chipped in to help pay for dinner, catered by Chef Enzo and Chef Claudia, who run the lunch service at Giordana's and the dinner service at El Rosal."

There was a wild round of applause, possibly from fans of their mole tacos, which were delicious.

"We're here to celebrate Joe and Brit's forthcoming nuptials," Gabe continued. "But before they get married, we'd like to put them through their paces and prove they're compatible by seeing how they stack up to the other couples in town."

"You know what that means," Duffy said to Jessica. He had a hand on the swell of her stomach. "That means we should lose on purpose to make Joe and Brit feel better."

"Oh, what a sweet idea." Jessica kissed her husband's cheek.

"Don't get any ideas about going soft," Mildred admonished her date. "We're in it to win it."

"It's darts all over again," Vince whispered in Harley's ear.

She shivered, not entirely from the evening chill, and didn't complain when Vince put his arm over her shoulders. What if they did well? What would it prove other than they'd been close once? Her shoulders tensed and she leaned into his warmth.

Gabe explained that each contestant would receive a large index card with numbers that corresponded to questions. He'd ask the questions quickly. They'd write their answers down quickly, and then he'd read all the questions by number again and they'd reveal their answers.

"If you want to back out, the time is now," Vince said softly.

"That would be wise." Mildred fluffed her snowy-white curls. "Hero and I know each other like the backs of our hands."

Harley noticed Mildred's beau didn't say a thing.

"We're staying," Harley said to Vince. "Living in the moment."

The questions came fast and furious. Gabe timed them on his military watch, which suited Harley just fine. She didn't want to overthink.

"All right, couples." Gabe waved his sheet of questions in the air. "Dinner is almost ready. It's time to find out which couples know each other best. We'll start with the ladies. First question, the answer of which is written on your card with a big, red, number one on it… What is your man's favorite food?"

Harley and Vince flipped their cards over. They'd both written the same thing. Vince looked perplexed.

The crowd read all the cards, groaning, chuckling and applauding.

"Mildred, chocolate is not my favorite food," Hero admonished, waving a card that said green beans. "It's yours."

"Ham with bananas and hollandaise." Duffy gave Jessica a kiss. "Spot-on." He'd written the same thing.

Gabe came to stand in front of Vince and Harley. "There's no way carrots could be my brother's favorite food."

"It's written on the card, my friend." Harley stacked the two cards together, unable to contain a triumphant smile.

"Moving on to the next question. This one is for the gentlemen. If you were home on a rainy day, what movie would your partner want to watch?"

The cards flipped over for the audience to see.

Harley and Vince's cards showed the same answer.

"Love Actually." Harley fanned her suddenly warm cheeks. "How did you know?"

"It has an architect in it." Vince lowered his voice. "And it was sitting on your DVD player when I came over to your apartment."

Harley was touched he'd remembered. She turned away, reminding herself this was just a moment, not forever. "What does yours say, Hero?"

"Days of Thunder." Hero sounded dejected. "I know you like Tom Cruise, Mildred."

"Honestly, that's my second choice." Mildred slumped. "I wrote *Cars*."

"We're moving on, people," Gabe said into the microphone, clearly born for the limelight. "Food is almost done, and we have eighteen more questions to go."

Before dinner was served, Vince and Harley racked up a total of fourteen matches. Joe and Brit beat them by two. Mildred and Hero only had ten. And Duffy and Jessica left in the midst of the game because Jessica thought she might be having contractions.

Gabe stopped by Harley's table while Vince was getting them bottles of water to drink with dinner. "Impressive score." Gabe lowered his voice. "Maybe you should stop pretending you aren't a couple and actually try being a couple."

How she wanted that to be possible. But love, like her balconies, was out of reach.

HARLEY WOKE UP DISORIENTED.

She'd had a dream she was a bride, except when she walked down the aisle, there was no groom awaiting her.

Her bed was harder than usual and her sheets felt as if they had too much bleach. She couldn't be home.

Her stomach gurgled.

And then she remembered where she was. Harmony Valley. A bed-and-breakfast. Vince.

She wanted to go back to sleep and re-imagine the dream, inserting a handsome groom with black hair and black eyes beaming at her.

Her stomach gurgled again.

There'd be no dreamland do-over.

She'd eaten too much salsa last night. Or overloaded her fajita with cheese and sour cream. Or realized that no matter how compatible she and Vince were on paper, no matter how much she and his family wanted their engagement to be real, it was a temporary fantasy.

Vince entered the room they shared, holding two mugs. One mug had a tea bag tag hanging from the side. Based on the smell, there must have been coffee in the other.

Harley sat up. "I slept in again."

"No need to apologize." Vince placed the tea mug on the nightstand next to her cell phone and then sat on his bed. "Take your time. You're on vacation. I'm going to tinker with the riding mower Gabe found and see if I can get it running."

"Thank you for the tea." Her stomach gurgled again. "Go drink your coffee in the dining room. I'll be out in fifteen minutes." She was going to Joe and Brit's house to tile.

"Don't mind me." He settled against his headboard. "I need to check my email."

"Vince. We're pretend engaged. I want a little privacy." In case she got sick.

He didn't look up from his phone. "Unless you were planning to dance naked into that closet they call a bathroom, there's nothing you're showing that I haven't seen before. I'm not looking, anyway."

"Yeah, but now we're just friends, remember? Vamoose."

He didn't say a word, feigning, she was sure, that whatever he'd found on his cell phone deserved his undivided attention.

She huffed, grabbed clean clothes from her duffel and headed for the bathroom.

SOMETHING HAD GONE wrong last night at dinner.

Everything had been fine with Harley until they'd eaten. She hadn't wanted to talk much afterward.

Vince lingered in their room, preferring the quiet to watching Gabe devour breakfast. Harley was in the shower. Every once in a while, he'd hear a bump. He knew about bumps and that shower. It was too small for anyone over the age of ten.

Her notebook was back beneath her pillow. He'd been raised in Harmony Valley where everyone was in everyone else's business. He took it out again and flipped through it, noting things he hadn't yesterday.

Staircases that ascended to clouds. Ribbons of walkway that curled around walls, as if they were catwalks designed for felines living in yurts.

Vince traced the lines of a house, wanting to be able to solve Harley's unsolvable puzzle.

A seed of an idea took root.

Not a solution, but a possibility, a compromise.

He'd worked on an ocean oil rig where creative architecture had sea legs.

Harley's phone was charging on the night-stand. It rang, shaking the idea for Harley's design concept loose. Her phone display read Dan Friedman.

Dan. Harley's old boyfriend. The man who'd smashed her saw. If Vince had known the guy was that vindictive, he'd have landed a few more punches before he'd let him go.

Vince nearly dropped his coffee in the rush to answer her phone. "For your own good, you need to quit calling, buddy." He ended the call without waiting for an answer.

He picked up her notebook again. That idea. He studied the drawing, trying to re-capture it. But the thought had slipped away.

The shower turned off.

Vince flipped back and forth through her sketchpad, listening to Harley dry her hair. No ideas appeared. At least, none that would help her. He was consumed with a mental photograph of Harley in Dan's arms.

That guy wasn't right for her. She needed someone who admired her work, appreci-ated her quick wit, accepted the fact that she'd go her own way and make decisions in her own time. All of which were impor-tant and had nothing whatsoever to do with how Vince could lose his hands in her thick hair when he kissed her.

She shut the hair dryer off, snapping him back to the present. He returned her sketch-pad to its rightful place.

Harley emerged, braiding her long, thick hair. She'd put on a pair of blue jeans and one of Jerry's company T-shirts, this one margarita-green.

"Why don't you ever let your hair down?" The only time he'd seen her take it out of the braid had been before she went to sleep at night. Or when he set it free.

"It'd get covered in grout, for one." She rummaged through her duffel, which seemed to hold more than Mary Poppins's magical carpet bag. "Or caught in a tile saw. Shed all over someone's new floor..."

"Get tangled in some guy's hands."

She hesitated only a second before firing back. "And then Jerry would tell me I'm re-ducing productivity at the workplace."

Their verbal banter always made him smile. If only things were different. If only *he* was different. "I could love you if—"

Harley half turned, half looked, half spoke. *"Wha...?"*

Vince hadn't meant to say anything. But

he was looking at her and the L-word was bouncing on the back of his tongue like a springboard diver readying for a reverse double somersault. Because she was great, really great. And talented. And beautiful. And it stank that he couldn't be the man she deserved.

But he could tell her how he felt about her, along with the parameters he had to live by. The rules that meant they couldn't be together. "I could love you if—"

She launched into his lap, knocking him back on the bed.

One kiss. Another. And...

Vince lost count. It was enough that Harley was in his arms. For the first time in days, he felt like he could breathe. He breathed in the scent of Harley—her soap, flowery shampoo, hardworking woman. He broke off the kiss. Set her aside. Sat up. "We need to talk." This time he'd try not to blurt out the L-word. "What I meant to say was—"

"I love you." She stared at him, blue eyes shining with the truth. "Don't mess this thing up again."

He drew back. "Love is serious." Loving him was serious, he'd meant to say.

She laughed, stopping when he didn't laugh with her. "What's wrong?"

"Let me rephrase. Loving me... You should consider all the consequences first."

"Consequences?" It was her turn to draw back.

He put his hands flat on the bed and leaned away from her to keep from reaching for something he shouldn't have—*her*.

"I could love you if...*if* you promised to let me go the moment I show any symptoms of—"

"No. Love isn't like that." Her head swung back and forth. "My love isn't like that. I don't need you to be perfect. No one's perfect. Perfection is overrated."

"But healthy isn't." He would not touch her again. He would not hold her. He would not kiss her. Something in his chest panged. "I've seen what happens to a healthy person in a relationship with someone battling schizophrenia."

"Which you don't have."

"But I could get."

"That's a risk I'm willing to take." She leaned forward, covering his hand with hers. "If it came to that, I could learn how to help you."

She was so young. So naïve. So hopeful. That hope wrapped him in its tempt-
ing, loving embrace, bringing him closer
to her. Closer to heaven. And everything
that frightened him in the night. She had
no fear. She looked at Vince and dreamed
about a full and happy life. With him. He
couldn't let her have that illusion. "I can't
have children."

Harley startled a little, like a kitten who
wasn't sure the sound she heard was that of
a predator's paw behind her. "Then why did
we use condoms?"

"I can have kids." At least, he assumed he
was biologically capable. The point he was
trying to make was about choice. "I told you
before. I don't want to have kids."

She'd grown wary, not to the point of de-
fensiveness. But she was looking at him in
that analytical way of hers.

He needed her to conclude that he was
not the right man for her. He needed it like
a drowning captain needs to know his crew
will be okay as he goes down with his ship.
"Let's say I never develop mental illness.
That doesn't mean my DNA couldn't be carrying something that passes the disease on

to a child. I won't do that to my kid or any kid."

"Has schizophrenia been proven to be genetic?"

"It doesn't matter. Lightning struck my dad against all odds." She was missing the point. "I won't take that risk. And you shouldn't, either."

"No kids?" The wheels were spinning. This had to be her deal-breaker.

He'd seen her smiling at his niece. He'd noted her chuckle as she'd watched Sam and Brad bicker. She liked kids. She wanted kids.

"We'll talk about it," Harley said carefully, fingers twining in her lap. She was just stubborn enough to believe she could change his mind. She'd probably taken a debate class in college. "Relationships are about compromise."

"No kids." He wasn't compromising on this. Ever.

"But…" Her fingers stopped moving. "We could adopt or find a sperm donor."

Vince should put an end to this madness right now. Before they fell too much in love. Before Harley refused to let him go when he became his father.

"I'm perfectly capable of taking care of kids and you, if need be."

He recognized the determined set to her jaw. Overlaid his mother's expression onto Harley's. Saw the path she'd travel. Saw her upbeat, positive personality deteriorate until she was a bitter, empty shell of the beauty before him.

"This can't work." Vince stood, charging for the door. Needing out. Needing to save her.

But Harley was quicker and reached the door before he did. She placed her hands on his chest. "What happened to small steps and learning how the simple things are done? What happened to not giving up after just one failure?"

She was using his own words against him.

She raised up on her toes, pressing her lips to his.

He was lost. Not lost as he'd been to his brothers when he'd left Harmony Valley. But lost to want. Lost to need. Lost to love.

And to his horror, he couldn't find the strength to insist Harley let him go.

Not until Gabe knocked on the door a

moment later, telling Vince what he already knew.

It was time to leave.

CHAPTER FIFTEEN

THE LONGER THE day went on, the sicker Harley felt.

Her head pounded. Her stomach churned. Her entire body sagged with fatigue.

She blamed it on Vince. On his fear of a disease he may never develop. But his fear affected his ability to love her freely.

It had taken a kiss to make him give them time. But Harley had no illusions. This was a temporary truce unless she could convince him their love was worth overcoming any doubt.

Vince checked on Harley before lunch, pressing a gentle, almost reluctant, kiss on her forehead before leaving. He was going to Santa Rosa for an engine part. He was determined to get the riding mower fixed to tackle the field they'd cleared for the wedding on Saturday.

The tile Gabe had found was cutting cleanly without cracks and going up without a hitch. That practically guaranteed something would go wrong.

"I brought lunch." Sam wandered in as Harley was finishing up the hall shower. She carried a plate with a turkey sandwich and potato chips. She wore her coveralls today, which sagged around her ankles. "It's so pretty." She took a picture of Harley's work with her cell phone.

"I still need to grout." But the black-and-white geometric pattern was stunning. "You can help with that tomorrow." Unexpectedly, Harley's stomach lurched. She ran for the front door, gagging, and spit up in the trash can on the front lawn.

"Should I get my dad?" Sam hovered in the doorway. "Or call Brit?"

Joe was in the garage. Brit was at the salon.

"Don't bother them." Harley turned on the garden hose and rinsed her mouth. The last thing they needed to worry about was a sick wedding guest. "I've been feeling... I don't know... Crampy? All morning."

"I always feel sick when I have my period," Sam said in a conspiratorial whisper. "Brit said I have to suck it up."

"Welcome to womanhood." Harley's insides contracted and she dry heaved.

"I should get Dad."

Geez. She was scaring the poor kid. "No." Harley dragged herself upright. "I just need a bottle of water and some air."

"Brit says learning to deal with cramps is how women get through childbirth." Sam made a face. "I'm never going to get pregnant."

Pregnant.

When was my last period?

Harley flushed with a heat that clogged her brain synapses. She couldn't remember. "I'm going to walk to the store and get something to settle my stomach." Because it was unsettled. Actually, unsettled didn't even come close to covering it.

"Walk? It's nearly a mile." Sam's youthful smile turned wicked. "You have a driver's license, don't you? Let's drive." She pointed to the tow truck. "Dad's got our truck up on the lift. I'm sure he won't mind if we take this beast for a few minutes." Before Harley could protest, Sam was off and running to get the keys.

Harley followed at a slower pace. She couldn't be pregnant. The only man she'd been with was Vince and they'd been smart about sex.

Nothing is 100 percent effective.

A baby. She couldn't kiss Vince into staying through that.

Ten minutes later, Harley parked the tow truck in front of the convenience store a mile south of the Messina garage.

"I'll be right back," Harley told Sam, because she wanted to buy a pregnancy test without an audience.

But Sam was already hopping out of the truck, oblivious to the situation.

A wave of nausea hit Harley again.

Nerves.

Breathe and deny. Breathe and deny.

I am not pregnant.

Harley climbed out of the tow truck as if she was eighty.

This was not how her life was supposed to go. She was supposed to be an award-winning architect by age thirty, married, and contemplating slowing down to have kids. If she was pregnant, her time with Vince would be over. And architecture? She could kiss that career goodbye. The high-powered niche that intrigued her required power lunches, networking cocktail hours, schmoozing dinners, not changing diapers.

She struggled to push through the heavy glass door.

"Edna says what you need is on the candy aisle." Sam leaned on the counter and talked to an older woman, presumably Edna.

Harley waved a greeting and moved slowly toward the candy. Just the thought of chocolate sent a wave of disgust up her throat. Opposite the candy were the antacid tablets. Pain relievers. Cough syrup. Tampons. Adult diapers. Condoms. And one lone pregnancy test kit.

Harley was afraid to pick it up.

Sam was telling Edna all about her bridesmaid dress.

Nausea rose like a helium bubble in Harley's stomach. Up, up, up. She swallowed it back down, not wanting to be sick in the candy aisle. Not wanting wasn't enough though, so she grabbed the test kit and raced into the bathroom. She'd figure out how to pay for her purchase later.

The bathroom looked like her grandmother's. A small white vanity with gold-painted trim. The molded plastic on the cold water handle was cracked. The toilet was running. If the test came out negative, Harley promised to open the tank and adjust the flapper.

The nausea receded. She opened the pregnancy kit.

The test stick was supposed to show results in mere minutes. One line for no. Two lines for yes. Harley completed the test, but couldn't stand to look at that stick while she waited. She set a paper towel on the vanity and laid the test on top, face down. And then she set the timer on her phone for one minute and paced.

Mom is going to be so disappointed in me.

She'd never be able to show her face in Birmingham again. It was as if being voted most likely to succeed had cursed her.

The timer went off. Harley peeked at the stick.

No blue lines.

She turned it back over and set the timer for another minute.

Bottles. Day care. Baby daddies.

Well, at least she knew who the father was. He'd been adamant he didn't want kids, so she'd have to come up with a plan to raise the baby on her own.

Stop thinking about it as if it's a done

deal. You have food poisoning from bad air-line peanuts.

She wasn't feeling sick anymore. It was more a numb feeling of terror.

The timer chimed. Harley peeked.

The stick might be too old to work. There was no blue line.

Or maybe I'm not pregnant.

She'd have to figure out how to pay for the test. Her wallet was at the bed-and-breakfast. She only had a five in her pocket. She'd much rather think about being arrested for shoplifting than about being a mommy.

She almost forgot to start the timer again.

Harley leaned against the counter and stared at a frilly cross-stitch hanging on the wall: Family Makes Any Place Home.

Houston felt like home to Harley. In that respect, she and Vince were on the same page. Neither one of them wanted to return to the place of their birth. She needed to take Brit's advice about cramps and deal with it. The sooner she finished cleaning up her workspace, the sooner she could crash at the B and B. Rest. That's what she needed. And water. Maybe a little chicken broth. Surely,

Reggie could bend the breakfast-only rule and fix her some of that.

The timer went off. Two minutes left.

It was going to be negative. Harley was going to feel better tomorrow. And in a few days, she and Vince would return to Houston and figure out their relationship once and for all.

Negative, negative, negative. If she thought it enough, it'd be true.

All she had to do was look and reset the timer.

Harley picked the stick up and checked her reflection in the mirror instead.

Was that a gray hair? Her eye makeup was smeared and she had no lipstick on. What had happened to the confident woman who'd landed a coveted job at a top-notch boutique architectural firm?

She'd disappeared along with Harley's ability to problem solve.

The door handle jiggled. "Harley?"

Harley startled. The stick flew out of her hand into the toilet. She shrieked.

Her fate floated facedown in the bowl.

Harley wailed.

"Harley?" Sam jiggled the door handle again. "Edna, come quick. Harley's sick."

"No, no. I'm fine." Harley lifted the toilet seat and fished around the toilet with the scrub brush until she got the stick high enough in the bowl that she could grab it. She tossed it into the sink, where it landed facedown.

The home pregnancy test gods must be having a big laugh at her expense.

But Harley planned to have the last guffaw because she wasn't pregnant. No way. No how. All she needed to do was to flip that stick over to make sure.

"I'm coming." An older woman's voice.

"No need. I'm fine." Harley ran soap and water over her hands and the stick. Only then did she register the results.

Two big bold lines of blue.

She went cold, staring at a piece of plastic the size of a thermometer and thinking there had to be a mistake.

A key inserted in the lock.

Harley fell to her knees and prayed.

To the porcelain god.

EXACTLY HOW POWERFUL was a pinkie swear nowadays?

Sam had given Harley the finger-locking oath that she wouldn't tell a soul about what happened in the bathroom at the convenience store.

Pregnant. If only it weren't true.

How was she going to tell Vince? Maybe they could discuss it while driving back to the airport. Yes, that was it. She should drive and he should be safely strapped in beside her, a captive audience for the two-hour trip. Or maybe she should wait until they were on the airplane. Four hours of forced togetherness. He couldn't run away from this. She'd promise to hunt down specialists and take whatever tests he could think of to prove that this baby would be healthy.

A baby...

Before her trip to the convenience store, Harley's nausea had been contained to her stomach. Now she felt a sickening sensation from her stomach to her ears. She pushed past it.

Harley was rinsing off the tiling tools with the garden hose when Joe strolled over from the garage.

"All done?" he asked, ducking inside before she could answer.

Was that speculation in his eyes?

Now Harley was just being paranoid. Joe couldn't know. Except...

Sam was in the nearby parking lot. She walked a white parking-space line as if she were balancing on a high wire.

Harley's pulse picked up, and not from the fear of Sam falling off the high wire.

Joe returned almost immediately. "That bathroom looks fantastic. Brit is going to love it."

"Thanks." Harley assembled a smile for Sam. Wasted, since the kid wouldn't look at her. "The tools are all here, ready to be returned." To wherever Gabe had found them. "Or to be used on your master bath. Sorry that Brit had to work while I tiled."

Joe held himself very still, reminding her of Vince. Except Joe's eyes darted from his daughter to Harley.

"What's wrong?" she asked. A new form of discomfort took over Harley's stomach. Dread.

"Um..." Joe kicked the tiling bucket with his work-booted toe.

"Dad! You are so *lame*!" Sam gesticulated with her hands.

"So much for pinky swears." Harley scowled at Benedict Arnold.

"I didn't tell him what happened in the bathroom." Sam scowled at her father. "I told him Uncle Vince was going to have a baby."

Joe touched Harley's shoulder. "If there's anything we can do for you…"

"Thank you, but…" She took note of the concerned lines framing his blue eyes. "You say that like I'm destitute." Well, she was close. "Or in need of help telling Vince."

Gabe putted around the corner in Rex's golf cart. *"Mamacita!"* He leaped out of the cart, letting it jerk to a halt on the road. He ran across dead grass to reach her, swinging her into his arms and spinning her around.

When her feet touched the ground, Harley's head kept spinning. Joe steadied her.

"Did Sam tell you, too?" Harley asked Gabe when she felt clear-headed.

"Sam?" Gabe looked over at his niece, who still stood a safe distance away in the parking lot. He shook his head. "I was at Rex's house watching *Jeopardy* when he got a call from the phone tree."

Harley's mind spun again. "Phone tree? The town has a phone tree?"

"Yep. Of which everyone in Harmony Valley is a member." Gabe laid a hand on her belly. "Hello, little guy."

Harley swatted his hand away. "I'm not into public displays of affection."

"Gabe." Joe seemed more comfortable chastising his brother than reacting to Harley's news.

"This is great." Gabe pushed Joe's shoulder. "Better get busy on that honeymoon, little bro, so there are two Messina cousins the same age."

"Gabe," Joe repeated.

"I know, you don't perform well under pressure. I saw your football games, remember?"

"Gabe!" Joe finally cut through his brother's joking. "Vince doesn't…"

"Vince doesn't know," Harley exclaimed. "Or want to have kids."

"OMG!" Sam crossed the strip of wild grass to join them. "What is Harley going to do?"

"Let's not tell him." Harley's suggestion met with three pairs of cold Messina eyes. "Or let's not tell him until it's official. You hear about false reads on those tests all the time."

"You threw up," Sam pointed out, helpful child that she was. "Isn't that morning sickness?"

Harley refrained from rolling her eyes. "A misnomer if there ever was one." She'd been feeling sick all day long.

"Anyway, I'd say you're pregnant." If Sam wasn't normally such a sweet kid, Harley would swear Sam would pay for this someday.

"Isn't that Vince's rental?" Joe pointed to the highway lined with trees.

Sure enough, a small, dark, SUV approached.

Harley's heart pounded. "Now's not the time to say anything." She'd wait until they got back to Houston. By then, maybe he'd have fallen in love with her a little bit more.

Gabe prodded Harley toward the road. "There's no easy way to do it, so just do it fast, the way you pull off a bandage."

"I'll have to say it fast or you or someone else in town will tell him before I have the chance." It wasn't fair. She was supposed to be married when she got pregnant. She was supposed to cook a delicious dinner for her husband, light candles, pour wine for him and apple juice for her. Why was nothing going as it was supposed to?

"I won't say a word." Sam held up her small right finger. "Pinky swear."

"I'm not falling for that again." Harley walked forward, but then stopped. "Just… Everyone stay behind me and keep quiet."

"She means you, Gabe," Joe whispered.

"I mean all of you," Harley whispered to them furtively.

CHAPTER SIXTEEN

VINCE HAD SPENT more than an hour alone in his rental. And he'd argued the whole time.

With himself.

There was no denying the love he felt for Harley. Just looking at her made him want to smile, to reach for her, to let his guard down. When he looked into her sky-blue eyes, happiness welled inside him, filling the dark, lonely places with light. But he'd never turned his back on responsibility without disaster striking. Thus, the internal dispute.

He should nip his feelings for Harley in the blooming bud.

He should be cautious and let love grow.

He should limit their time together.

He should spend as much time with her as possible. Their scam was almost over.

And then he pulled into the repair shop parking lot, where his family stood waiting with Harley.

Waiting for what?

No one cracked a smile, not even Sam and Gabe.

Harley stood apart from the rest of them. Her arms were wrapped around her waist and her cheeks were pale.

No good news ever came from a somber welcoming party.

Fear slid its forearm around Vince's throat and squeezed. He shouldn't have left her here alone. He jammed the SUV into Park. If she'd been injured working in that house. If someone had hurt her...

He got out of the SUV, and held the riding mower's new fuel filter hose like a weapon. "What happened?"

No one greeted him. Sam looked like she might cry. The air grew as stifling as a Houston summer.

"Somebody say something." Vince swept the parking lot with his gaze, looking for arterial blood. "Where's Brit? Is she okay?"

As one, his family stared at Harley.

"Brit's fine." Some color returned to Harley's cheeks. "It's, um, is that the part you needed for the mower?"

"The part?" Who cared about the part?

"Look, Vince..." Gabe stepped forward, as if assuming command.

"Gabe." Joe pulled him back.

"Joe..." Gabe warned, swiping his hand aside.

"Guys." Harley turned and held out her arms as if she was herding his brothers backward. She should've known they weren't herd-able.

Brit's truck squealed around the corner and didn't slow down until she skidded into the parking lot. She threw open the door and ran across the asphalt toward them. "I just heard! Congratulations!" She wrapped her arms around Harley and squealed.

"Congratulations?" Vince glanced around the group once more.

Had Harley come to her senses and decided Vince was a complete and total crap shoot? Was she leaving on the next flight back to Houston?

A freight train was thundering around a track in his head, drowning out sound. He didn't know whether to be happy or sad, or angry or glad.

"What is wrong with you guys? Harley is pregnant and..." Brit held on to Harley's arms, but Vince no longer heard what she said.

The freight train roared into high gear. Vince couldn't hear what his future-sister-in-law said next. Nor did he see how Harley reacted to the statement—was there shock, denial or happiness? He may have spent the last few hours fighting with himself, but he'd been knocked out by a phantom blow.

The next thing Vince knew, he was sitting on the asphalt, surrounded by his family, who seemed to be arguing about phone trees and pinky swears.

Why weren't they talking about the baby?

"Hold up. Quiet down, everyone." Vince searched the crowd for a set of elegantly sculpted cheeks and calming blue eyes. "Where's Harley?"

The crowd parted and there she stood. The pregnant woman. Looking neither elegant nor calm.

She swayed from side to side as if she was on a pitching ship. Her eyes were a dark, stormy blue and as restless as a rough sea.

She needs me.

And yet… *Pregnant.*

Vince struggled to stand. "Are you going to have a baby?"

Harley's uneasy gaze landed on him. "It's hard to say. There were two little blue lines."

She held her thumb and forefinger close together. "And then everyone got excited." Harley wasn't excited.

Because she knew they'd finally found a deal-breaker.

Vince, who'd avoided attachment all his adult life, stumbled back. He stared at the redwood picnic table. At Joe and Gabe. At Harley. And all the while, the chest that had felt hollow for so long, tried to cling to a heart that was breaking. His.

A hopeless effort, a vindictive voice inside his head whispered.

Vince clung to it anyway. To love. And possible happiness.

The afternoon sunlight bounced off the new finish on the redwood picnic table, revealing the tracks of splits and scars in the wood, wounds that Joe had tried to fill. His little brother should've known that was futile.

A hopeless effort.

More blood drained from Harley's face and she wavered like a strand of tall grass in the wind.

"The dad. Is it that—" Vince caught sight of Sam out of the corner of his eye and reconsidered his word choice "—*loser* Dan?" An image of Dan's smarmy face swam before him. He suddenly couldn't stand the thought of Harley having Dan's baby. "Tell me the truth."

"*If* I'm pregnant..." Harley's voice shook. "It's yours."

"But we were always so careful."

"I never slept with Dan." Harley's voice hardened. "He used to be my boss."

Vince envied that strength. He was still too far off kilter to process anything properly.

"It's only been you." Harley didn't sound pleased about that at all.

Widening his stance, Vince shored up his legs, which happened to be rebelling, like every cell in his body, to the idea of parenthood. "Do you know what you've done?"

"What I've done?" Her eyes narrowed. Her arms unwound from her waist and her hands came to rest on her hips. "Please, tell me."

"Brit, get Sam inside." Joe took Vince's arm, not to steady it, but to try to yank some sense into him, as if Vince's arm was the emergency shut-off valve connected to his mouth.

Vince wrenched his arm free. "I'm not good husband material and I can't be a father. You know this." Bitterness formed in

Vince's stomach. It erased every bit of control and rational thought he had left. "I spent years making sure my life wouldn't be as hurtful as my father's was. And that child…" He pointed at her flat belly, but couldn't complete the sentence.

"It scares you," she spoke softly. Those blue eyes…they registered pain, loss. They mourned love's passing. They punctured the bitterness in Vince's stomach.

Not enough to get rid of it completely. "You're damn right it does," he wheezed. "And it should scare you, too."

One of Harley's slender hands drifted over the waistband of her jeans. She was choosing sides. Her gaze returned to Vince. Her chin came up a notch. She hadn't chosen him.

This was wrong. Everything was wrong. Her being pregnant. Him saying hurtful words. The situation. The redwood table. He almost sank to his knees and begged forgiveness.

A sound to his left drew his attention.

Brit had turned the knob on the door from the service bay to the sales office. The sound sent him back in time.

Mom turning the doorknob, carrying

a suitcase. Her eyes red from crying. *I'm sorry. I'm sorry. I'm sorry.*

"Go. Just. Go. No one wants you here."

Her expression hardened. "You're just like your father."

Brit swung the door open.

"Apologies won't make things right." Bitterness swelled inside Vince, roughening his words, hardening his stance.

You're just like your father.

Vince forced himself to meet Harley's gaze squarely. Forced himself not to think about love or lifetimes lost. "I can't be the person you want me to be."

"You mean you won't try." Harley's hand remained at her waist.

"That's right."

"Hey," Joe spoke to Vince in a calm voice. "Take a minute to think about this."

But Vince's head was shaking, his hands were shaking. Heck, his brain felt shaken. How could Harley stand there and deliver the news with such composure? "The Messinas, without warning, could follow in their father's footsteps and lose their grip on reality."

Like now, he thought, feeling completely out of control, consumed by resentment toward his father's DNA.

"Vince, how about you and I go to the bar and get drunk?" Gabe stepped between Vince and Harley. "I'm buyin'."

Vince shoved him to the side. "Dad was fine when he was younger. Just as sane as you or me." A distant part of Vince's brain noted he wasn't making a case for sanity. He ignored it and snapped his fingers. "And then everything changed. Dad was paranoid. Depressed. Suicidal. That could be any one of the three of us. Any time." He caught sight of Sam lingering at the door in the service bay with Brit. "And Sam... She could wake up one day and—"

"Shut up!" Normally, Joe was the quiet one in the family. Not when his daughter's feelings were threatened. His face was red and his words on fire. "Brit, get Sam inside! Now!"

"Vince." Harley's voice was placating, but she hadn't moved a step toward him.

Her distance was just as well. Vince was past the point of reason. "I can't predict if a child of mine is going to be right as rain or mad as a hatter. No one can tell. No one can predict."

Sam wailed, turning to bury her head in Brit's shoulder.

Vince cast his gaze around the assembled group, trying to make them see the truth of it. "You can't run away from this, Harley, not like you run away from a bad day on the job. You have to grow up sometime. I can't protect that baby from the possibility of me being a danger to those around me."

"Stop." Harley choked on the word. She raised her watery eyes to the sky while her hands dropped to her sides and her mouth worked. Not that she found any words. Not for several painful seconds. And then her hands fisted and she put Vince in her sights and words shot out like buckshot. "You don't need to say any more. You don't need to hurt me. Or Sam. Or your brothers. You don't need to lash out at us because you can't stand to hurt alone.

"Schizophrenia is a disease, like cancer or Alzheimer's." Harley glared at him. "Did I tell you breast cancer runs in my family? I could get it at any time." She laid her hands over her breasts before resting her hands on her hips once more. "You do not own the what-if-I-get-a-disease card."

"She's right," Gabe said.

Vince might have agreed if he wasn't so afraid for that baby she was carrying.

Harley drew a deep breath and the hard shine in her eyes softened. She tilted her head to one side and looked at Vince the way she had this morning. With tenderness. But also with sadness and regret, emotions so powerful they pressed in on Vince.

"I'll love this baby the same whether you want to be a part of its life or not. I'll love this baby whether it comes into this world healthy or with mental challenges. I'll love…" Her breath caught in her throat. She drew another, set her shoulders back, and took aim one more time. "I'll love this baby exactly as I could've loved you." And then she turned on her heel and ran toward the bridge.

Leaving Vince shot full of holes. He sagged on his feet.

This is how Dad felt when Mom left.

His father had told the boys to never speak of her again. That hadn't kept Vince from thinking about her or missing her or waking up in the middle of the night with a pain in his chest that wouldn't go away.

This is what I tried to avoid.

Except, in his mind, he hadn't thought he'd feel like he'd been tied to a tow rope and dragged up Parish Hill and then left to rot. He hadn't imagined he'd be the one who was left. Again.

"Consider your next words carefully, Vince." Joe crossed the parking lot to comfort Brit and Sam, who still stood huddled at the office door.

"Congratulations. You didn't just hurt Harley." Gabe stared at Vince like he didn't have the proper credentials at a hostile checkpoint. "You hurt your family."

Harley reached the bridge. Her steps faltered. She bent over, as if she were breaking.

He almost went to her. He almost gave in. But Harley was tough enough to recover. He had to be strong enough to let her go.

"I'm not sorry." Vince watched Harley gather herself and continue over the bridge. "I'm scared for Sam. And I'm scared for us."

"You can't turn your back on your child," Joe said in a more controlled voice, having finally gotten Sam to go inside.

"I'll give her child support." He tried not to watch Harley's retreating back, tried not to think about what-ifs and rolling with the punches. "I don't want to make Harley or that baby suffer. I don't want to push Harley to the brink of a breakdown, until my own child tells her to go. To get away. To leave her babies and save herself. It was too hard with Mom."

Joe and Gabe didn't say a word. They stared at Vince, processing his admission.

His final secret was out.

"You told Mom to leave?" Joe's voice had the sharp edge of a diamond blade.

"I drove her to the bus station," Vince admitted. Surprisingly, the weight on his shoulders didn't feel any lighter.

"With your blessing?" Gabe's hands fisted.

"Yes."

"Is that why you don't spend time with us?" Gabe's voice was unfamiliar. Rigid. Severe. "You chose her instead of us?"

"I chose to protect you." Vince's words were a betrayal unto themselves. "And her."

Gabe's brows were so low they almost seemed a part of his black eyes. "Why? She could have kept Dad from killing himself."

"Get out." Joe's words were harsh and raw. Vince had just used the same unforgiving pitch with Harley. "You're not my brother. You're not *family*. You have no idea what family means. What loyalty means. What love means." Joe pointed toward the highway with a hand that shook. "Leave.

Don't come back. Don't call. Don't come to my wedding."

Vince didn't need to be told twice. He'd known for years Joe and Gabe wouldn't approve of what he'd done.

He drove back to the bed-and-breakfast, gathered his things and was out the door before Harley returned to their room.

If Harley had meant to return to their room.

It didn't matter. Vince left town to be alone.

Just like Mom had done.

CHAPTER SEVENTEEN

IF HARLEY WAS SMART, she'd go directly to the bed-and-breakfast, shove everything in her duffel, and beg for a ride to the airport from Reggie. But she wasn't thinking as she ran away from Vince.

She was hurting.

Harley crashed through brush along the river's edge. Her T-shirt ripped. Her hair yanked. And yet she didn't stop to be careful. She couldn't stop.

Vince didn't want to be a daddy.

Vince didn't want *her*.

Harley had suspected he'd break up if the cautious love between them grew stronger. She'd suspected he'd need space. She hadn't anticipated a rupture that laid waste to hope and made ashes of her heart.

She had no idea how long she'd been running when she stumbled into a tree, this one an oak. The bark was rough but the circumference sturdy. She wrapped her arms around it, not caring that its bark scraped her skin. It was a small discomfort compared to the pain she couldn't bring herself to face.

Someone cleared their throat.

Immediately, her heart leaped toward the possibility of Vince having a change of heart and having miraculously found her. She lifted her head and...

There was a man, all right. She should have known it wouldn't be Vince.

She'd reached a small park. Tall trees. Sparse grass. Picnic benches.

"I suppose you don't want to hear me ask if there's anything I can do for you." The mayor stood a few feet away. He wore black tights and a yellow tie-dyed tank. He carried a green rolled-up yoga mat and looked serene enough to have been using it. He held out his arms. "But I'm a lot better at hugging than that tree."

The man was a stranger to her. But in that moment, she accepted his offer of solace, ran into his arms and cried on his shoulder. And cried. And cried some more.

She shed tears for lost dreams. A stellar career. An unrequited love. A handsome, supportive husband. A child doted on by two adoring parents. Every tear was like a piece of her heart falling into the river and being swept away.

When her tears had subsided, Mayor Larry pulled back to look at her face. "That's rock bottom. You've got no place to go from here but up."

It would be rude to roll her eyes, so Harley closed them instead.

"Open your eyes, Harley. You've got to face it. It could be worse." The mayor towed her to a picnic table, set her down and sat beside her, laying his yoga mat at his sandaled feet.

She drew a shuddering breath. "You heard through the phone tree?" Had it already spread that Vince had left her?

"I did get the message that you're carrying." He said it as if she was toting a gun.

"Vince…left." The words, said out loud, only made her hurt more.

"Some men have a hard time dealing with mortality." He put his elbows on the picnic table behind him and stared at the river. "When my wife told me she was having a baby, I was terrified."

"But I bet you didn't reject her." Harley laid a protective hand over her abdomen.

"I told her I wasn't ready. Still had things I

wanted to do with my life." He stretched his legs out in front of him. "Wasn't my proudest moment." He fixed Harley with a knowing look. "She kicked me out of the house. Wouldn't let me back in for two weeks. It forced me to think about who I was and who I wanted to be." He shrugged and looked at the river again. "Mostly, it made me realize who I wanted to spend the rest of my life with and if I deserved her."

"Vince doesn't deserve me." Harley's eyes burned with tears, but she had to say it, even if it was only out of loyalty to the little one growing inside her. "He doesn't deserve this baby."

Harley hoped Vince would have a change of heart, but she doubted it. It was going to be hard to face him, but she was ready. "Thank you for not running away when I was hysterical."

"I have daughters." The mayor had the kindest eyes. "I wouldn't want them to be alone at a moment like this." He slapped the tops of his thighs. "Now. Tell me you've thought more about our downtown projects. I could open up the doors for you if you need to get inside and measure."

"Today?" Harley didn't want to. And yet

it might be just the distraction she needed. Not to mention she'd have an excuse to give Vince some breathing room.

"Not today." Mayor Larry brushed a tear from her cheek. "You need a good rest to be creative."

"Tomorrow, then." She needed to talk to Vince tonight.

She pulled herself together and returned to the bed-and-breakfast, prepared to reiterate to Vince his opinion didn't matter. She was having this baby with or without him. Hopefully with him.

But apparently without him.

Vince was gone.

His things were cleared out of the bathroom and his suitcase wasn't in their room.

Admittedly, she'd crumbled. Vince hadn't just rejected her. He'd left her. His fear of hurting someone was greater than the love he felt for her.

I could love you if...

Harley stayed in her room, not answering when Brit and Reggie knocked. She needed time to grieve.

Hours without solid food made her feel a bit weak the next morning, but not nearly as nauseous. She took an apple from the dining room sideboard and made her escape without anyone seeing her. She had a meeting with Mayor Larry to keep.

The morning was bright. The air crisp. Perfect weather for love and happiness. Heartbreak? Not so much.

Mayor Larry met her outside the old locksmith shop. He'd brought her a green tea from Martin's, opened the doors to all four spaces, and left her alone. But she wasn't alone. She saw Vince everywhere.

Harley wandered around the empty stores the mayor wanted for his tie-dye shop, but couldn't bring herself to sit still and sketch. She kept seeing Vince's features soften as he'd complimented Mildred's driving skill.

She went across the street to the grocery store. Nothing interested her in that spider-webbed building, either, except for the empty train trestle around the outer walls. Its wire support reminded her of a suspension bridge.

This was hopeless. She was being paid good money to bring the town council's vision to life. And all she saw, all she heard, all she felt, was Vince.

Dutifully, she entered the tall building Rose wanted for the main theater, convinced nothing would inspire her enough today to take her mind off Vince. The building was a box. A blank slate. Her brain was just as empty.

Fresh air billowed inside the open space. She sat against a wall close to where Vince had stood yesterday, and contemplated the hard decisions ahead of her. She needed a better job, a better place to live, a good babysitter. She couldn't afford to wallow, or worse, run away as she'd done with Dan. Vince had been right about that, at least. She needed to face her problems like an adult, even if it took her baby steps to get her life on track again.

She flipped open her sketchpad, but not to an empty page. She'd flipped it open to the spread of the theater with its ribbon of balconies. "I didn't need to see you today." She began to flip to something else when she noticed a set of bold lines fringing her balcony. Lines she hadn't drawn. At the edge of the paper was a small set of neat initials. *VM.*

Vince just couldn't resist. He had to try to fix the unfixable balcony. She hadn't asked him to. She hadn't even given him permission to look at her sketchbook. He'd butted in and done it, the same way he'd taken on responsibility for everyone else he cared about.

There was no pattern to his lines. They were drawn like a poorly constructed cat's cradle, the child's game with string, one finger-move from flipping into a single loop and losing the game. Nothing webbed or regularly spaced, which meant...

Harley bent for a closer look. She'd thought Vince's scribbles would be as unproductive as a starburst cable design, blocking everyone's view. But the way he'd positioned the cables allowed for the curved box seats to be at different heights, clearing the view of the stage.

"This could work." Out of habit, she raised her eyes upward. Instead of sky, she stared at the ceiling above. Almost in the same spot Vince had been looking at yesterday. The side wall. He'd mumbled something about a balcony. But his design...with a few properly placed thin lines...made a balcony possible. She and Dan had talked about suspension as a possibility, but he'd drawn straight predictably placed cables. Vince knew Harley favored unpredictable lines.

How had he known? She thought of the answer as soon as she thought of the question. The train track. It'd been right there in front of Harley but she'd been looking sky-ward. She hugged her sketchpad, wanting to hug Vince.

Rose's balconies were going to be beautiful. And like Brit's mermaid art display, it would be unique enough to attract visitors.

Vince had left her a gift. She'd much rather have had him sitting next to her explaining it. She'd much rather have been hugging him. But having a solution was better than him fixing her tile saw. With this, she could get her job back with Dan.

And, oh, ugh, no. She didn't want that job back.

But she had leverage to break her contract. She could move back to Birmingham and get a job with an architectural firm near her parents. For the first time since Vince had walked out, Harley felt all wasn't lost.

She took a picture of the balcony drawing with her phone and sent it to Dan.

An old truck and a golf cart pulled up across the street. Joe and Brit got out of the truck. Gabe and Sam got out of the golf cart.

"I hope Harley's all right." Brit shaded her eyes to peer in through the glass at the former locksmith shop. "Your brother is a jerk."

"A total turd." Sam wore baggy blue coveralls and dragged her booted feet onto the sidewalk. Her brown hair was dull and limp, as if she'd slept poorly. "He's my least favorite uncle."

"Then things are as they should be, munchkin." Gabe slung his arm over Sam's small shoulders. "We've disowned him."

No. Harley dropped her sketchpad. Her pencil clattered nearby. Vince needed his family or he'd truly be alone.

"We're putting Harley and the baby in Vince's place," Joe confirmed, staring across the street to where Harley was. He wore his work uniform: navy slacks and a blue-gray button-down with his name stitched on the pocket. True to Messina male form, his hair wasn't dull or limp. It was a beautiful, shaggy work of art. "There she is."

The Messinas descended upon Harley in a wave of Vince-fueled disgust.

"Forget Vince. He's a deadbeat. Always had been." Joe didn't waste any time disparaging his brother. "We think you should move to Harmony Valley."

"I'll make sure your kid shows up to school every day." Gabe sat next to Harley on the floor, stretching out his jeans-clad long legs. He wore a dingy white T-shirt and too much musky cologne. "By the time your kid is ready for school, I'll be retired."

"Our house will be finished in a few weeks." Brit was dressed for work at the beauty parlor in a pink polka-dot slim skirt and a white lace blouse. Her smile was strained and there were bags under her eyes that matched Harley's. "You can move in above the garage."

"I can babysit," Sam said.

Harley's stomach did a slow barrel roll. She'd lost one Messina and picked up four. Much as she appreciated their support, what she wouldn't give to have her original Messina back.

"That's a very generous offer but…" Harley opened her sketchbook and stared at the lines Vince had drawn. It was just like him to do something good and leave without taking credit. "You can't just excommunicate him."

"We can." Joe drew Sam into a hug, tucking her face into his chest as if she needed protection.

"You'd do that? After all he did for you?" Anger thrummed in her veins. "He wanted to go to college. Instead your parents used him to keep a roof over your heads. And you wonder why he developed a fear of mental illness, while you didn't."

Brit glanced from one brother to another, seeking answers that weren't forthcoming.

"I refuse to feel guilty." Gabe stood and backed away, looking displeased with Harley. "I'm thinking about what he said to Sam and what he said to you."

"He drove our mother away. Literally," Joe said. "There were a couple of months there where we had to deal with Dad by ourselves."

"Before your uncle came and let you run free? Without much discipline?" Harley tossed her braid over her shoulder just as she'd tossed Joe's protests aside. Vince's brothers didn't contradict her. "I bet Vince still worked more hours in the garage than you did."

"Regardless," Joe said gruffly, not quite meeting her eyes. "Our offer stands." He left, followed by Sam and Gabe.

"Why are you sticking up for Vince?" Brit had tears in her eyes. "He left you."

"Other than the fact that I love him?" Harley's hand drifted to her abdomen. "Because he's always sticking his neck out for someone else and no one ever does the same for him."

"I… Joe…" Brit considered her words before speaking again. "Are you staying for the wedding?"

Harley sighed. She had to stay in town until her flight on Sunday. She couldn't afford the exorbitant change fee. "If you don't think my being there will ruin the day for Joe."

"Of course not. Just… Vince can't come. Joe is adamant about that."

"Vince left yesterday." The words clogged her throat. "I'm not sure where he went."

Brit bent down and hugged her quickly. "He'll be back."

Harley lifted her gaze to the point at the top of the wall where Rose's balconies would go. Vince had done all he could for Harley. He wasn't going to return.

Gabe drove off in the golf cart with Sam. Joe backed out, calling for Brit.

"Vince loves you," Brit reassured Harley. "I could tell from the first. It was in his eyes."

His googly eyes. Which had all been an act for a family that didn't appreciate what he'd done for them.

Harley reached for her sketchpad. She wouldn't take Vince's sacrifice for granted. She'd make him proud.

If she ever saw him again.

CHAPTER EIGHTEEN

VINCE PARKED IN front of a brick home in Sugar Land, Texas.

It was one of the grander houses on the block. Jerry could afford all the trimmings. It was a far cry from the small ranch-style home in Harmony Valley. Of all the men his mother had dated in the last decade, Jerry was the most successful.

Vince's mother had gone to work for Jerry as a temporary bookkeeper while Jerry's permanent employee was on maternity leave. When her stint there was over, they'd begun dating. And a few months after that, Vince's mother had moved in. That's when Vince had noticed an opening at Jerry's company and applied for a job.

Vince had driven to the airport and flown home the day he'd told Joe and Gabe about the past. His brothers thought he'd done the wrong thing with regard to his mother. Vince had to find out if Mom felt the same.

And so he'd put on his best pair of slacks and a new blue polo shirt, and showed up at his mother's door. Along the way, he'd glanced at the Houston skyline and thought of Harley and of a child he couldn't raise, for their sake, not his. He hoped Harley would find his scribbles. He hoped those few hurried lines would help inspire her to find a solution for the elegant curving balconies and return to the profession she loved. He'd send her child support and she'd find another man to love their baby like it was his own. Vince vowed to stay away, even if he had to move far away to do so.

The Texas heat had turned the grass a brownish green. But the lawn was neatly mowed and the walk clear, edged with white rosebushes. There was a bass boat on a trailer in Jerry's driveway next to his dually truck. A large silver SUV sat next to it with a license plate frame that read Proud Soccer Mom. That had to be Jerry's daughter's vehicle.

Vince reached the front porch and knocked on the door.

Jerry opened it. He had the sun-bleached blond hair and tanned leathery skin of a man who lived his life working and playing outside. The sound of a child's squeals and water splashing drifted from within. Jerry had grandkids. Five soccer-playing prodigies.

"Vince, what are you doing here?" Jerry looked perplexed but opened the door, ushering him inside. He was a good man and a fair boss, if a little cheap when it came to purchasing new equipment.

"Is Gwen home?" Vince's mother's name felt awkward on his tongue. He couldn't pretend any more about their relationship and didn't care if Jerry fired him. "I need to talk to my mom."

"Vince?"

Jerry's house was open concept. A sunken living room led to a formal dining room and then to a kitchen. The walls facing the backyard were floor-to-ceiling windows. A large blue pool sparkled out back.

Vince's mother stood at the kitchen counter in front of a blender. Her straight, dark brown hair was pulled back from her tanned face. She wore Texas makeup, which was always a tad heavy for Vince's taste, and a green-and-white sundress. But all in all, she looked well-preserved for fifty-eight and a hundred percent better than the last time he'd seen her in person.

"Vince?" She didn't rush forward to hug him close or kiss his cheek or take his hands and thank him for setting her free.

There was his answer. Vince crossed his arms over his chest. He'd made a mistake coming here now, not to mention letting her leave all those years ago. It'd cost him two brothers. "Mom."

His mother's hands hovered above the blender, as if she'd forgotten what to do next. She wore wide silver bracelets on both wrists. "How did you—?"

"It's hard for anyone to stay hidden nowadays." Vince's words seemed to echo across the cavernous distance between them.

Out back, blond kids in brightly colored swimsuits bobbed in the water on noodles. If that had been the Messina boys, they'd be using those noodles like swords.

"Do you know this man, honey?" Despite being a good guy, Jerry was a little slow to catch on. He moved to stand between Vince and his mother, which earned him points in Vince's book. "He works for me."

"I should be going." Vince half turned toward the door.

"You'll do no such thing. Come inside." His mother charged across the living space to reach him. Only when she reached the hardwood foyer did she slow to a screeching barefoot stop. "Jerry...honey..." She didn't take her eyes off Vince. "This is one of my boys. Did you say he works for you?"

"Not for long." Jerry wasn't as tall as Vince, but he managed to look down his nose at him anyway. "He's got some explaining to do."

"Let me talk to him first." She whispered something to Jerry that Vince didn't hear, kissed his cheek, and then led Vince to a small office at the back of the house that overlooked the large swimming pool.

The pool was one of those spectacles that cost as much as a small house. Miles of rock waterfalls. A slide and grotto. Hot tub. Sunken bar and poolside grill.

Jerry joined his grandkids outside, sitting near enough that he could hear Gwen cry for help and come running if need be.

Instead of sitting behind the desk, Vince's mother sat in a pink club chair and indicated Vince should sit opposite her in a matching one. The house smelled fresh. No one smoked here. On the credenza behind the desk, there were pictures of her and Jerry, along with pictures of blond kids hugging her while they clustered around a birthday cake.

She seemed to be taking an inventory of Vince's features, looking happy if not exactly smiling. "You're so handsome. There was always the promise of it when you were younger."

He hadn't come to exchange pleasantries about his appearance or hers.

But it wasn't all pleasantries. She held on to the arms of the chair with white knuckles. "You look…"

Vince expected her to say *good*.

"…like you've had a hard time lately."

"Lately? I had a hard time after you left. We all did." Why sugarcoat his reason for coming?

Tears welled in her eyes. Her fingers dug into fabric. "I'm sorry." And that was all she said.

Vince couldn't handle all this civility. Anger burst past the shock of seeing her. "Did you ever look back? Did you ever think of us?"

"Sure, I did. I called once. I talked to Turo."

"Once." She'd known where her children were, just as Vince had known where she was. And she'd only reached out once? They were even.

"I... I had to get counselling after I left you."

A child squealed happily behind her, but her focus remained on him.

"What made you decide to change your name and start a new life?"

"Self-preservation. I took back my maiden name after your father died." She was so calm, as if she'd rehearsed this conversation many times before.

Vince had rehearsed it, too, but it wasn't going at all to plan. He'd expected her to be defensive and twitchy, the way she'd been when he'd last seen her face-to-face. He'd imagined he'd be superior, accusing her of abandonment. Or the benevolent son, forgiving his weak, lost mother. She may have left Harmony Valley lost and defeated, but she'd found herself.

"I loved your father." Her smile was tender. "I met him when I was waitressing in San Antonio, attending college and trying to figure out what to do with my life." Her gaze drifted to the credenza. Tucked behind the recent, more colorful pictures was a small, faded, family photo of the Messinas. "Tony was in the Air Force and swept me off my feet. And then Gabe came along…"

"And the rest is history."

"You're angry." She frowned, the tanned wrinkles making her look ten years older. "And you should be. I took a vow and broke it. I wasn't strong enough to commit my husband so he could get the help he needed." But she'd been strong enough to leave her babies behind and seek solace for herself. "You know, your father never gave me permission to access his medical records. I couldn't refill his prescriptions. His psychiatrist wouldn't talk to me about his condition." Her words rose higher and higher, until they bounced off the ceiling and echoed around them. "I was supposed to be Tony's support system, but he wouldn't let me support him!"

"So you had me do it." There was the bitterness he'd harbored for years, out in the open where it belonged.

"You were the only one he'd let help in the garage." She squeezed the armrests. "You kept us going."

"I was a kid. You were supposed to protect me." Admitting it made him feel small.

A cascade of giggles erupted outside. Jerry held one of his smaller grandkids above the water and was blowing raspberries on the boy's belly.

Vince straightened in his chair, his shoulders as stiff as green wood. He couldn't remember being given such unabashed affection, but he bet Harley would be generous in lavishing it on their child.

Mom glanced over her shoulder, but didn't smile. "You think you were denied a childhood like that?"

Vince was having trouble filling his lungs with air. He could only nod.

"Maybe you were too young to remember going to the fair. You ate cotton candy and it got all over you. Gabe tried to eat it out of your hair." Her blue eyes warmed. "Or the time I took you three boys for pony rides at a ranch in Cloverdale. Gabe wanted the biggest pony, only when he got on, it would only walk forward if I held a carrot in front of its nose. You wanted to ride a pony with Joe sitting in front of you. You hugged him so tight, he nearly squirmed right off the pony." Her voice softened. "And there was the time your father made me try to bowl for the Pumpkin Queen Crown in Harmony Valley, except I missed all the pins. You three boys ran over and knocked them all down." Her eyes filled with tears. Their boyish antics had meant something to her.

"I wish I could recall those happy times." He kept his voice carefully neutral. He didn't want to like her and he hadn't planned on forgiving her. He'd only come for answers. And maybe selfishly to vent some of his frustrations to her about the man he was today because of her choices. "I remember Dad's mood swings and the chain smoking and some of your last words to me."

Mom leaned forward, tilting her head slightly, encouraging him to share.

Didn't she remember? Did he really have to say it out loud?

"You said I was just like Dad." All neutrality slipped away. His words felt heavy and hard, like an overinflated radial tire barreling toward a target. "You told me there was no hope for me."

She sat back as if slapped. "I wasn't well."

"Apparently no adult in the household was." It was time to go. He'd spoken his piece. She hadn't apologized or refuted her words. He slid his feet back, preparing to stand.

"Vince." She reached over and clasped his hand, not hesitantly or lightly, but with the familiarity of a mother who cared. "Forget what I said. Take a good look at the man you've become. Other than looking exhausted, you seem well balanced, healthy, okay."

Vince blew out a breath he hadn't known he was holding. "For now, you mean."

Her brow furrowed. "You don't think you'll develop a mental illness, do you? It seems far too late. Your father was diagnosed in his teens."

No one had told Vince that. "But…"

"He self-managed his mood swings for many years. It wasn't until Joe was born that he needed meds. And only because I begged him. Taking medicine ate at his pride." She wiped a tear from one eye. "If it hasn't happened to you by now, it most likely won't. You shouldn't live in fear."

Vince gripped her hand tighter as he tried to process what his mother was saying.

"I've been thinking about you boys. Jerry asked me to marry him." She waited to see if Vince would say something. When he didn't, she sighed. "I said no. I do love him, but I'm not the trophy wife he should have."

She was just like Harley, holding herself to unrealistic standards. "Who are you to judge what Jerry wants? If he loves you…" Vince stopped himself from finishing the thought.

If Jerry declared his love for Vince's mother, he had to know what he was in for. Jerry knew about her past and he loved her anyway. He trusted their love would take care of any bumps in the road in the future.

Just like Harley had offered to do with Vince.

Vince couldn't advise his mother to trust in love if he couldn't do so himself. He wanted to move past his fears. He wanted his mother to move past her fears.

Mom stared at Jerry with love in her eyes. "How long have you been in Houston?"

"More than a decade."

Her gaze snapped back to Vince. "And yet, you never approached me before?" She leaned forward, those blue eyes demanding an answer. "Why now?"

Vince had planned to mention Joe's upcoming nuptials. Instead he blurted, "I'm going to be a father."

"You say that like it's a bad thing, when, in fact, it's a gift." Her eyes saw too much, more than Vince wanted to let on. "Ah. You took my words to heart about being ill like your father."

He nodded. "I'm sorry. I wasn't in a good place. I suppose neither of us was that day." She stared out the window at Jerry sitting with his feet in the pool surrounded by grandchildren he spoiled with love. "I can't take those wedding vows again. I can't trust myself not to break them." She reached for Vince's hand once more. "But you can. You can be the father yours wasn't capable of being."

Vince had a feeling it might be too late for that. "I said some pretty horrible things to Harley. I don't think she'll take me back."

"Do you love her?"

He didn't hesitate. He nodded. "Too much."

"You can never love too much. You are like your father, you know." Mom released him. "In the ways that count. He was an honorable man, so determined to do what was right. You'll win her back. She and the baby will need you. You, of all people, know how hard it is to raise a child alone."

He'd been so determined not to try, if only because he might be a danger to Harley and the baby. Visiting his mother gave him hope.

"You need to marry Jerry. He's a good man, too." But so were the others. Dave from the oil rig. Warren from the heating and air-conditioning company. Tim from the marina. "If you love him, that is."

"I do." Her gaze roamed the photos behind her desk. "He's the only man I've dated since your father who I can see myself growing old with. He doesn't judge me for my past. He values me for who I am today."

Vince could only hope that Harley had it in her heart to do the same thing.

CHAPTER NINETEEN

Vince wasn't coming back.

Two days had passed. It was time to face facts.

Harley sat up in bed unsure if she was out of sorts due to morning sickness or heartache.

At least when the mayor'd had a negative knee-jerk reaction to being a father, he'd fought his way back into his wife's good graces.

If only Harley and Vince had been married before this happened.

Harley patted her tummy. "I would never blame you, little one."

Still, she couldn't find it in her heart to blame Vince, either. She understood him too well. But understanding and missing were two different things.

Harley approached Gabe during breakfast about finding tile for Joe and Brit's master shower.

"I need something to do so I don't sit around and focus on how I feel." Overall, the morning sickness was more manageable now that she was eating like a pregnant woman with a picky digestive tract. No greasy food. No rich food. No sugary food.

She'd finished the sketches for the town council yesterday morning. She'd been bored yesterday afternoon.

"You could maybe find a new date for the wedding," Gabe said with a twinkle in his eye. "You'd have a great time with me, if you weren't in love with my brother. Why, we could even get married."

Harley refused to take Gabe seriously. Making sure Reggie wasn't around, she whispered, "You should ask Reggie to be your date."

His fork splashed in his syrup-filled plate. "Reggie hates me."

"Hate is such a strong word." Harley smiled. "Go find me some tile."

"Your wish is my command," said Gabe, the miracle worker, returned his attention to the plate of syrup-drenched waffles.

Harley walked to the bakery, enjoying the mild, dry weather.

Conversation ground to a halt when she

entered Martin's. Apparently a Messina baby was just as noteworthy as an adult Messina.

"Any word from Vince?"

"Is he coming back for the wedding?"

"Does she look like she's showing?"

"No. She looks like she's glowing."

"I wish." Harley stepped up to the counter.

"The usual?" Tracy was on duty this morning. Her short blond hair was as perky as her smile.

Perkiness was an enviable quality nowadays, at least to Harley.

"Green tea and carrots," Harley confirmed. The bakery kept baby carrots and peeled apple slices in stock for younger patrons. "To go." She planned to walk the river. Maybe she'd get lucky and find something Brit could use in her sculpture.

"I think she's showing," someone said behind her.

Harley sucked in her gut and hunched her shoulders to minimize her breast size.

"She's not showing," Tracy chastised. "But she is glowing."

"That Messina boy will regret it if he doesn't come back for her."

"If he comes back for the wedding, I'm going to give him a piece of my mind."

"You can't spare more than a small piece, Georgia."

Harley made her escape amid peals of laughter.

Next, Harley stopped by Phil's, which was where Brit worked. Phil's used to be the town barber shop. Now it catered to the female crowd.

The day was just beginning, but the bride-to-be was elbow-deep in perms and old ladies under hair dryers. Phil was busy, as well, applying color to an older woman's hair.

Rose sat in the waiting area, tapping her feet. She looked like she was ready for safari in khaki walking shorts and a zebra-print blouse. On the wall above her, a metal mermaid swam above an antique bicycle. "I'm debating a color change." Rose waved Harley over. "What do you think of red?"

"Your hair is lovely as is," Brit interjected. She wore silver tights beneath a shimmery silver dress.

Phil wore a traditional barber's white smock. His hands shook as he painted an auburn tint on the woman's short hair. No one seemed to mind the tremor. Phil was rumored to be a whiz at mixing hair colors. "I've been told I can't color your hair."

"Poppycock and nonsense." Rose stood, not a white hair in her tight chignon out of place. "Every woman should be a redhead once in her life." She looked to Harley for agreement.

Harley raised her hands. "My mother always said, 'Hair color is like a good pair of shoes. Once you find a pair that fits, you stick with them.'"

"We should put that on the wall somewhere." Brit whisked the drape from Mrs. Edelman's neck. "All done."

"Darn." Vince's third-grade teacher eyed Harley. "I wanted to hear the news about Vince."

"No news," Harley said a tad less than good-naturedly. Did everyone have to ask about Vince? "He's still AWOL." He hadn't answered her text from a few days ago asking if he was okay. "I'm here to ask Brit if I can tile her master bathroom. That is, if Gabe finds tile."

"Are you redoing the bathroom here?" Mrs. Edelman counted out bills to pay Brit. "It's more gas station than spa, if you ask me."

"No one asked you, Carly," Phil snapped. "Things are fine here as is."

"It's for our house." Brit swept Mrs. Edelman's gray hair on the floor into a dustpan. "Yes, I'd love you to do it, Harley, but you'll have to ask Joe, too."

Rats. She'd been avoiding Joe, aka the Vince Hater.

The front door flung open. Irwin stepped in. He wore a tan sports coat, khakis and a blue pinstriped bow tie. He carried a bouquet of daisies and looked like his white comb-over had been treated with too much hair gel.

Gabe stood outside on the sidewalk, watching intently. He had an up-to-something smile on his face.

"Rose!" Irwin shouted above the whirring hair dryers.

"Yes?" Rose turned to face him, as did four other elderly women.

Irwin froze. And not the hesitation or pause kind of freezing. This was the choking kind of freezing.

Harley waved at Gabe and pressed a hand to her throat, letting Gabe know his dating prodigy was crashing and burning.

Sans grin, Gabe pushed the glass door open a crack and whispered, "Irwin, like we practiced."

Irwin nodded. Eyes wide. He swallowed and said less confidently and at a lower volume, "Rose?"

"Yes?" Rose arched a white brow.

Irwin sucked in air like a dying air compressor. "Bemydateforthewedding?" The question tumbled out of Irwin's mouth like one long strung-together word.

"Please," Gabe whispered through the crack in the door.

"Please," Irwin added dutifully, thrusting the daisies toward her.

All eyes swiveled to Rose, who stood silently.

"Rose," Gabe whispered. "Say yes."

Rose suddenly seemed to come back to her senses. Or perhaps not, because she said simply, "Yes!"

The shop erupted in applause.

"Idiot," Phil mumbled, but he was smiling.

"That was romantic. Now…are you going to take Vince back?" Mrs. Edelman sat in her walker near Harley. "He was the kindest boy. I know he'll return to rescue you."

Harley wasn't holding her breath. At first, she'd thought he'd left for Cloverdale or somewhere else nearby to cool down. Now she suspected he'd gone back to Texas. Besides, he'd been banned from the wedding. Joe still refused to talk about him. "I'm not sure I need rescuing."

Funny how just saying the words aloud reinforced what she'd been trying to tell herself. She was going to be okay.

"We're still trying to adopt Harley ourselves." Brit checked the curlers on a woman under the dryer, and then ushered another elderly client into her chair. "What does she need Vince for?"

Love, comfort, stability. Cold nights in the winter. Someone to help me breathe in the delivery room.

Sadly, Harley's list could go on and on.

Irwin was still standing in the midst of the shop.

"Kiss her cheek." Gabe was still standing at the crack in the door.

Irwin darted toward Rose, raised up on his toes—because she was taller than he was—and pecked her cheek like a chicken going for seed. And then he practically ran out the door and into Gabe's arms.

"Idiot," Phil said, louder this time.

There was laughter and mention of phone trees.

"Oh, Harley, dear…" Rose carried her bouquet two-handed, like a bride. "I forgot to tell you that yesterday Mayor Larry found an architect interested in your ideas for the theater."

"That was fast." And a little depressing. Someone else would be attempting to bring her balconies to life. It was bad enough that Dan was ecstatic back in Houston because the mechanical engineers had been thrilled with Vince's solution. Well, not exactly bad. Dan had torn up her contract, accepting her offer to own the rights to the balcony design in Texas.

Harley made polite mention of how happy she was for Rose and the mayor. That, at least, was true.

"You know, this architect was wondering if you'd be interested in an apprenticeship." Rose showed her bouquet to Mrs. Edelman. "I told him you were having a baby and moving on."

"She should consider working from home," Mrs. Edelman said firmly. "So you can raise your baby and provide for yourselves."

"You should get out before they start planning the rest of your life." Brit tilted her head toward the door.

Before Harley could make her exit, Sarah entered the shop. "Harley!" She charged forward and hugged Harley the way she'd hugged Vince, sans the pinch. "We should have drinks or dinner or something to commiserate." She smiled at Brit's patrons each in turn. "We both got dumped by Vince."

"The way I heard tell," Mrs. Edelman said primly, "you dumped Vince for Gabe, who dumped you."

"Oh, semantics." Sarah's smile didn't waver. "We both got dumped by a Messina."

Harley didn't think that was anything to celebrate. She hurried out the door and headed for the garage.

House painters had taped off the ranch house windows and doors and were starting up the paint sprayer. Gabe and Irwin had wheeled the riding mower out to the parking lot. Irwin had taken off his sports jacket and tie.

"Harley!" Gabe grinned and got down on one knee. "Are you overcome with Irwin's display of romance? Did you come to hear my proposal again? Unlike my brother, I'm willing to beg you to marry me."

"The intent is much appreciated, but the answer will always be no." Harley peered into the service bays. "Is Joe around?"

"He's underneath Agnes's Buick." Irwin pointed toward the left bay.

"What do you want with Joe?" Gabe got to his feet and blinked, as if he'd gotten a head rush.

"We need to ask him if I can tile their bathroom." At Gabe's eye-roll, Harley added, "Brit's orders."

"Good thing I haven't started on that request yet." Gabe returned to the mower. "We're going to take the mower on a test drive first."

"And see how fast it'll go." Irwin was clearly enamored with speed.

And the riding mower was probably just his speed.

The painters were giving the ranch house a soft shade of blue. It wouldn't matter what color they painted it. The house would still be boxy and plain, unless...

"Gabe, do you think you can find shutters for those front windows?"

He laid a hand on his chest. "I can find anything, anywhere."

"Shutters would be great. I'll let you know if the man in charge approves tile."

"He better." Gabe turned the key in the mower ignition. It clicked but didn't start. He poked around the engine, much the same as Vince had done a week ago to Harley's truck engine. "Brit wants it. And you know what they say. Happy wife, happy life."

Harley entered the garage. "Hey, Joe. Do you have a minute?"

"Sure." Joe slid out from underneath the green Buick on what looked like a man-size red skateboard.

"I need a huge favor." On her way over, she'd come up with a plan. "I'm bored to tears. Help a girl out, will you? I'd love to do the tile in your master bathroom."

Sam rolled out from under the Toyota in the right service bay. "Holy smokes, Dad. She must think you were born yesterday."

Joe chuckled.

"Hey." Harley pretended to be deeply offended. "Whose side are you on?"

"Mine. My shower is done." Sam rolled back underneath the Toyota.

Joe reached for a bottle of water and took a drink. "Harley, you know how I feel about freebies. We pay our way around here."

Backup plan number one. "That's fine. You can pay me." Harley hoped her tone wasn't too casual. "I'll bill you when I get back to Texas."

A few days ago, before she knew Joe, she'd have looked at him and thought how much he looked like Vince. But Vince's features were a bit more pronounced, less tame. And the dark eyes. They went better with that devilish Messina smile.

Joe shook his head. "Messina's pay their own way. This is non-negotiable. Besides, that much tile isn't in our budget until next month. Maybe the month after that."

Backup plan number two. "But Gabe will be gone by then, right? Where will you get the supplies from?"

"Brit is perfectly capable of negotiating a lower price."

"Just not as low as Gabe, I bet."

Joe hesitated in their back-and-forth. "We've got to get through this wedding without going broke, buy Sam back-to-school clothes—"

"Thanks, Dad!"

"—and then we can finish the house."

And for the third and final backup plan... "And you'll be asking your new bride to live in the apartment upstairs, which is very *très* chic. Kind of...the-furniture-no-one-wanted-at-a-garage-sale chic." She paused to let that sink in. "Or you could let Gabe work his magic—with receipts, of course—and do this girl a solid so she doesn't get bored sitting around waiting for her flight to leave, and you can get moved into that lovely re-model of yours that much sooner."

Joe's mouth worked.

"Hey." Sam rolled out from under the Toyota again. "Think carefully before you delay my school clothes shopping in any way."

Joe's mouth worked, all right. It worked into a smile. "You have plenty of clothes. Didn't we just take you bra shopping a couple of months ago?"

"Dad!" Sam shot to her feet, wiping her hands with a blue rag. "Why would you say that? Gah! Parents are just so...so... *impossible*!" She disappeared into the sales office. Her feet pounded the stairs and then doors slammed above them.

Joe rolled under Agnes's Buick.

"And I'm assuming that's a yes?"

"Tell Gabe that tile needs to be nearly free or he's buying Sam school clothes." Joe chuckled. "And he can take her shopping. I bet she needs more new bras."

"Gladly." Let the big man sweat that one out.

VINCE PUT ON his dark blue suit in a hotel room in Cloverdale with sweaty palms.

He was crashing his brother's wedding.

He had apologies to give and amends to make. To his family. To Harley.

He didn't know if anyone would listen.

He arrived early at the family property. The house had been painted robin's-egg blue. White shutters had been added to the windows and fresh grass had been rolled on the front lawn. Vince almost didn't recognize the place.

Someone must have fixed the riding mower. The field once filled with dilapidated cars was now mowed to a civilized height. White folding chairs had been placed in neat rows on two sides of a white gazebo. White ribbons and bows had been placed down the aisle. And on the garage parking lot there were more tables and chairs than ever before, many beneath pop-ups to provide shade.

Vince parked on the road and went in

search of his brothers. He found them inside the upstairs apartment, along with the best man, Will Jackson, Joe's best friend from high school.

His reception was frosty.

"No," Gabe said when Vince closed the apartment door behind him. He hadn't yet put his suit jacket or tie on. His tie hung loosely around his thick neck and his biceps strained the cotton material of his shirt sleeves.

"Hear me out." Vince held up his hands in surrender.

"We're not doing this now." Joe was attempting to knot his tie. The last time he'd tried to do so had been his first wedding day. He'd needed Vince's assistance then, too.

"Hey, Vince." Will spoke like the voice of reason. His blue suit was a cut above those worn by the Messinas, but then again, he'd made his fortune in the tech world. He could afford nice things. "Let's go outside and talk."

"Maybe later, golden boy." His childhood name for Will.

Vince came forward. "At least, let me get your tie right."

"Fine." Joe lifted his chin. "But don't talk."

"And tie mine before you leave." Gabe buttoned up his collar.

Will glared at Vince and leaned against the wall.

There was no way Vince wasn't talking. "Mom left here and had to get professional help to sort herself out," Vince said simply. "She'd been smoking two packs a day and steadily losing weight and her mind. I had no idea she was that sick."

Joe's eyes clouded with pain, but he wouldn't look Vince in the eye. Gabe swore under his breath. Will's glare reduced to a hard stare.

"Mom wanted me to drop out of school." That had been her cry for help. He'd been too young to recognize it. "And when I told her no, we argued."

"Those hall passes…" Joe's voice trailed off, still refusing to look at him.

Gabe was looking at Vince, but he wasn't really seeing him.

Will went to the window, his turned back giving them a small measure of privacy.

Vince finished tying Joe's tie and turned to Gabe. He hesitated, mouth dry.

His older brother looked lost. He never looked lost. "You should've told me." Gabe's voice was rougher than sandpaper on rusted metal. "I was the oldest."

"You took my girlfriend." Vince moved in to tackle Gabe's tie. "You snuck out of the house at night more than I snuck out of school during the day. You were so busy carving trees in Harmony Valley, who could talk to you?"

"You should have told me." Joe's brows were crowded together on his forehead. "I was here. I was here the entire time."

"I should leave you guys alone to hash this out." Will moved toward the door.

"Stay." Joe pleaded. "You lived through this with me as much as they did, probably more."

"Ouch," Gabe said.

Vince finished with Gabe's tie and faced Joe. "Mom moved to Texas. She's using her maiden name. She's dating a good man… My boss." Might just as well get all of the messy details out on the table. "And I finally worked up the nerve to talk to her this week."

"You mean you hadn't before?" Joe's skin was turning a blotchy red.

"No." Vince thrust his hands in his pants' pockets. "I couldn't bring myself to do it. I was…" No sense denying it. "I was afraid she'd be angry that I tracked her down."

"And was she?" Gabe asked. There was a bottle of whiskey on the counter. Gabe poured himself a shot and downed it.

"No. She was sad. Apologetic. At peace in a way that I wasn't."

"Well…" Gabe laughed, but it lacked his usual humor. "You're a mess. We all know that."

Vince shrugged.

"What about Harley?" Joe pinned Vince with a hard look. "What about the baby?"

Vince couldn't speak.

Joe didn't let up. He moved in closer and his tone turned mean. "If you went to all those lengths to protect Mom, you need to work twice as hard to protect that baby. I know first-hand how hard it is to be a single parent."

"I offered to marry her. It was the least I could do." Gabe took his suit jacket off the hanger.

Vince scowled. He should've known better than to trust Gabe around Harley.

"Don't get your pants in a wedgie." Gabe

slid into his jacket. "Just so you know, she turned me down both times I asked."

"You asked her more than once?" Vince might have slugged Gabe if he wasn't afraid of getting blood on his shirt before the wedding.

Gabe straightened his lapels. "To my enormous surprise…she remains loyal to you."

Vince had to stop himself from sagging with relief.

"I'm beginning to regret having a meeting in the city these last few days," Will said. "I missed out on all the good stuff."

"You need to patch things up with her." Joe laid his hands on Vince's shoulders.

Until that moment Vince hadn't been sure Joe would forgive him. "I don't think I can fix this." He'd said some awful things. Some truly awful things.

"I've never seen anything you couldn't fix." Gabe slapped him on the back. Hard.

"Even Mom called you the Fixer." Joe released him, beginning to smile.

"You had some skill in the repair department," Will allowed.

They were joking with each other again. In that moment Vince knew he and his brothers were going to be all right. That is, if they could get past one more surprise.

"There's just one more thing."

Gabe rolled his eyes.

"I'm going to pour everyone a shot." Vince reached for the whiskey. "Mom's downstairs."

CHAPTER TWENTY

"WHERE SHOULD MY horseradish potato salad go?"

Harley had been put in charge of organizing the dishes dropped off for the potluck reception that was to follow the wedding. She turned to face the woman carrying the horseradish potato salad.

It was Eunice, the elderly woman with purplish-gray hair who quilted in the window seat of the bakery and watched over the toddler boys. She wore a pink-flowered dress and white feathered mules. "I wanted to make my famous ham, hollandaise and banana casserole, but my neighbor, Duffy, said that should only be served to family. I'm not entirely sure what that means."

Harley's stomach turned at the unappetizing combination. "It means he wants to keep that special recipe a family secret."

"Oh." She smiled and blinked her eyes in that Kewpie doll way of hers. "Yes, it does."

She patted Harley's flat stomach. "And how is the baby today?"

Harley stiffened. This wasn't the first time she'd been touched inappropriately like that in Harmony Valley. Being pregnant was like a license to touch in this town. "I'm feeling good."

Eunice leaned in close, widening her blinking eyes, which were an interesting shade of brown, almost violet. "I've been in the labor room. You need to keep up your strength." She squeezed Harley's bicep. "Although you are a wiry one. Are all architects that strong?"

"No." Harley took possession of the horseradish potato salad and backed away. "You should find a seat, before all the good ones are taken."

"Harley?"

A very tanned middle-aged couple stood at the door to the garage sales office. The man was blond and fit, and wore a simple gray suit that looked expensive. The woman wore a blue sheath with beaded trim. Her brown hair was pulled back in a neat ponytail. Her makeup was flawless. She wore wide silver bangles along with a simple white corsage on one wrist.

The man started to laugh. "You don't recognize me without my sunglasses and baseball cap?"

"Jerry?" Harley rushed over to hug him. "I don't recognize you because you're not yelling. What are you doing here?" And then it sunk in. Vince's mother was dating Jerry. Harley introduced herself to her baby's grandmother. "Do Joe and Gabe know you're here?"

"Yes." Gwen's cheeks deepened in color. "I was nervous. I haven't seen them since..."

"I'm sure they were happy to see you," Harley said hopefully, dragging the corner of her lips up. The fact that she was still here and no one was yelling had to mean something positive had happened. "I'm happy to finally meet you."

"Vince told us you were expecting," Jerry surprised her by saying. "You need to be careful about what you carry on the job site from now on."

"Jerry, now isn't the time to talk about work," Gwen scolded her beau. She hugged Harley, kissing her cheek. "I'm so happy for you. We both are. I'm a wonderful babysitter and I'll be in your corner if Jerry pushes you too hard."

It was telling she said nothing about Vince. He'd been banned from attending the wedding and it was probably too expensive for him to fly all the way back from Texas.

"It's all right." Harley's smile felt easier, because Gwen was very sweet. "I've been thinking about making a career change."

Jerry's eyebrows went up. "Not before the Randall job. It's herringbone everywhere. No one does herringbone like you do."

"Maybe not before the Randall job," Harley allowed. She still had rent to pay.

"Good." Jerry seemed pleased. "By the way, I'm hoping Gwen gets wedding fever and finally agrees to marry me."

"You don't have to tell everyone." Gwen blushed a fiery red. "I don't know what's gotten into you today."

"Wedding fever," Jerry repeated, chuckling. "Let's go find a seat on the groom's side." He glanced at Harley. "Do you know which side is the groom's side?"

"No clue."

"It's the right side," Gwen said. "Maybe we should hide somewhere until the ceremony starts. I don't want to be recognized and have to explain where I've been."

That wasn't such a bad idea. "You can

walk over by the bridge. The bride created the art on display. She's quite talented." Harley pointed out the mermaid riding the surfboard above the garage doors. "She made that mermaid, too."

"She welds," Jerry said with a gleam in his eye.

"That doesn't mean she's going to go to work for you, Jer." Gwen took his hand and led him toward the bridge.

The guests began coming in droves, dropped off by the party bus or walking from cars parked along the road. Harley was busy for several minutes grouping salads together on one table and entrees on another.

"Harley?" Sam rushed up in a tea-length, gray satin dress, wearing make-up and carrying a small, pink-flowered wreath. "Brit wanted you to wear this in your hair."

Harley accepted the delicate circle of flowers. "Why?"

"She said all family members are wearing flowers. Gotta go." She hitched up her skirt and scampered off.

"Harley." That voice.

It traveled up her spine like a slow hand on a cool night.

Harley shivered. She wasn't supposed to

see Vince today. She wasn't ready to see him today.

Harley turned slowly.

Vince looked like he hadn't slept in the days since he'd been gone. There were bags under his eyes and lines crossing the bags. His cheekbones looked hollow, as if he hadn't been eating, either.

Harley didn't think she looked much better. "Vi-*ince*." His name came out in a half-broken squawk. "Does Joe know you're here?"

He nodded. "I wanted to talk to you before the ceremony." He wore a nice blue suit and a gray tie with white polka dots. His hair was the only thing that had held up to the stress and still looked fabulous.

"Harley?" Vince said her name as if she hadn't been paying attention.

Which she hadn't. "Yes?"

"Come with me." Vince took her by the arm and led her into the ranch house. He probably wanted to smooth things over with her before the ceremony so as to avoid a scene.

Not that she'd make one.

Mayor Larry caught her eye and gave her a thumbs-up. He'd misread the entire scenario.

Vince wasn't here for her. He'd brought his mother back as a wedding gift to Joe.

The kitchen cabinets had been put in yesterday. The countertops wouldn't be added until next week. The house was beginning to look like a home built in this century.

Vince stood in the middle of the living room, looking sad and uncomfortable. "I'm sorry."

"For what?" There'd been so many harsh words exchanged between them, Harley wasn't sure what he was apologizing for.

"I've been a fool." Of all the truths he'd told, this one rang clear as a bell. He believed it.

"I understand." She sighed. "You can't rationalize fears. I just… I hope we can find common ground and parent together."

He scowled at her.

So. Harley's stomach knotted. He hadn't gotten over his aversion to being a parent. She wouldn't talk about this here. Not now with the entire town ready to bear witness to him tearing what was left of her heart to pieces.

"Thank you for the idea for my balconies." She forced herself to smile, even if she only smiled at a spot over his left shoulder. "It could work out."

"I don't want to talk about balconies." His words were as flat as her putty knife, but sharper edged.

"Oh." She had to get some distance between them if she wanted to avoid crying. Harley walked down the hall. "Do you want to see what I've done in the master shower?" It was simple traditional subway tile on the walls and classic small-octagon black and white tiles on the floor.

"No." He grabbed her arm, bringing her to a halt. "I want to talk about us."

"There is no us." He'd made that very clear earlier in the week. "Don't let Gabe force you into something you don't want."

"Gabe couldn't force me…" He ran a hand through his hair, making the bangs stick straight up. "Can we start over?"

"Completely over or just today over?"

He claimed her hands. His were big and warm and released butterflies in her chest. "I'll go back as far as you let me."

Harley held her breath, trying to hold in butterflies.

"I talked to my mom. About my father's illness. Turns out…he was diagnosed much earlier than I thought. His teens. She thinks I'm fine." He spoke in fits and starts. His discomfort was almost a tangible thing in the air. "But she's not a doctor, so I went to a psychiatrist. He said I was fine."

"Do you believe them?" Because he didn't sound confident. And his eyes. They were darting around in panic mode.

He didn't want to be a father. He was trying to patch things up because it was the right thing to do.

Harley felt sucker punched.

"I doubt I'll ever shake the fear that I might develop the disease." He straightened and met her gaze squarely. "But I truly want to pursue a relationship with you. And have our baby." That last statement came out more like an afterthought.

She nodded absently.

"For years I've been under the assumption that my fate was grim." His dark eyes seemed deep and endless. "For years I kept people at arm's length."

She was unable to look away, although it felt like she was seeing a train barreling toward a barrier. She being the barrier and he the careless train.

In the days after Vince left, this had been

the conversation she'd longed for. But it lacked one thing. Heart. She remained unconvinced of his sincerity of feeling for her and the baby.

"But then you came along and I told you so much I'd kept hidden away… I couldn't keep it inside when I was with you."

"You only told me because we struck a deal. Between friends."

"You know we're more than friends. We should get married. Because we love each other." His voice was flat. His patience had worn thin.

Hers was entirely gone, buried beneath the remains of the relationship they'd once had. "I've had days to think about what we had."

The corners of his mouth turned up hopefully.

"And days to think about what we didn't have." She held up a hand when he would have said more. "Most relationships launch slowly. You get to know someone. And then you…*get to know someone*." She whispered this last. "You learn to know their boundaries. How they like to have fun. What makes them feel loved. How to trust each other. To know your lover's reaction in times of stress. We have none of that."

"What are you saying?"

"I'm saying I don't know you. I can't trust you to be there when I need you." She placed a hand on her belly and tried to say these last words without letting on her heart was breaking. "I'm saying that we shouldn't get married."

"YOU LOOK LIKE—" Gabe peered at Vince's face when he returned to the apartment above the garage "—you've been kicked in the teeth by Harley."

"She turned you down?" Joe stopped pacing in the upstairs apartment and put his hands on his hips. "What did you say to her?"

"The truth. I told her I'd finally got my act together and—"

"Oh, come on!" Gabe tossed his hands. "That's not what a woman wants to hear."

Will nodded.

"Stay out of this." Vince glared at the best man.

"What you said…" Joe moved to Vince's side. "That's like saying you're more important that she is."

Vince eyed the bottle of whiskey on the counter. "Aren't we of equal importance?"

The other men in the room shook their heads.

"You gave away equality when you had that meltdown." Joe's smile was rueful.

"That's not fair." Even as he said it, Vince winced. He sounded like one of Jerry's tired grandchildren after a day in the pool.

"It may not be fair," Will said, all holier than thou, "but now you've got to make up for it."

"How, genius?"

"With a really grand gesture." Joe answered for his best man. "Women want to be swept off their feet." Easy for him to say. He'd built a Volkswagen out of stone to win Brit back.

"I could propose again." Vince had a ring in his breast pocket.

His advisors shook their heads.

"Not without the big apology first." Will turned a wedding ring on his finger. "I got down on my knees in front of the entire town during the Spring Festival."

The back of Vince's neck began to sweat.

"What you need is something flashy." Gabe brightened. "Something in red."

"Red? The only thing I've seen around here that's red is… No." Vince practically dove for the whiskey. "That was supposed to be Brit's wedding gift."

"You're going to give Harley my bride's wedding gift?" Joe's brows lowered. "Regifting drops to new lows."

"Who said anything about *giving*?" Gabe chuckled. "I'm talking about borrowing. Taking it for a test drive, so to speak."

"There's just one problem." Vince had poured a shot but couldn't bring himself to drink it. "The chopper doesn't run. What am I supposed to do? Roll it out, straddle the seat and ask her to ride on my very slow steed?"

"You aren't the only one with mechanical skills, bro." Gabe waggled his eyebrows.

"This is the antique chopper Gabe's got hidden downstairs?" Joe looked torn. "I thought you were giving it to Brit for her art display."

"We are. Leave everything to me." Gabe went out the door.

Vince rested both hands on the kitchen counter and tried to steady his breathing. Everything would be all right. Gabe was on the case.

Gabe to the rescue?

Vince downed the shot.

"Gabe ignored me." Joe reached for the whiskey bottle, then decided against it and set it back on the counter. "Why does he always ignore me?"

"Other than the fact that you're his baby brother?" Will came over and straightened Joe's tie. "He only ignores you when he has a really good idea."

"If I were you—" Joe pinned Vince with what looked like their mother's blue eyes "—I'd be afraid. Very, very afraid."

CHAPTER TWENTY-ONE

THE WEDDING WAS BEAUTIFUL.

The bridesmaids wore tea-length gray-satin dresses. Sam fidgeted, alternating her gaze between her father and Brad, who sat in the second row.

Brit wore a vintage lace gown with princess sleeves. Her hair was in a sophisticated updo and she cried happy tears from the moment her grandfather gave her away until she and Joe sealed their vows with a kiss.

And Vince? He didn't look Harley's way once. That was the only thing that wasn't beautiful about the wedding. But how could Harley complain? She'd told him they were through. And, just like after Waco, her heart was protesting her head's decision.

Harley helped Rose and Agnes get guests settled with food and drink while the wedding party took pictures. Rose took her seat next to Irwin. They both blushed. The wedding party sat at a table near the closed service bays. There were toasts and kisses and laughter.

Harley's laughter felt as hollow as her mother's Easter egg chocolates. She wanted to leave and was just waiting for the right moment to slip away when an engine rumbled in the garage. One of the service bay doors slid open.

A man in a blue suit rode the monster motorcycle that was Brit's wedding gift out of the garage. He rode past the wedding party and brought the bike back around to the curb.

"Harley." He held out a hand. "Let's go for a ride."

"Vince?" Harley stood at her table, three tables away from the curb. "Vince?" She had to say his name again. He didn't ride motorcycles. He was a carrot-eating, careful man.

"I haven't ridden a motorcycle in years. I used to think it was the most fun a person could have. Freedom and the open road."

"Amen," Irwin piped up.

Harley pushed her chair back and moved toward the aisle between the tables. "What are you doing?"

"I'm telling you how I used to have fun, back when I had too many responsibilities." He revved the motor. "Doesn't mean I wouldn't like to ride every once in a while. An old man likes to relive his glory days."

"You're not old." There was an odd feeling in Harley's chest, and it wasn't indigestion from Eunice's horseradish potato salad.

Vince smiled at her. Not in the desperate, forced way he'd done in the house, but with confidence and caring. Like he loved her and he wasn't afraid anymore. "I'm not perfect. I've tried to tell you what choice to make concerning your life and career. Those choices are yours to make, not mine."

The odd feeling in her chest increased. She recognized it now. It wasn't the wild flutter of young butterfly wings, but a quickening heartbeat of a woman in love.

"Do you know when I feel most loved?" he asked.

Harley shook her head, edging between guests to reach him. Past Rose and Irwin. Past Jerry and Gwen. Past the smiling mayor.

"I feel most loved when I'm in your arms."

The wedding guests let out a collective *ahh*.

"I want to share that love with our baby."

The *ahhs* got louder.

Sarah had moved her chair too far back, blocking Harley's way.

"You can trust me." He spoke with confidence, but there was vulnerability in his eyes, as if he didn't realize why Harley had stopped, as if he wasn't sure he'd addressed all the concerns she'd voiced in the house earlier.

"If you don't take a ride, Harley," Sarah said, half rising from her seat. "I will."

"That thing is a death trap," Sam said, but she sounded like it was an invitation to adventure.

"It's a chick magnet," Irwin said, his voice ringing with pride. "That bike got me a date with Rose."

"Idiot," Phil muttered.

Harley was working her way around the other side of the table, barely able to walk and keep her eyes on Vince at the same time.

Vince ignored their audience. His tender gaze was only for Harley.

"I love you, Harley O'Hannigan. I love the way you outthink me. I love the way you outwork me. I love the way you take care of everyone else before yourself." He revved the motorcycle engine.

She was close enough that its rumble reverberated in her chest. She'd forever associate the sound with the newly discovered strength Vince had discovered in love.

He stared at her with loving eyes. "I want to be the one that makes sure you're taken care of. I want to be the one that loves that baby to the moon and back. Take a chance and get on this thing."

Somehow, she had come to stand next to him. "I…" Her brain was kicking in, filling her head with protests because she'd been hurt by Vince before.

"You're scared." His voice had the deep, slow cadence of the river rippling past the bridge. "Don't worry. I won't go fast. Not at first. Not until you're comfortable." He wasn't talking about a motorcycle ride. "Small steps. Together."

Her hand found its way into his. He gave it a reassuring squeeze.

"I'm more comfortable with some things. You're more comfortable with others. We can face anything head-on." He leaned forward, giving her enough room to climb on.

"Don't go too fast." Or her dress would fly up. Or she'd fall off.

She wrapped her arms around his waist.

MELINDA CURTIS   373

"Just a short ride. Baby steps, remember? Trust me."

And she did.

To Vince's credit, he went slow, which disappointed Irwin but made Harley the happiest woman on the planet.

Well, next to Brit. It was her wedding day, after all.

He rode down Main Street. He rode over the curb onto the town square, parking beneath the spreading oak next to the lone park bench.

There was a bouquet of roses on that bench.

Harley nearly fell off the big bike.

But Vince's hand was there, steadying her. And then somehow he had her off the bike, sitting on the bench and holding the roses.

He dropped down to one knee and held out a blue-velvet box and a princess-cut ring. "That baby is going to be the luckiest baby alive, because its mother and father are going to love it, no matter what." His eyes were bright and his hair was perfect.

Harley had no illusions as to the state of her hair. She'd worn it down today and had no idea how the wreath was still on top of her head or how it looked. Her hair didn't matter. But her heart… It seemed to beat just for one man. *Mr. Vince Carrots Messina.*

"I love you, Harley. I can't say it enough." He was the prince she'd dreamed of. The one who would love her forever and ever. It was there in his eyes, the ones that shone with love. His love had been there all this time, communicating with her heart in secret, keeping her from falling out of love with every setback they faced. "A man needs three things in life."

"Three things?" She'd only ever heard him mention two.

"Just three things. Pride, honor, and you. Will you marry me, Harley?"

"Yes." She ignored the ring and embraced him. "I love you." She kissed him once, sweetly, for never giving up on his fears. And if they came again, they'd battle them together. "I'll marry you because I can't imagine loving anyone else more."

And because his hair didn't lie, after all.

EPILOGUE

"HARLEY! HURRY!" VINCE ran around the small apartment and gathered the things they'd need—pacifier, baby bottle, blanket, diapers. "They're going to have the ribbon-cutting ceremony without you."

Life was good. A joy. Not a test of survival.

Harley was close to finishing up her first year of an apprenticeship with an architect in Santa Rosa. Vince was working as a part-time carpenter for the contractor the town council preferred. He was a full-time student studying civil engineering at Sacramento State University. And a full-time dad. To save money, they were living in the apartment over the family's repair shop in Harmony Valley.

The theater and tie-dye shop were finally finished with renovations and ready to open. Harley's ideas had been embraced by the architect Rose and the mayor had chosen.

His wife should have been floating on air like the theater balcony. Instead she was dragging her feet in the bathroom.

"Harley, I'm packing up Colton." He lifted their three-month-old son out of the playpen where he'd been fascinated with the brightly colored butterflies dangling from a mobile above him.

Colt put his hands on Vince's cheeks and squealed. On cue, Vince blew the thick black hair on top of Colt's head. His son giggled as if this was the first time they'd ever played that game.

He was a beautiful, healthy boy. Every day, Vince counted his blessings.

"Vince." Harley stood in the open door of the bathroom. "Do you remember the day you asked me to marry you?"

"The day I asked you to marry me twice?" Vince jiggled his happy son into the car seat and buckled him in.

"Yes, that's the one." She smiled, tentatively at first and then wider. Motherhood and marriage agreed with her. She was always smiling, always gracious, always beautiful. Today she wore a slim pair of black slacks, fancy half-boots and a white sweater that draped off one shoulder. She looked good enough to kiss long and slow and make them miss the ceremony entirely. "Do you remember what you said that day about taking small steps?"

"Sorry, honey. We don't have time to go slow or we'll be late." Although he wouldn't mind being another minute late if it meant he could steal a kiss. He walked over and put his hands on her slender waist. "We have time for just one kiss."

"Baby steps." There was a dazed look in her eyes, like the one that greeted the morning some days lately. She was busy and the baby didn't always sleep through the night.

Vince captured her lips for a tender kiss. He pulled back and drew her across the room toward the diaper bag, the baby and the door.

"I'm pregnant." Harley wasn't smiling when she said it. But then she grinned and said softer, "*We're* pregnant."

"But… I'm just getting used to having one." *Another baby?* He gazed down on the drooly, gummy, sweet-faced grin of his son. Another baby. It was going to be awesome. "I love you." He pulled her into his arms. "I love you both. I love you all."

"Tell me the truth. It scares you a little,

doesn't it?" Harley grabbed Vince's hands and swung around so she was nearest the door, dancing the way Sam did with him sometimes.

"It's getting hot in here." Knowing Harley would get the joke, he picked up Colt's car seat and diaper bag. "But…a little fear can be exciting, if you're by my side."

She gave him a quick kiss and her smile turned wicked. "Always."

* * * * *

USA TODAY *bestselling author*
Melinda Curtis has written other
HARMONY VALLEY *romances.*
Please visit www.Harlequin.com
for these great titles:

SUPPORT YOUR LOCAL SHERIFF
LOVE, SPECIAL DELIVERY
MARRYING THE SINGLE DAD
A MEMORY AWAY
TIME FOR LOVE
A PERFECT YEAR
SEASON OF CHANGE
SUMMER KISSES
DANDELION WISHES

Get 2 Free Books,

Plus 2 Free Gifts—

just for trying the
Reader Service!

Love Inspired

HOME on the RANCH

YES! Please send me the **Home on the Ranch Collection** in Larger Print. This collection begins with 3 FREE books and 2 FREE gifts in the first shipment. Along with my 3 free books, I'll also get the next 4 books from the Home on the Ranch Collection, in LARGER PRINT, which I may either return and owe nothing, or keep for the low price of $5.24 U.S./ $5.89 CDN each plus $2.99 for shipping and handling per shipment*. If I decide to continue, about once a month for 8 months I will get 6 or 7 more books, but will only need to pay for 4. That means 2 or 3 books in every shipment will be FREE! If I decide to keep the entire collection, I'll have paid for only 32 books because 19 books are FREE! I understand that accepting the 3 free books and gifts places me under no obligation to buy anything. I can always return a shipment and cancel at any time. My free books and gifts are mine to keep no matter what I decide.

268 HCN 3760 468 HCN 3760

Name	(PLEASE PRINT)	
Address		Apt. #
City	State/Prov.	Zip/Postal Code

Signature (if under 18, a parent or guardian must sign)

Mail to the **Reader Service**:

IN U.S.A.: P.O. Box 1867, Buffalo, NY. 14240-1867
IN CANADA: P.O. Box 609, Fort Erie, Ontario L2A 5X3

* Terms and prices subject to change without notice. Prices do not include applicable taxes. Sales tax applicable in NY. Canadian residents will be charged applicable taxes. This offer is limited to one order per household. All orders subject to approval. Credit or debit balances in a customer's account(s) may be offset by any other outstanding balance owed by or to the customer. Please allow 3 to 4 weeks for delivery. Offer available while quantities last. Offer not available to Quebec residents.

HRCBPA18

Get 2 Free Books,
Plus 2 Free Gifts -
just for trying the **Reader Service!**